The women of La___
share an uncommon gift that
will lead them to days filled with
danger—and nights of desire.

Faye Nettles seems like just another beguiling ingenue. But Faye came to Lavender House seeking refuge from a tragic past, a past she fears may find her at any moment. So though she finds lying detestable, she must keep her dark secrets—especially from Rogan McBain, the towering, muscle-bound Scotsman she has been tasked with investigating.

Rogan McBain seems like just another brutish soldier. But though he served admirably in His Majesty's army, Rogan has far more on his mind than fighting—like the golden-haired angel who's shown up at his door. Faye could bring even the strongest man to his knees, but she thinks he's a downright devil. If only he could find a way to charm himself into her delicate heart . . .

By Lois Greiman

Lois Greiman

CHARMING THE DEVIL

AVON
An Imprint of HarperCollinsPublishers

AVON BOOKS
An Imprint of HarperCollins*Publishers*
10 East 53rd Street
New York, New York 10022-5299

Copyright © 2010 by Lois Greiman
ISBN 978-0-06-184933-6
www.avonromance.com

First Avon Books paperback printing: February 2010

Avon Trademark Reg. U.S. Pat. Off. and in Other Countries, Marca Registrada, Hecho en U.S.A.
HarperCollins® is a registered trademark of HarperCollins Publishers.

Printed in the U.S.A.

10 9 8 7 6 5 4 3 2 1

Prologue

London, England
1813

S haleena was naked. Absolutely exposed from the top of her fiery head to the tip of her ridiculously pointy toes. Not a bonnet. Not a stocking. Not a stitch.

She must feel silly, Faye thought. Not to mention chilled.

Summer had yet to visit the soggy streets of London, and no one had stirred a fire in the hearth an arm's length to Faye's left. The hearth that housed a secret compartment where one could hide, a compartment where she rather longed to closet herself away so she could no longer see Shaleena's demmed pointy . . .

"And what of you, Mrs. Nettles?" Lord Gallo's voice broke through Faye's reverie with a jolt, though, in actuality, she'd been watching him the whole while. Far better even to concentrate on the man in their midst than to stare agog at Shaleena's oversized . . .

"Do you still feel prepared to take on this mission?"

Panic struck her like a bolt of lightning. *Mission? There was a mission? What mission?* Had she agreed . . . But yes. Of course she had, even though she was as mad as a wild hare. Or, perhaps, because of—

"Mrs. Nettles?" Gallo said again, and Faye focused with an effort, calming her mind before something went awry, lifting the delicate teacup carefully from its saucer. It was hand-painted. Imported through the East India Trading Company. She took a refined sip.

"Of course, my lord," she said, pinky just so, not too stiff, not too limp. She was not, after all, a barbarian. Or so she had been told. "I shall learn who, if anyone, caused the death of Lord Brendier. All will be well."

There was a moment of silence before Madeline spoke. Some might have felt a bit of breathless anxiety in that silence. "You understand you'll be expected to speak with . . . men."

Faye kept her grip light on the cup's delicate handle, for they had been known to snap off with the slightest provocation of late. "Of course," she said, and forced a genteel smile.

"We've reason to believe a Mr. Rogan McBain may somehow be involved. It is said he visited

Brendier some hours before the baron was found dead," Madeline added.

God help me. "Valuable information," Faye said.

Madeline's lovely brow furrowed a little. "McBain is thought to be something of an intimidating character. He was a decorated lieutenant."

"Ahh."

"And there are rumors that he killed someone in a duel some years back. A Mr. Winden, I believe."

"Then I shall certainly avoid drawing pistols at dawn."

Madeline's scowl deepened. "So that's acceptable to—"

"Oh for Christ's sake!" hissed Shaleena, and jerked to her feet. Her bosoms bobbled as she pointed a finger at the fireplace. Flames popped like firecrackers on the nearby logs.

Startled from her carefully varnished pretenses, Faye jumped, nearly jerking out of her chair. Shaleena laughed.

"I'm sorry, little witch, did I frighten you?"

For a moment, terror ran rampant in Faye's soul, riding roughshod over her senses, firing up ashy memories, but she forced herself to remain as she was, forced her lips to move, her grip to loosen.

"Not at all. I'm simply—"

"What?" Shaleena asked, and laughed again. "Frightened out of your wits? I'm sorry if my little bit of magic startled you. But that's what Les Chausettes do. That's what all those who are gifted do," she said, and swept her hand sideways to encompass the handful of others who occupied Lavender House's elegant parlor. "We freeze and concoct and *enflame*," she said, and, lifting her arm again, made the fire burst dramatically upward.

Faye felt her heart thunder in her chest, but when Madeline spoke, her tone evidenced no tension whatsoever.

"Yes, that's very nice, Shaleena. You may well equal Ella's pyrotechnics if you continue in your studies, but we did not call this meeting to enjoy your fire show. Indeed, there was something else entirely we hoped—"

"I will challenge your sister," Shaleena hissed through clenched teeth, "to a match of powers anytime she wishes to humiliate herself and prove to everyone—"

"We have hired a gardener," interrupted Lord Gallo. All eyes turned to him. His tone, Faye noticed, was somehow bland but assertive all at once.

"A gardener?" questioned Darla. She was not the oldest of the witches, yet her hair, hip length and swaying with a life of its own, was as silver as mercury. "Do you think it wise to bring another into the fold? We have already welcomed the boy named Cur and—"

"Cur!" Shaleena snapped, and turned sharply away, red hair bouncing over fleshy buttocks.

"Have there been troubles with the boy?" asked Gallo, skimming the faces of the women before him.

"No," Darla said. "He's . . . impetuous at times."

"I'm rather fond of him," Beatrice said. But Bea had an unearthly bond with the beasts of the field, so it made some sense.

"He's quite gifted," said Heddy. She looked like nothing so much as someone's grandmother. Few suspected the astounding physical strength she could conjure. "For a young male, he is marvelously—"

"Gifted! What can he do?" Shaleena stormed.

"He has quite a talent for changing his voice."

"Voice. Any jackanapes in Cheapside could do as much," she argued, and grabbed a fistful of locks near her left breast. "He set my hair on fire."

There was a moment of stunned silence.

"Well, I believe that answers your question, then," Madeline said.

"I don't want him here," Shaleena rasped.

"His visits are sporadic at most," Madeline said. "And as you said, this house is for the gifted. Surely you can accept—"

"I *cannot* accept. Either he goes or—"

"I would recommend caution," Gallo said. His voice was almost inaudible, yet it seemed as distinct as sunrise.

Shaleena turned to him with a snarl. "He can barely invoke the simplest of spells."

"Perhaps you've yet to learn all there is to know of our young friend."

"He is not my friend. Indeed, I am not entirely

certain he's human. There's something . . . disturbing about him. What good is he to us?"

"What good were you when first you came to us, Shaleena?" Gallo asked, and for the first time in her memory, Faye saw Shaleena falter, but she rallied quickly.

"Even then my powers were clear. You said as much yourself."

"And I am saying the same of the boy. He's searching for understanding. For a family of sorts that will—"

"Family!" Shaleena spat, and laughed. "What are you trying to tell us, Jasper? That he's your newly discovered by-blow?"

Perhaps Lord Gallo's mouth pinched the slightest degree; but if he was angry, he showed no more signs than that. "I am saying some compassion might be in order. Most of you were well aware of the source of your powers long before you could control them. Is that not so?"

"Grandmother's abilities were far different than mine," Beatrice said. "But she was clearly gifted." Others nodded. Faye remained silent. Conjuring memories was a dangerous thing these days.

"Cur was a foundling," Madeline said.

She and Lord Gallo had been wed less than two full years, but they worked well as a team. "He has no idea of his heritage. No way of knowing—"

"Then he's among the lucky few," Shaleena said, "for family . . ." She stopped abruptly, teeth clenched.

"What of family?" Madeline asked softly, but Shaleena raised her chin, defiant in the face of would-be compassion.

"He's had fair warning to stay clear of my path," she said.

"Very well then," Gallo said, and, rising to his feet, touched his bride's shoulder, his hand almost hidden from view, as if he had no wish to be thought affectionate but could no longer bear the distance from her. "Then let us discuss the gardener."

"I only worry about exposing ourselves to too much scrutiny," Darla said. "Thus far we have got on with a minimum of outside interference, and I would—"

"I think it a fine idea," Shaleena said, and tossed her hair with vicious verve over her shoulder. "It will be pleasant having a true man about. He *will* do more than trim the hedges, won't he?" she asked, raising one brow in a suggestive manner.

"He seems capable of a good deal," Gallo said dryly. He had long ago become adept at maneuvering the battlefields of conversation. "We have planned for him to care for the stables and act as driver as well."

"Ahh, an accomplished man," Shaleena said, preening as she glanced at Madeline. It had been abundantly clear for some time that Shaleena had set her cap for Lord Gallo. Gallo's burgeoning interest in the soft-spoken Madeline, however, had come as something of a surprise. "How refreshing."

"Can we trust him?" Darla asked.

"We would not consider him otherwise," Madeline said. "As I'm sure you're aware, Jasper has a way of sensing these things."

Heddy scowled. "Are you saying this gardener is gifted?" Lord Gallo's ability to "feel" power was what had gained him the unenviable task of gathering the members of the coven, of guiding them, though he claimed no real powers of his own.

"A small amount, perhaps," Gallo said. "He seems to have the ability to change his appearance somewhat?"

"How unusual," Darla said, "that we would find *two* gifted males at once."

"It is indeed rare," Gallo admitted.

"Unprecedented here at Lavender House," Ivy said. She was tall and willowy, with a round face and pretty eyes.

"I don't care if it's unheard of in all of Christendom," Shaleena said. "I am only interested in his . . ." She slanted her gaze toward Faye. "How shall I say this without making our little faerie there swoon? *Physical* nature," she said finally. "Tell me, Madeline, is this gardener handsome?"

"I believe you may have met him in the past," Gallo said.

"Truly?" Shaleena sounded intrigued. "Well . . . I've nothing against old lovers so long as they know their—"

"He calls himself Joseph. I believe he might be Hungarian. Or Rom. As you may remember, he was Madeline's butler for the short while she lived apart from—"

But Shaleena stopped him with a hiss.

Faye turned to her in astonishment, for even from Shaleena, she had never heard such vehemence.

"Is something amiss?" Gallo asked.

"Why would you invite that foreigner here?" Shaleena's violet eyes narrowed in her alabaster face.

"Because he was brought to us," Gallo said. "And he needs a place in the world."

"Find him another place."

"What have you against him?" Gallo asked.

Shaleena shook her head, eyes wild. "There is something about him."

"Something . . ."

"Dark. Evil."

Gallo's usually implacable expression evidenced the slightest hint of curiosity. "What makes you think—"

"Hah!" she crowed. "And you are supposed to be the one who knows these things. Who *feels* these things. The one chosen by the committee to care for us."

Silence erupted in the room, but Lord Gallo had already recovered from his overt display of emotion. "Feel free to broach my regrettable shortcomings with the committee if ever you feel there's a need," he said.

She glared at him for a seeming eternity. "Keep him from my sight," she hissed, and, turning, stormed from the room.

Silence fell around them.

"Well," Madeline said finally. "Are there any other concerns?"

There were none, other than Faye's fervent wish that she *truly* belonged among Les Chausettes. Wished she possessed a fourth of Shaleena's fire. A smidgen of Madeline's wisdom. A nugget of Heddy's strength. Good heavens, she'd settle for Darla's *hair*. For she knew beyond a shadow of a doubt that she could not complete the mission set before her. Not now. Not ever.

Chapter 1

"**M**rs. Nettles, you say."

"Yes," Faye said, and almost managed a smile though the ballroom milled like a chaotic whirligig about her. "I believe I heard you speak of Lord Brendier's death."

The golden-haired gentleman raised his brows, rocking back on his heel to skim his gaze down the tangerine flow of her gown. "I am Lord Rennet, Baron of Siltberth, but all my corky friends call me Lord Rex." He tilted toward her with a conspiratorial air. "What shall I call you, my dulcet dove?"

Every burning instinct demanded that Faye hit the pretty lord with a chair and make a dash for the nearest exit, but sometimes her instincts were wrong. They certainly had been with Tenning. For months without end she had believed he wanted the best for her. That he cherished her as a daughter of sorts. That he kept her locked away for her own protection. Perhaps she was equally mistaken this time. "Mrs. Nettles," she said, and he smiled jauntily as if she'd said something vastly amusing.

"So tell me, Mrs. Nettles, did *Mr.* Nettles accompany you?"

"No," she said, and felt relief sluice through her; the truth was ever a balm for her nerves. "Lord Brendier . . ." she urged, impressing herself, if none other, with the steady, almost prissy sound of her own voice.

"Ahh yes. 'Tis a terrible tragedy. You know that his opponent, a Mr. Daimmen, I believe, died on the spot," said Rennet. "I am still reeling from the news."

Faye stilled the tremble of her hands, let the innocuous lies buffet her, and reminded herself that none knew her dark secrets. To those of the glittering *ton* she was naught but what she appeared to be. A wealthy widow, well dressed, perfectly coifed, refined. Her high-waisted lawn gown hid the unsteadiness of her knees just as effectively as the tulle lace above her bodice veiled the pounding of her heart. "You knew him well then?"

"Indeed, yes." Rennet drank from the silver flask he had drawn from an inner pocket of his carefully fitted tailcoat. He was an attractive man, she supposed. Stylishly dressed and immaculately groomed. He was also a liar. Rich and shallow and terrifying. But who among this assemblage was not?

For a moment she was once again tempted to

scan the mob that crowded Mrs. Tell's ballroom like burrowing ants, but she did not, for she was certain Rogan McBain had not yet come. She would notice his arrival, know him by the pewter brooch pinned to his lapel.

"We were dearest friends," Rennet continued, but it was another lie. Faye felt it like a pinprick to her temple.

"You were present for the duel then?" she asked.

"For the duel? Indeed not," he said, and executed a delicate shudder, which shook even his elegant hands. His hair was thick, golden, and carefully brushed away from his brow. His eyes were blue and bright and false. "Had I known his intent, I would surely have warned against such a bag of moonshine."

"You think duels foolish things?" she asked.

"Lady Mullen—*Charlotte*—has proposed to do away with them forever."

"Lady Mullen?"

"Surely you've heard the phrase, 'mild as Mullen.' 'Tis said she's ever so kindly and quite pretty. But it's her autumn fetes that have made her famous. They're most instrumental in raising funds each year for the Foundling Hospital. At any rate, she abhors duels ever since her husband was killed some years ago."

"Thus you abhor them, too?"

"Most certainly," he said, then grinned sheepishly, flashing perfect teeth as he leaned infinitesimally nearer. "If you're going to get yourself winged in the process."

"So Lord Brendier was only struck in the . . ." she began, but suddenly her eyes caught a flash of metal. Or maybe it was more subliminal than that. Maybe she didn't notice the man's brooch at all. Maybe it was his eyes, as gray and somber as a wolf's. Maybe it was his steely expression, or his clenched hands—or his sheer size!

He stood in the doorway, towering over his contemporaries, and there was nothing Faye could do but stare, breath caught in her throat, heart pounding like a trapped animal's. And suddenly all her refinement, all her careful training sloughed away like water from a gargoyle's roaring maw, and she was young again. Young and small, with Lucifer's heavy footfalls pounding on the forest floor behind her.

She spun about, ready to flee, to run as she always had. To beg for forgiveness. But something caught her arm. She stifled a scream.

"Mrs. Nettles," Rennet said, and a modicum of sanity settled into her reeling brain. "Are you quite well?"

She nodded once, though every quivering instinct insisted that she escape. Sheer power of will allowed her to stay, though the nape of her neck was already damp with chilled perspiration. She should have thought to bring a handkerchief, but she had never yet remembered one, though she perspired like a Thoroughbred when nervous.

"You look as if you've seen a ghost."

Not a ghost. He was real. Would always be real. At least in her mind.

"You're as pale as alum."

Behind her, the bewigged orchestra played a sweeping waltz, but it only sounded discordant to her pounding head. Conversation swirled around her as elegant couples gossiped and conversed, flirted and lied.

She could feel the deceit boiling around her like acid.

Her captor tilted his golden head at her and smiled. "Perhaps you should lie down."

Off to Faye's left, a man bellowed a laugh. The noise sounded maniacal, echoing in her brain.

"There are empty beds aplenty above stairs," he said, and winked. "Not that I would know."

She'd been a fool to pretend she was prepared for this. A fool to pretend she would *ever* be prepared.

"Perhaps you are overwhelmed by my manly charms," he said.

She should answer. That much she knew. She should smile, converse. Perhaps flirt a bit. It was far more likely she'd turn into a speckled rock and fall off the face of the earth.

Across the room, the giant stood alone, surveying the room. His eyes were deep-set and intense, his hair sable, his skin dark. And his body . . . Beneath the midnight green of his fitted coat, his shoulders looked as wide as a carriage, his thighs as broad as cannons. How the devil had she ever thought she would be able to approach him?

Her captor laughed. The sound was happy, lighthearted.

She stifled a wince, knowing she should emulate that gaiety. Should laugh, tease, *lie.* She managed an arched brow. When scared witless, try haughty; it was, perhaps, Madeline's most practical advice.

"Perchance some fresh air is in order," Rennet said, and, clearing his throat, steered her toward the open double doors.

But just as she turned, *he* found her, speared her with his eyes, caught her. She felt the contact like a strike to her heart.

"Tell me, Mrs. Nettles, where *is* Mr. Nettles?" She heard Rennet's words like nothing more than a mumble in her mind, for the giant Scot was watching her. Did he know she'd been sent to ferret out his secrets? Did he know already that she suspected him?

"Mrs. Nettles?"

"Yes?" She yanked her gaze from McBain and pulled her tattered decorum around her like a cloak.

"Your husband—"

"Is dead." It was part of the story she'd been given. The story she'd painstakingly memorized. "Drowned."

"I am—"

"Fell through the ice while returning to our modest but happy home in Imatra."

Rennet drew a deep breath. They were still moving toward the doors. Beyond the arched portals, the darkness of the garden called to her. "So you're a widow."

Across the room, the giant stepped toward her.

Panic reared inside her, striking with flinty hooves, but Rennet had a hold on her arm, and she dare not bolt. Dare not cause trouble. Not again. Not after the oboist. But how was she supposed to know woodwinds would make such an ungodly racket when they were mysteriously flung into the percussionists behind them? She'd only been trying to escape a madman. Or perhaps he had just been a suitor. It was so demmed hard to tell.

"Here we are. Hold up now," Rennet said, tugging her to a halt, and she managed, just barely, to remain where she was, for the greatest threat seemed to be behind her. The noise, the lies, the peopled, opulent ballroom looming like an ogre in the background.

Here, the gardens stretched quietly around her, garbed in vast, soothing darkness, dappled with compassion, imbued with hope. Faye filled her lungs and tugged her arm carefully from her self-appointed escort's. The minty scent of pennyroyal calmed her, drew her in, enticed her to step deeper into the darkness, to drink in the night, to let it shiver across her senses. It was quiet here, away from the madness of the crowd. Thick, contented hedges grew in a curved row. Blooming vines twined cozily over arched arbors, and potted palms stood sentry atop the stone wall to her right.

"Forgive me. I fear I've been quite rude," said Rennet and eyeing her, took another sip from his flask. It gleamed dully in the moonlight. "I should have thought to bring you out of doors as soon as you began looking as if you were about to swoon."

She glanced toward the lighted doorway behind her. No demons poured out to devour her. Indeed, the yawning entrance was empty, but that hardly meant she was safe. "I was not about to swoon." Perhaps.

"Ahh, how disappointing," he said. "I do so love to catch angels as they fall."

Maybe McBain hadn't even seen her. Perhaps he had been looking at another, and it was simply her own "highly developed survival skills," as Madeline called them, that had made it seem as if he were bearing down on her like a wolf on its prey.

"That was a compliment," Rennet said, and, grinning, bent slightly at the knees to look directly into her eyes. "Deserving of a smile. You *can* smile, can't you?"

"Yes," she said, and scowled a little, trying to remember what she had planned to ask Rennet should the opportunity present itself.

"Good." His lips quirked up even more. He was probably charming, but she had known such men in the past. Tenning had been as cultured as a pearl, lavishing her with gifts, with compliments. There was, after all, a reason for her fears; she wasn't completely mad. Perhaps.

"I simply do *not*," she said, and dared him to think her eccentric. Better that than the truth.

Rennet stared at her for a moment, then, "You don't . . . smile."

"Not generally."

"How do you feel about laughter?"

It was often false and therefore made her head pound like a smithy's rounding hammer. She knew it was strange. Good God, she knew *she* was strange. No one had to tell her. But they had. Though the vernacular changed: odd, gifted, magical. It all meant the same thing.

"So, you don't smile, and you don't laugh," he surmised. "What *do* you do, then, Mrs. Nettles. When you are not setting men agog with your astounding beauty?"

"I . . ." *What? Tried to forget? Tried to remember? Tried to survive?* "I . . . read a good deal."

"Read?" His brows were raised again, his lips quirked up in an expression that some might find beguiling. But she wasn't beguiled. Terrified, maybe. A little nauseous. But definitely not beguiled.

"Yes."

"And what does a rare beauty like you read? Sonnets to match your beautiful countenance?"

"The *Times* mostly," she said and glanced

toward the house again, lest someone spurt from the doorway and pounce on her. "Politics. But journals too."

"Journals."

"Yes." It was why she was here, after all. Why she had forced herself from Lavender House, her home, her sanctuary. Because there was evil. And perhaps Madeline was right. Perhaps she could make it better. Negate a bit of the sort of pain she herself had caused.

"What kind of journals?"

"Those regarding battles mostly," she said, and glanced behind her once again.

"Ahh . . ." He laughed. "A bloodthirsty little pixie are you?"

She snapped her eyes to his. Wondering if he could somehow sense the truth in her. Wondering if he was right.

"Not at all," she said, and hoped to God he couldn't hear the terror in her voice. "I am merely interested in the goings-on of the world."

"Good God, you're not one of those dreaded bluestockings, are you?" he asked, drinking again, and at that, she almost *did* smile. For that was exactly what Les Chausettes were.

Of course, they were also witches.

"As I said, I'm merely interested," she repeated.

"Well really, lovey, I would think you could find something more intriguing than all those ghastly battles."

She raised a brow at him. "Such as?"

His grin cocked up. He reached for her hand. She was tempted to step back, but there would be little point. The stone wall was only inches away. She had nowhere to go, thus she stood very still, letting him encircle her cold fingers with the heat of his. "Are you certain you were once wed?"

"Why do you ask? What—" she began, but managed to stop herself. He was only teasing, after all. Thinking himself clever. Therefore, she must stick to the story she'd been told time and again: She was the widow of a wealthy merchant, now self-sufficient, able to make her own way in the world.

But there were days she could barely manage to piece together two coherent sentences. Today would not be one of those days though. It would not.

"Quite certain. He was called . . ." she began, but suddenly the fictional name was gone. Completely erased from her mind.

"*Mr.* Nettles?" he guessed.

"Albert," she said, remembering suddenly and managing to imbue her tone with a smidgen of wryness for his foolish wit.

He lifted her hand to his lips. Panic spurred through her as he kissed her knuckles, but she didn't yank her arm away. Didn't scream. Didn't even kick him in the groin, though she had been trained to do just that should the situation call for it. Surely such restraint was a reason for some pride, but she could feel that restraint crumbling, and covered with words.

"He was seven-and-twenty," she said. "Born the third day of June in the year of our Lord, 1782. Died on January twenty-first, 1807. He inherited his father's shipping business five years before. He had no brothers. His sisters were named Edna and Ivadel."

"Indeed," Rennet said, and kissed the underside of her wrist. But there was something funny about the way he spoke. Almost as if he were amused.

She winced but held steady, stifling the fear.

"He had fair hair, blue eyes, and stood five feet, nine inches in his stocking feet."

He kissed the inside of her elbow and glanced up. "I myself am a bit taller then," he said. "But that's hardly the true measure of a man, is it?"

"I believe one would have to take his mass into consideration as well," she said, and glanced about, hoping to God that Madeline was near. Or Ella. Or any of her coven sisters. Anyone to wrest her from this pounding misery.

"I believe we both know what matters to a woman."

If only that were true. "Do we?"

He laughed, low and private. "It's length, not height," he said, and, stepping up close, pressed his crotch against her thigh.

Terror shot through her, paralyzing her throat. She tried to yank away, but he held her arm.

"Or is it girth that concerns you?"

"Only if it fastens my saddle," she said, and he laughed.

"A witty minx, aren't you?"

"Absolutely." Her voice sounded breathy. "But I fear I must go now."

"Go? Don't be silly. The night is young. Young and beautiful. Like you," he said, and wrapped an arm about her back.

"Release me." She tried to jerk back, but a hedge was to her right, the wall behind her.

"Come now, don't be so standoffish. I understand you might be shy after . . ." He leaned back, but still held her hips to his. "How long has it been since your husband's passing?"

"Please—" she began, and he laughed.

"I love it when women beg," he said. "Try this, 'deeper Rex. Harder.' "

Terror wafted over her in deep shades of the past. "I'll be of no use if I'm defiled," she rasped.

"What?"

"I'll . . ." she began, but fragments of reality came drifting back. She was no longer a child. No longer bound. No longer defenseless and scared and used like a weapon to ruin the lives of others. "Release me," she said again and tried with all her might to inflict her voice with the gruffness Ella could conjure on command. But she did not have that lady's astounding gifts. Only unpredictable powers of her own.

"Never fear," he said, and kissed her neck. "I shall make certain it is as pleasant for you as it is for—" he began, but suddenly he was ripped away, torn from her as if a strong wind had taken him.

One minute he was standing before her. The next he was stretched out beside the wall like a tossed caber.

And in his place was Rogan McBain. His eyes struck her like a lance, freezing her to the ground.

He knew the truth! She could see it in his ungodly eyes. He had heard that she suspected him and had come to silence her.

He loomed over her in the darkness, shoulders so broad they shadowed the moonlight, blocked her escape.

Panic sliced her, ripping through her reality, throwing her into turmoil. She reached for the wall, longing for support. She had no wish to harm anyone. No wish, and yet the potted palm flew from the ledge like a launched cannonball.

The clay pot struck the Highlander directly in the face. He staggered backward, but she didn't wait to see if he'd fall. Didn't wait to see if he'd follow. Instead, she fled, leaping past him, scrambling like a hunted hare through the pennyroyal and away.

Chapter 2

"You what?"

"You what?"

Lord and Lady Gallo sat very still, watching Faye as if she had suddenly sprouted fangs. They'd remained in the evening finery they had worn to Lady Tell's, he in his formfitting breeches and cutaway coat, she in the powder blue gown that flattered her comely figure and contrasted nicely with the ivory divan occupying the north wall of the parlor. Beside it, a scrolled hatrack reached toward the ceiling, bearing a trio of frilly chapeaus.

Despite its somewhat unorthodox uses, including mock battles and conjuring spells, it was an extremely elegant room. Still, for a moment, Faye was tempted almost beyond control to hide beneath the delicate Queen Anne chair in which she sat. That, however, might be considered a bit odd for a woman her age. Thus, she straightened her back, cleared her throat, and glanced toward the hearth with the hidden compartment.

Stopping in the doorway to Faye's left, Shaleena glanced in, then smirked and entered. Faye refrained from closing her eyes, though the other was sky-clad yet again.

"I struck him with a potted plant," she said, for the truth was too seductive to be ignored. It drew her, pulled at her, though she managed to refrain from admitting that she had not meant to harm the towering Scot. Failure to control one's powers was a serious threat to all of Les Chausettes. "A fan palm, I believe."

"But—" Lord Gallo began.

"Why?" Madeline finished.

Shaleena chuckled.

"I simply . . ." Faye shot her gaze to Shaleena, then dropped her attention to her hands. The knuckles looked rather pale. "I'm not entirely certain," she said, and loosened her grip somewhat.

"Not certain." Lord Gallo's voice was steady but low, so perhaps Faye only imagined the frustration in it.

"I believed him to be . . . evil, " Faye said, and indeed, he had seemed to be the very embodiment of Tenning's threats. He seemed to be Lucifer himself, come to find her once again.

Shaleena smirked as she sauntered nearer. "Better evil than scared out of your wits," she said.

"Shaleena," said Lord Gallo.

"I'm not scared," Faye said, but her voice was faint. Even the least gifted would know she was lying.

"You're a timid little field mouse who doesn't—"

"Shaleena." Gallo said again. He never raised his voice. Indeed, his tone rarely varied, but his warning vibrated through the house. "Leave this room."

"I'll not—" Shaleena began, but he stopped her.

"This moment or forever," he said. There was finality in his tone, firmness in his expression.

Naked and angry, she left.

Faye fiddled with a fold in her skirt. The silence was as heavy as ash. "She does *own* clothes, does she not?"

"Yes," Madeline said, and let the corner of a smile shine through for a moment.

Lord Gallo muttered something. Faye couldn't quite decipher it, but it almost sounded like a curse, which was ridiculous, of course, because Lord Gallo did *not* curse. Not when out and about. But not in the privacy of Lavender House either. And that fascinated her. For in her experience, men were often entirely different in private than in public. Tenning had treated her like a coddled child when with others. Like his cherished pet. None knew the atrocities he forced her to perform. Just as none seemed to know of the beast he kept in his employ. Lucifer, he called him. Lucifer would come for her if she did not obey, if she did not garner the secrets he wished to know of others.

"I beg your pardon?" she asked softly, but he stood and turned away.

"Perhaps we should return to the business at hand," Madeline suggested, not glancing at her husband.

Faye stopped her fiddling and forced herself to sit still.

"Maybe you could explain to us why you felt the need to strike Lord McBain with a potted palm."

"As I've said, I believed him to be evil."

Lord Gallo lifted the teapot from its place on the sideboard, freshened his wife's cup, then seated himself again. Faye glanced at him and forced herself to relax. Though she had spent more than four years under his protection, his nearness still made her twitchy. But perhaps he was aware of that fact. Perhaps that was why he tended to remain in the background during these discussions.

"And what brought you to that conclusion?" Madeline asked.

Memories slid up Faye's spine like phantom wisps of smoke, but they were not memories she would share. Not today. Not ever. "He's . . ." she began, and felt her throat freeze up.

"A man?" Madeline supplied. and Faye zipped her gaze to Lord Gallo and away. "Is that why?" Her voice was quiet.

"You yourself said he may be involved in Brendier's death," Faye said.

"We know the Scot paid the baron a visit shortly before his death," Madeline said. "But that hardly proves culpability."

"No, of course not," Faye agreed, nerves tangling. "But he's . . ." She stopped herself.

"A man?" Madeline asked again.

Faye remained silent a moment, but finally forced herself to speak. "It seems likely," she said.

"Faerie Faye . . ." There was humor in Madeline's voice, but perhaps there was more. Disappointment maybe. The possibility steeped Faye with a soft infusion of sadness. "Not all men are evil."

Faye shifted her gaze to Lord Gallo again. The sight of him made her stomach twist. "I realize that."

"Do you?"

She dragged her attention back to Maddy. "I know it in my head."

Madeline smiled as she crouched beside Faye's chair and reached for her hand.

"But not your heart."

Faye refrained from flittering her attention to Gallo again. "I'm having a little trouble convincing my stomach, too."

Madeline laughed.

"And what did your stomach tell you about McBain?"

"He was large," she breathed.

"He was that," Madeline agreed, and there was something in her voice that made Faye search the older woman's eyes.

"You do not think large a bad thing?"

"Well . . ." Madeline seemed flustered suddenly. Almost embarrassed. "Not in every . . . I mean, no. Not necessarily."

Faye nodded. She could learn. She could change. She was sure of it. "I'm sorry. Truly I am. I know I should not have injured him."

"That's not our concern. Not principally, at any rate," Madeline said. "I doubt you did him any great harm. He's built like a stone garrison, after all. Legs like pillars. And did you notice—"

Lord Gallo cleared his throat. He was scowling a little, a rare expression on his usually stoic countenance. A mischievous smile almost seemed to flit across his wife's classic features. "The point is, you cannot simply strike men whenever they frighten you," he said.

"Yes," Madeline agreed, but there was something in her eyes again. That intriguing spark of mischief as if she were playing some sort of incomprehensible game with her standoffish husband. "That is exactly what I meant to say."

"But neither do we want you to take undue risks," he added.

"Also true," Madeline said. "Was there some reason you felt particularly at risk?"

The truth trembled on Faye's tongue, but she held it there. Hid it there, though the similarities between Lucifer and the Scot loomed in her trembling soul. "It occurred to me . . ." Quite recently. This very instant, in fact. "That perhaps Luci . . ." She stopped herself, searching wildly for his name. "Mr. . . ." What was it? MacDoom? MacDeath? Mac . . .

"McBain," Madeline said.

"Yes." What was wrong with her? She had the social skills of a shrew mouse. "Perhaps Mr. McBain struck Lord Rennet to keep him from speaking to me."

Now they were both scowling at her.

She refrained from clearing her throat. "That is to say, if Lu . . . Mr. McBain is, in fact, the murderer, and Rennet knows something of his crimes, then would it not make sense for him to try to keep the other quiet?"

"By knocking him unconscious," Jasper said.

Faye nodded.

"However," Madeline said, "it would also make sense for McBain to strike if he were attempting to protect you from some perceived threat."

"Protect—" Somehow, in the near hour since the garden incident, Faye had never considered such a possibility.

"As Lord Gallo protects you," Madeline added.

"But—" It wasn't possible. That wasn't how the world worked, Faye thought, then skimmed her gaze to Lord Gallo. He sat perfectly still, watching her. And for the hundredth time she wondered why he had found her. Why he had brought her here. To teach her, he said. To help her. And maybe it was true. Maybe. For never had he touched her or gained a farthing at her expense. Not in all the months since he had brought her to Laver '

House. Still, some men had patience. No souls. But patience.

"But what?" Madeline asked.

"I do not think that was his intent," she said.

"And why is that?"

She shook her head, trying to explain without explaining. "He was so . . . large."

"Indeed," Maddy agreed, leaning closer conspiratorially. "Did you happen to notice the width of his—"

"I believe we've already discussed his size at some length," Lord Gallo said, and Faye skittered her gaze to him.

Gallo was not a large man, though sometimes he seemed so. Large and intimidating, but his bride had never shown even a modicum of fear where he was concerned. Indeed, at the moment she almost seemed to be enjoying the unfamiliar terseness in his tone.

"Big does not equate bad," Madeline said. "You must remember that."

"Sometimes it does," her husband argued, and now she laughed out loud though she didn't turn toward him.

"They are not one and the same, Faerie Faye. Therefore . . ." Maddy paused, maybe to think, maybe for dramatic emphasis, but if that was the case, the pause was hardly necessary for her next words fairly knocked the air from Faye's constricted lungs. "You must go to him and apologize."

"What?" Faye rasped.

"I don't know if—" Gallo began, but Madeline held up her hand, halting his objections.

"You struck a perfect stranger for no good reason."

"I doubt he's—"

"Not a genteel slap, mind. You hit him in the face with a potted plant."

"A palm," Faye whispered, though even in her own mind she wasn't certain why that made a difference.

"For no good reason," Madeline added. "A celebrated soldier who might very well have been trying to save you."

Faye scowled, saying nothing, but it would have hardly mattered if she had. She was certain she would not have been heard over the erratic pounding of her heart.

"Rennet was trying to take liberties, was he not?" Madeline's voice had softened.

Faye managed a nod.

"He'd drawn you out into the darkness of the garden."

And the darkness had been lovely. It was the pretty golden baron she'd found frightening. But not as frightening as the towering Highlander. Never that frightening.

"Were you trying to escape?" Madeline asked. Her voice was little more than a murmur, as if she loathed belaboring the point. And yet she did.

Faye nodded again, desperately wanting the entire episode behind her.

"Did you tell him to stop?"

"Yes." Her throat felt tight. She couldn't look up, knowing she was not to blame yet feeling in the very depths of her being that she *was*.

"Might the Scotsman have heard you?"

She thought about that for a moment, tried to swallow her fear. "Perhaps."

The room went quiet, then, "Faerie Faye," Madeline murmured.

Faye forced her gaze to her mentor . . . to her hero.

"Have you forgotten that you made us a vow?" Her chest ached.

"You said you would become a full member of this coven. That you would embrace your powers, work for good, find the man who murdered Lord Brendier."

"I know," she whispered.

"Brendier was well thought of by the committee," Madeline said, "and we've no way of knowing what might have caused his death."

"Perhaps he truly did die of the wounds sustained in the duel."

"Perhaps, but we cannot go to the committee until we've exhausted every possibility. It is they who fund Lavender House, after all. Indeed, they hold this sisterhood in the palms of their hands."

"Perhaps Shaleena could go to his estate," Faye said, suddenly hopeful. "Touch his belongings and divine—"

"Brendier has been dead for more than a week

now. His killer's imprint, if indeed he left one, has grown cold. Besides, Lady Onyx has been . . ." She shook her head and scowled. "Unpredictable of late."

It was true. During the last few months, she seemed less focused. And even though she was still as sharp-edged as a saber, at times Faye would see her staring into space. Or stranger still, Shaleena would stare at Cur. Not in that way she stared at other men, as if she intended to devour them whole. But as if she was thinking, remembering. True, Cur was young, not yet twenty years of age. Still, that had not curtailed Shaleena's flirtations in the past. And it had certainly not caused her to remain clothed.

"What of Ella?" Faye asked.

"My nephew is not yet walking, and Ella is a mother even before she is a witch."

"Rosemond then. Or Heddy or—"

"The committee is counting on you," Madeline said, and the room, always so comfortable, always her haven, suddenly felt too small. "*I* am counting on you," she added, and Faye caught her gaze. Her mentor's eyes were solemn, as green as smooth-cut emeralds and wise beyond Faye's wildest hopes. "You are stronger than you know," she said, and, rising smoothly to her feet, left the room.

Not half an hour passed before Jasper turned down the gas on the bedchamber lights and eased onto the mattress behind Madeline.

She remained as she was, staring dismally at the wall in front of her, worry gnawing her gut like a rabid hound. "Was I too harsh with her?" she asked.

Jasper sighed. "You are the one who insists she is stronger than we realize. That she has yet to trust her own powers."

She rolled onto her back and found his face in the darkness. He had a beautiful face. But it was not necessarily his best feature. Not when he was naked, as he was now.

"Maybe I was wrong," she said, and refused to be distracted by his chest or his arms or his other attributes, equally astounding but not quite so visible. "Maybe I pushed her too hard. After all, the mission is . . ."

"Simply a means of coaxing little Faye to realize her potential?"

She covered her eyes with her hand. "What have I done?"

"I believe you have forced her to face her fears."

"What if she gets hurt?"

"She already hurts," he said. "The question is, who else might be injured while she learns to control her powers."

"She's so very gifted. Much more than she knows. But her past . . ." Maddy lowered her hand, found his gaze with her own. His eyes looked old and calm, even in the darkness. "What happened to her? Why won't she tell us?"

He touched her face, etching her cheek as if memorizing the lines. "*You* rarely speak of the past."

She closed her eyes to the feel of his fingers against her skin. "It's too terrible," she said. "Her past, it's too awful to face, isn't it?"

"She's here with us now," he said, and swept a lock of hair behind her ear. Feelings, soft and mellow, skittered like rainbows along the course taken by his magical fingertips.

"Because of you," she said.

He smiled a little, that rare gem of contentment that made her world right. Safe. "I brought her here. She stayed because of you."

Turning onto her side, she kissed his fingers. "Thank you," she said.

"For what?"

Tears blurred her vision. "For saving her. For saving Ella." She closed her eyes to the memories, to the pain.

"The committee pays me to find the most gifted," he said. "You know that."

"*I* was not the most gifted," she murmured, and opened her eyes, finding him in the darkness. Finding peace.

"Perhaps not then," he said.

"I can never repay you," she whispered, and at her words his ancient eyes grew more solemn still.

"You have already given me more—" he began, but she placed a finger to his lips, stopping him.

"I *want* to repay you," she said, and ran her hand down his chest. It was as hard and smooth as glass. Strong and dark and beautiful.

"Ahh, well . . ." His words were little more than a sigh. "If you must."

She moved closer, felt his desire shift against her. "I must."

"Though I suppose it will not be as pleasant for you as if I were as large as say . . . . a Scotsman."

She smiled at the lovely edge of jealousy in his voice. She supposed she was petty. She also supposed she didn't care. It had taken him years to reveal any emotion at all, and she could not help enjoying watching his eyes darken, hearing his breathing change. "Ahh, McBain," she said, and sighed.

"God help us," he groused, shifting away, and she laughed as she wrapped her hand around him, capturing his full attention

"I wouldn't trade you for a dozen Scots," she murmured, and kissed the corner of his mouth.

"Are you certain?" he asked.

"Unless they were as large as—" she began, but in that moment he kissed her, making her forget that Scotsmen even existed.

Chapter 3

Rogan McBain's eye was throbbing.

He stood alone in the kitchen of his rented town house and gazed out on the street below. The sun was just now rising from its rosy slumber. The time that always made him introspective.

Perhaps he should not have returned to London. He had seen enough trouble here in the past, and God knew he didn't belong amid the preening *ton*. Hell, he barely belonged *indoors*. But where *was* he to be these days? He had been a lieutenant in His Majesty's Army for more years than he cared to count, but it was no secret that some called him the Celtic Beast.

Below him, a bright chestnut clopped past, bearing a man in a scarlet waistcoat and blue greatcoat. A Redbreast, he was called, a member of London's newest attempt to curb crime. But this city would forever revel in chaos. Perhaps the same could be said for the world at large.

Cupping his right shoulder with his left hand, Rogan rolled the joint backward, trying to alleviate the pain, but it was there to stay. One of a dozen aches to be expected after a score of years on the battlefield. The Anglo-Mysore Wars, the Battle of Boxtel, the Storming of Badajoz. He winced at the bloody rush of memories. What had those battles gained him? Gnarled scars, burning nightmares, aching limbs, and an eerie ability to sense the advent of trouble. Yet, despite his oddities, good men had died. Good soldiers and others. Innocents. And for what? So some foreign hunk of soil could be exchanged among the English hierarchy? Aye, his father had been English, but his mother's kin had been Scots to the very roots of their brawny beings. His mother's brothers, who had initiated him to battle, and who, in later years, had followed him into more than a few. His mother's brothers, who had given their lives a thousand miles from their beloved Highlands.

They should never have ventured onto Spanish soil. Should have understood the curse that stalked Rogan McBain. But they had refused to turn back. When a Celt set his mind, there was little one could do to change it.

On the street below, a scruffy lad trundled a barrow of parsnips down the darkened lane. London was forever filled with ragged children. Cheap labor, they were, and little more. Chimney sweeps, millworkers, parish apprentices. McBain winced as memories marched in.

"Bain!" Connelly's voice boomed through the house as he banged the front door shut and strode through the foray, boots rapping on hardwood as he passed through the great room, with its sparse furnishings. "Bain!" He came nearer, glanced into the narrow sitting room, then turned into the doorway of the kitchen. "What the hell happened to you?" he rasped.

"Nothing to concern yourself with," Bain said, and in that second the carefully guarded concern fled Connelly's eyes, replaced immediately with a spark of mischief as if he already guessed at the embarrassing cause of the other's pain.

McBain scowled, scrunching the skin around his damaged eye. Despite the fact that it had blossomed into a dozen vibrant colors even before he'd found his bed, he had almost forgotten its existence. Just another benefit of too many battles. Or too much introspection.

He poured tea carefully into a ridiculously small cup and lifted it to his lips. It was hotter than Hades, so he set it gently onto its matching saucer to eye his so-called friend. "She must have been something special," Bain rumbled.

Connelly gave him an arch look as he retrieved a walnut from the basket on the table and tossed it in his hand. "Who?"

"Someone else's wife," Bain guessed. Although Connelly was happy enough to share the town house's rent, he rarely spent a full night in his own bed. But neither did he generally linger elsewhere, even when there *wasn't* an angry husband involved. Which was, most probably, a rare occasion.

"Ahh, yes, well, Marguerite is a unique . . . and very umm energetic . . . woman. But . . ." He smiled at Bain's battered eye. "Don't distract me. Tell me the tale."

Nonplussed, Bain poured water from a pitcher into a basin, then squeezed the excess from a saturated rag. He had no desire to discuss the previous night, but before he could apply the cloth to his eye, Connelly had snatched it from his fingers.

"Dare I hope *you* were involved with an angry husband?" he asked.

Bain increased the intensity of his glower. "Hand over the rag, Connelly, or be gone from my sight," he growled. Introspection—who needed it?

"Sight!" Connelly laughed and waved a well-manicured hand in front of Bain's face. "Are you saying you can still see, old man?"

"Give me that," Bain said, and, snatching the rag back, put the cloth to his eye. It felt wet and cool and soothing against his heated flesh as he lowered himself into a chair, which groaned beneath his weight.

"So honestly . . ." Connelly settled his lean hips against the table, crossed his long, booted legs, and grinned happily. He was a champion at playing the dandy to the posh London crowds. "Who struck you?"

"Go sleep it off," Bain suggested, and tilted his head back against the wall behind him with a sigh.

"Or perhaps it was a *what*," mused the other tapping his cheek. He had a long face and long fingers. In fact, according to Connelly himself, everything about him was long. He stroked his chin, making a show of looking thoughtful. Generally, it was his second-most-irritating expression, the first being happiness. "But I thought trolls were just a thing of old tales."

"Why are you not yet absent?" Bain gave Connelly the evil eye from his left orb and spoke past the cloth now draped across most of his face.

"Or maybe it was an inanimate object. Might a house have struck you, my friend?"

Bain didn't respond. It was usually best not to encourage the vociferous bastard.

"Well, whatever the case, I can see that apologies are in order. It seems I should have stayed at Mrs. Tell's and looked after you, but the lovely Marguerite was not only energetic. She was *impatient* as well." He shrugged. "Still, I would have sworn it would be safe to leave you unchaperoned. None of the fashionable pinks there looked especially fearsome. But wait . . ." His voice was musing again as if he'd come upon some great insight. Bain refrained from rolling his eyes lest the right one pop from its socket and roll across the floor. He had no wish to do anything to cause Connelly that much unfettered glee. "Perhaps the culprit was the gaffer with the cane. True, he was older than the Almighty Himself. But he did look decidedly grumpy."

Bain clenched his jaw and wished to hell he'd never met Thayer Connelly, but it was damned hard to turn back the clock. Besides, the cocky Irishman had come in handy on more than one occasion. Not that Connelly didn't owe Bain. Indeed, he did, for when they'd first met, a cuckolded little Italian had been threatening to castrate the other with a hot poker. Bain might well have let the irate husband have him, but at that precise moment Bain's brigade had been a few men short, and rumor was that Connelly was fair to middlin' with a blunderbuss. The rumors had been true. Had Connelly not joined their ranks, Bain's corpse would still be rotting on some distant field. Although, at that precise instant, that possibility didn't seem to be the worst of all options. Once the mouthy Irishman learned Bain had been bested by a lass no bigger than a wood sprite, death might well seem preferable.

And how the hell had that transpired anyway? One minute Bain had been minding his own affairs, glaring out at the dance floor and the next, he'd been staggering across the garden like an inebriated Spaniard.

Memories tingled through his brain. Very well then, perhaps a little something had happened between the glaring and the staggering. Perhaps there had been a woman.

Breath caught tight in Bain's throat at the memory. For she had been more than a woman.

She had been a golden-haired angel with silken-sand cheeks and eyes like an amber promise, or so it had seemed at the time.

"But no. Hold up," Connelly was saying. "I do believe that old man was knocked flat by an onerous draft of wind. Last I saw of him he was trying, rather valiantly I might add, to rise to his feet. Hmmm." He canted his head to the side, eyes narrowed. "Might he have trounced you *after* he gained his balance?"

Bain steadied his breathing. He was acting like an infatuated dolt. And why? She had hardly been a woman at all. Just a slip of a lass, really. Except she hadn't seemed like a lass either, for her eyes spoke of things only the ancients should have seen.

A shiver coursed through his body.

"Or might it have been the wee lad what took the ladies' wraps?" Connelly continued. "Might you and *he* have had an altercation?"

"It appears as if I might have been wrong," Bain rumbled past the cloth, keeping his body carefully relaxed.

"About the fact that you could best the wrap boy?"

"About the fact that you were judicious enough to know when to be reticent."

Connelly laughed, uncrossed his legs, and stepped forward. "Well, I'd be worried about in-citing your wrath, big as you are, but knowing you were felled by a girl little bigger than a spring hare . . ." He paused, letting his words fall into silence.

Bain sat up slowly, allowing the rag to drop from his face as he found the Irishman with his eyes. "I should have let him have you," he said.

Connelly raised a mercurial brow. "The Italian?" he guessed.

"Perhaps you would be less irritating as a gelding," Bain explained, and Connelly howled with laughter.

"So I'm right!" he said, and slapped his leg as if no greater news had ever been shared. "You *were* bested by a maid."

McBain refrained from gritting his teeth and rose slowly to his feet, careful to keep his movements casual, to remain cool. So Connelly had only been guessing. He should have known. The Irishman thrived on these foolish mind games, and though there may be proper circumstances for such cerebral sport, there was, from time to time, nothing more fun than putting Connelly's head through a wall.

"I thought you had learned your lesson about drinking to excess," Bain said, and Connelly laughed again, ignoring him.

"I, too, saw the lass," he admitted, still grinning. "A tempting armful, I'll grant. But she was already taken by the fair-haired fop, or so I thought. Rogan McBain, however . . ." Drawing an imaginary hat from his head, Connelly swept it in front of his too-tight breeches to bow dramatically. "Far be it from that great warrior to leave a bonny lass to a lesser swain."

"Now might be a fortuitous time to learn to shut your mouth," Bain suggested, but to no avail, for Connelly's eyes were as bright as a zealot's on a binge.

"I could barely believe my eyes when I saw you follow them into the gardens."

He shouldn't have, of course. That much was now obvious. Surely he'd learned better years ago. But beneath the maid's polished veneer he had thought he'd sensed something else. Something fearful and fragile. He'd had little choice but to follow them. Or so he'd thought at the time. Though he'd know better from this point forward. Next time he saw a damsel in distress, he'd hie himself in the opposite direction as fast as his timber-sized legs could carry him. He was fair fast for his size.

"I admit I meant to go out myself just to watch the action, but by the time I extricated myself from the charming Marguerite, the girl was already fleeing past the front door. And I thought to myself, Thayer, you winsome devil, you should go see to matters in the gardens. Your good Scottish friend might once again be in need of assist. But when I arrived out of doors, Goldie was laid out flat, and you were gone. Which got me to thinking—"

"It seems unlikely," Bain said, and, rising, pushed his way past Connelly to the pantry.

"Thinking . . ." Connelly added, turning to watch him, "that perhaps you made some sort of advance toward the lass."

Bain gave him a glare over his shoulder. Connelly raised his brows.

"Though, I'll admit," he said slowly, "you've not been much of a ladies' man in the past."

Retrieving a loaf of oat bread and a pot of honey, Bain pushed his way past Connelly as he moved toward the table.

"And why might that be, I wonder." He was musing again. The bastard. "I mean, true, you've not the good looks and charm of myself, but then, you're not Irish." He shrugged his shoulders. "So that is surely to be expected. Still . . ." He canted his head quizzically. Bain stared balefully in return. "You're not half-ugly. Well . . ." he corrected ruefully. "You're *half*-ugly. But some maids will trade good looks . . ." He motioned toward himself, then stepped closer to Bain. "For sheer"—he trailed his right hand through the air—"freakish size."

Bending, Bain pulled a long-handled knife from the top of his boot. "If you're wanting to retain that hand, you'll be keeping it out of my face," he warned, then sliced a chunk of bread thick enough to use as a discus before sitting to drizzle honey carefully on top and take a good-sized bite.

Connelly grinned ecstatically. "Which brings me to wondering . . . might my giant Scottish friend be an even better friend than I realize?"

Bain swallowed, put his bread down, and settled against the back of his chair, motionless as he waited for new foolery. "And what might you be meaning by that, laddie?" Sometimes when his ire was up, his brogue deepened, and he forgot all the fine words he had learned while reading through the eve of battle.

Connelly was grinning like a Syrian monkey. "Tell me true, McBain, have you been coveting your neighbor's arse?"

Bain's chair scraped ominously against the floor as he rose to his full height. He curled up his right fist. It still ached from the time he'd spent in Ceylon, but that hardly mattered. "Spoiling for a bit of sport, are you, lad?"

"Not your sort." Connelly laughed and backed away.

"And what kind of sport might you be thinking that would be?" he asked.

"Two men, one bed, and—" he began, but in that moment, McBain reached for him.

Connelly tried to dodge away, but McBain had already curled his fingers into the Irishman's shirtfront.

They stood face-to-face.

"Demmed, you're ungodly fast for such a big freak of a man," Connelly rasped.

"You should have deduced that before now if you've a wish to live out the day," Bain rumbled.

"Oh, I'll survive the day."

"Aye? And how do you plan to do that?"

"I'm thinking a knee to the groin."

"Perhaps ye shouldn't have preceded the action with a warning, then."

"I always forget that," Connelly quipped, and, grabbing the pitcher's handle, swung with a good deal of force. Had the blow landed, it would have rattled the Scot's head like an empty gourd.

Instead, Bain caught Connelly's wrist in his broad palm.

"Oh hell," Connelly breathed.

"You were ever a dirty fighter," Bain rumbled.

"But I saved your hide on more than one occasion."

"Mayhap you should be more concerned about saving yours," Bain retorted, and drew back his other fist.

"What was that?" Connelly rasped, and turned his head as if listening intently.

"That," Bain said, not bothering to listen, "is you acting like an imbecile."

"Not that." He paused, then, *"That,"* he explained, when a scratch of noise came from the front door.

Bain scowled.

Connelly grinned. "I believe we have visitors."

"At dawn?"

"Maybe Marguerite told her friends of my charms."

"Maybe Marguerite came to complain about some unexplained itching."

Connelly laughed. "A problem you'll never have if you continue to live like a demmed—"

The noise came again, a little louder now and definitely issuing from the front door.

Releasing Connelly's shirtfront, Bain pushed the Irishman backward with a scowl and strode toward the entry hall. His boots sounded heavy against the hardwood. The door handle felt small in his hand.

He opened it with a snap and stopped abruptly, for a pixie-sized angel graced his stoop.

Chapter 4

The door creaked open like the cover to a crypt, then he was there, Lucifer, stepping from the snarling shadows of her childhood. His eyes were gray, his sable hair unruly, his cheeks stubbled. He was dressed in an open-necked tunic and dark tartan. It crossed at his shoulder, was pinned in place with the miniature sword that passed through his pewter brooch and belted snugly about his waist, but she dared not look lower. Indeed, she dare not speak, for he looked too formidable. Too large and powerful and *angry*. But she had made a vow to Madeline. And that she would keep.

"Good morning," she said, though even those simple words were all but impossible to force from her lips, for he was staring at her with those grim-reaper eyes, the left of which was rimed in magenta turning to puce. "Mr. McBain, isn't it?"

His brows lowered even farther, though she would have sworn they could not.

Faerie Faye tightened her grip on the little paper-wrapped item in her hand and tried not to vomit.

She would do what she must. Would keep her secrets while ferreting out others'. For her cover. For the sisters of her heart.

"Who is it?" someone called, then the door opened farther, and another man stepped into view.

It was then that Faye tried to turn and run, but her legs refused to do her bidding. Refused to do so much as budge.

"Good God, McBain," said the smaller fellow, and banged his companion on the back with a hearty whack. "Look who we've got here. Lady . . ." He turned to her expectantly, but her breath was caught fast in her throat, and she was wrong about her legs. They *were* moving, trembling like chimes in a windstorm. "Lady . . ." He canted his head a little and tried again.

"*Mrs.*," she corrected, and raised her brows in haughty challenge as she'd seen others do.

"Ahh well . . ." He shrugged, grinned, as charming as a serpent. "I've no prejudices, Mrs. . . ."

It took everything she had to remember her supposed name. "Nettles."

"Mrs. Nettles. How very nice to meet you. I'm Thayer Connelly, and this is . . . Well . . ." he chuckled. "I believe the two of you became acquainted last night. Did you not?" he asked, and glanced from one to the other.

Faye could feel his attention shift from her to the giant, but she dare not turn her own gaze from the brooding Scotsman. She'd wounded him, injured him, a seasoned warrior, a celebrated soldier. Until this moment, she'd not thought of the humiliation that might cause him.

"Oh, where are my manners?" Connelly asked. " 'Tis all but a crime to leave such beauty languishing on our doorstep, is it not, McBain?"

The giant remained mute.

"Please, Mrs. Nettles . . ." Connelly straightened. "We were just about to . . . have some tea," he said, and skipped his merry gaze to his companion as if they shared some jolly secret that had nothing to do with tea at all. "Won't you join us?" he asked, and motioned toward the interior of their home.

The ironbound door yawned like a dark maw ready to devour her.

"I just stopped by for a moment," she said, and managed to keep from leaping into the surrounding topiary.

"Then we must surely enjoy every moment with you even more," Connelly said, and reached for her hand.

She remembered to breathe though it was a close thing.

The Scotsman turned his attention to his friend, brows lowering still farther.

"Well . . ." said the Irishman, and, raising her hand, pressed a slow kiss to her knuckles. It was all she could do to refrain from launching herself from the stoop and bolting for the carriage Joseph kept waiting by the curb. "Tell us, please . . ." He straightened, then cupped her palm with his own.

It felt large and cool, like manacles against her skin. The Scotsman was standing perfectly still, staring at their hands. Just as Lucifer had watched from the darkness of her window, silent, looming, waiting until she could tolerate no more. Until she fled the house and Tenning's toxic care. "To what do we owe this unusual pleasure?"

She searched for her voice, but memories were crowding in, crushing her larynx.

"Perhaps you had some unfinished business with the oversized Scotsman here. Or . . ." He smoothed his thumb over hers. "Maybe—"

"Irish." The giant's voice was no more than a rumble.

"Yes, my friend?" Connelly looked as happy as a puppy. As merry as a songbird.

Their gazes met like sunlight on steel.

"Mayhap your new whip has arrived at Master Balmick's."

"I only ordered it a few days past."

"But you insist on going there each day regardless."

"I am certain I can miss one—" he began, but McBain interrupted.

"Might you be prepared to mend that wall?"

A moment of understanding seemed to stream between them. Connelly remained absolutely still for an instant, then grinned, dropped her hand, and backed away. "My lady," he said, and bowed. "It has been a rare pleasure meeting the lass who can—"

McBain cleared his throat. The sound rumbled like thunder in the morning air.

Connelly laughed out loud. "Until next we meet," he said, and grinned as he disappeared into the house.

Faye's heart beat like a drum in her chest. The enemy had been reduced to one now. But for the life of her she couldn't decide if that made matters better or worse.

She clenched her empty hand and dredged up every molecule of courage she ever hoped to possess. "I wished to apologize."

He said nothing.

She was holding her breath but managed to force out a few more syllables. "Usually I'm . . ." *. . . safely hidden away in Lavender House.* " . . . as mild as Mullen."

His brows lowered even farther.

"Surely you've heard the term," she said, mimicking Rennet.

"Aye," he said. His tone was devilishly low, frightening in its intensity.

"I didn't mean—" she began, but words failed her, so she thrust the package at him, pushing her arm out to its full length. "Here."

He didn't reach for the package, didn't move at all, but remained exactly as he was, like a burly predator planning his attack.

Her hands were beginning to tremble. She steadied them and lifted her chin. "Please. Take it."

He did so finally, slowly, engulfing it with his hand.

"It's a gift."

He raised his gaze to her.

She tried to think of something clever to say, but his steady, quicksilver eyes had driven every potential witticism clean out of her head.

He shifted his weight. "I've not received a gift from an adversary before."

"An adversary!" she said, and almost bolted, but he motioned languidly toward his eye.

"Oh." She contained a wince. "I just . . ." It looked so horribly painful, so hideously raw. "Sometimes I become a bit skittish in social circumstances."

Silence pulsed around them, broken by naught but the distant sound of a baying dog.

"Skittish," he said finally.

"Yes."

"Were that all me Tommies were so capricious."

She blinked.

His expression didn't change in the least, but there was something in his haunting silver eyes. Something that almost spoke of humor. "Surely we would rout our enemies in a matter of minutes."

The world went quiet, focused, cleared. And she realized suddenly that he almost seemed . . . uncertain. Yet he stared at her, as solemn as a dirge, not moving closer, not retreating.

She cleared her throat and lowered her eyes. "You should open your gift."

Silence again. She tried a tentative glance. He was gazing contemplatively at the package in his hand.

"Might it contain a wee warrior even smaller than yourself?"

She scowled. "No."

He tilted his head the slightest degree. "Are you familiar with black powder?"

"Do you think I mean to harm you?" she asked.

"For reasons entirely unclear to one such as meself, the possibility did cross me mind," he said. Despite herself, Faye felt her lips twitch the slightest degree, but she had learned better long ago than to be charmed. Learned, ached, paid.

"Here," she said, and, reaching out, took the package back. Their fingers brushed. And with that quick exchange came a flash of errant feelings that tingled through her system like static electricity. Not quite painful, but almost.

Her breath hitched up tight, and in the pit of her being, she felt a strange, shooting star of something. But it was only her cowardice, she was sure of it. Unwrapping the package, she lifted the contents for him to see.

He peered at the gift, unspeaking for a moment. "A rock," he said finally.

Their gazes met with a velvet clash. "Bloodstone," she corrected, and lifted the russet amulet by its leather thong. Her heart felt strange. " 'Tis said to be a warrior's friend."

"Then mayhap you'd best wear it." He was staring at her again, making her chest feel too tight for her heart.

She shifted her gaze away, then forced herself to meet his eyes again. "Ancient healers believed it to be advantageous."

Behind her, a horse trotted down the street, the two-beat gait sharp and staccato in the fresh-stirring day. McBain glanced up, looking over her head. Like his chest, his throat was broad, she noticed. Broad and dark and corded with unquestioned strength.

"You should not converse with the likes of Rennet," he said, his words slow and cadenced as he brought his attention back to her.

Startled by this change of dialogue and frightened by his . . . well *everything*, it was all she could do to hold his gaze. But amid the fear there was a spark of something else. Something never before felt and therefore unidentifiable.

His eyes were as sharp and low-browed as an osprey's. "Terrible things occur even in the best of houses. You should not risk yourself beyond your husband's protection."

She drew a careful breath and forced herself to speak. "I have no husband."

He stared at her a moment, then shifted his gaze back to the street behind her. "I am sorry."

Interesting. Not a spark of pain sounded in her head. Not so much as a dull throb to suggest an untruth. Why? Did he find her so unappealing that her widowed status prompted not the least bit of interest? "That I am not wed?" she asked.

He was silent for a long moment, but finally he lowered his attention to her face again. "That I made you revisit tender memories."

"I've been alone for quite some time." She was skirting the issue, avoiding the pain, but his next question forced her hand.

"How is it that he died?"

"He drowned." She refused to wince. "Broke through the ice while returning to our modest but happy home in Imatra." She'd mimicked that particular lie enough times so that it should no longer spark an ache in her brow, and yet it did.

He watched her in silence, and there was something about his expression, something about his solemn, silvery eyes that sounded a warning bell in her head, that jumbled her nerves and forced her litany.

"His name was Albert. He was the youngest of three, born on the third of June in 1782. He had fair hair and blue eyes and was but seven-and-twenty when he . . ."

She fell silent, though it was all but impossible to do so. What would she give to be normal?

"Your father, then," he said.

"What?" Her voice was barely audible to her own ears.

"Mayhap your sire could accompany you if you feel it necessary to commune with men in the dark of—"

"My father is dead." The truth. It had escaped. She felt panic bubble up like a fountain inside her. But wait! All was well, for this once the truth meshed with the lies she'd been fed with such cautious regularity.

"Certainly, you have a guardian." He looked grimmer still. Enraged almost, and that anger seemed to fuse her tongue to the very roof of her mouth.

But she had made a vow. Thus she raised her chin and struggled for haughty. But truly, normal would be a welcome surprise.

"Can I assume you do not trust Lord Rennet?" she asked.

He nodded solemnly.

"May I ask why?"

He didn't blink. Possibly ever. "He is a man."

She felt her eyebrows lift of their own accord. Curiosity edged off fear. "You don't like men?"

"It would be imprudent to trust them."

Then she was certainly no fool, but she *was* intrigued. "Them?" She canted her head a little, trying to figure him out, to see through his mask. Everyone wore a mask.

"Us," he corrected.

The rumble of his voice sent an odd, inexplicable shiver through her. Part fear, part something else, but she held her ground. "Do you always warn your victims, Mr. Mc . . ." And dammit, she'd lost his name.

"My victims call me Bain," he said.

"Bain." It suited him. Not as well as Lucifer, but well enough.

He nodded. "How do yours refer to you?"

"I have no victims," she said, and for a moment he only stared, studying her face as if it were a portrait to be memorized. The sight of his colorful eye made her want to squirm, but she squelched the weakness.

"I am surprised they are not strewn about your feet like fodder," he said.

She scowled, but he didn't explain.

"Your friends then," he said. "What do they call you?"

"Faye." It was not her given name, but none but a very few knew that.

"Faye." He said the word slowly. "As in wee folk?"

"Wee folk?"

"Pixies and their contemporaries."

"I suppose so," she said though she had no wish for him to associate her with anything otherworldly.

He nodded curtly and backed toward the door. "My thanks," he said, "for the . . . rock."

"Wear it," she said.

He paused, broad fingers folded over the stone, which he glanced at before bringing his stormy gaze back to her. "Your pardon?"

"Against your skin," she said, and touched her own throat. His gaze followed the movement, but his body remained absolutely still. The air seemed suddenly motionless.

"Very well," he said, and bowed as he backed away.

"Now." The single word came out too sharp, too panicked. She almost closed her eyes against her own foolishness. "If you please."

He was staring at her again. Perhaps he thought her beautiful. Entrancing even, she thought breathlessly, and knew all the while it was far more likely he found her odd.

"It has healing powers," she said.

He scowled. He was, without a doubt, more accomplished at scowling than anyone she'd ever known.

"According . . ." she added hastily, "according to the ancients."

Their gazes welded, then, "Very well," he said, and, bending his brawny neck, slipped the leather over his head. It caught on the dark length of his hair, and he lifted it, baring the masculine strength of his throat for just a moment.

He'd folded the billowy sleeves of his simple tunic back from his wrists, and the muscles in his enormous forearms bunched as he pushed his hair aside. The neckline of his shirt shifted, revealing a few hard-honed inches of his chest. She watched the movement, feeling strangely breathless as the umber stone brushed past the soft fabric of his shirt and bumped gently onto his skin. The string was longer than she'd intended. Perhaps she'd thought, as she'd spent the sleepless night preparing the stone in the light of the gibbous moon, that he was even larger than he was. But that hardly seemed possible, for in the broadening light of day he looked as if he'd been hewn from stone, every muscle chiseled just so. His shoulders were bunched, his chest summer-tanned and mounded, his—

He cleared his throat, and she dashed her gaze away. Good heavens! It was clear now. She had entirely lost her mind.

"Thank you," she said, then jerked her gaze to his, for even she wasn't entirely sure what had prompted her appreciation. Surely it couldn't be the fact that he had bared a few inches of his chiseled person. He was, after all, the enemy. "For . . ." She motioned stiffly toward his chest. A man like he would have nothing to fear. Nothing at all. And how wonderful that would be. " . . . agreeing to wear it. It looks . . ." She stopped, unsure where her thoughts were headed. "It will help mend your wounds."

"A pity it wasn't gifted to me years ago, then. 'Twould have come in handy on the battlefield. But . . ." His silver-frost eyes almost seemed to sparkle for a moment, and she found, once again, that she was holding her breath. "I did not expect London to be so fraught with dangers."

"My apolog—" she began, but he interrupted.

"There is a hunt." He blurted out the words.

She stopped, breath held, lips still parted. "What?"

He looked peeved, at himself or her, she wasn't sure which. "There is to be a foxhunt tomorrow." He paused. A muscle ground in his powerful jaw. "They ride at dawn from the Black Swan."

She should breathe soon, she thought, but she didn't.

He scowled over her head and into the distance. " . . . me."

She allowed one careful breath. "I beg your pardon."

He lowered his gaze, and suddenly she wondered if he, too, was holding his breath. "Perhaps you would deign to join me." He said the words clearly now, succinctly, as if he was being ultimately careful to force out each syllable. And at the meaning of his invitation, the world seemed to give way beneath her feet. She couldn't join him. She didn't like men. Didn't understand men. Didn't trust men. But he looked almost . . . almost as if he were blushing. And . . . well . . . she had vowed to see this mission through to the end.

"I . . ." she began, but he was already shaking his head.

"My apologies," he rumbled. "I did not mean to . . . A lady such as yourself . . . Horses. Odiferous beasts that . . ." He drew a breath. It made his chest swell, made the brooch lift and fall. He nodded his head curtly. "My thanks for the stone," he said, and turned toward the house.

"I enjoy the smell of horses," she said.

He stopped. Turned back, scowling again. "A frail lass such as yourself can certainly find more appropriate pursuits than—"

"I am not frail," she said though in truth she was. Had always been. Tenning had told her as much, but for reasons she could not explain, she had no desire to lie to this man. "I've no *wish* to be frail."

He stared at her, expression so solemn it all but broke her heart. "I'll not have an injury on me conscience," he said, and reached for the knob behind him.

"I shall be there," she said, shocking herself with her own ridiculous words.

The tendons tightened in his throat as he turned toward her, casting the leather thong out in sharp relief. They stared at each other for a hundred lifetimes. "Do you have a mount, then, lass?"

"Well . . . no."

"Then it seems—"

"She'll ride Antoinette," said a voice.

They turned in unison toward the door, but it remained firmly closed.

Faye turned her questioning gaze to McBain, but he said nothing.

"Antoinette?" she asked.

"The Irishman's mount," he rumbled.

"Why is she named—"

"I've thought it unwise to ask," he said.

She searched his eyes for humor; but if he

thought himself funny, he gave no indication. "I've no desire to put him out," she said.

"If only you could."

She scowled, but he shook his head, unwilling to explain. "The mare is large and—"

"I've no trouble with large . . ." she began, then caught herself. The blush started from her toes. "Horses!" she said quickly. "I have no trouble with large horses."

She almost thought she heard someone chuckle from the far side of the door. She lifted her chin.

"I'm an excellent equestrienne."

McBain was gritting his teeth. "I do not think this a good idea."

Why? What did he have to hide? "Then I shall find my own mount."

"I did not mean—"

"I will be there," she said again, and managed to turn away without passing out.

Chapter 5

Why would a woman of Faye Nettles's faerie-like quality, a woman of beauty and refinement, agree to ride with the likes of Rogan McBain? True, initially, he had thought her nervous around men. But she had come to his house unescorted at dawn. Surely that spoke volumes. But what did it say exactly? No one in this bloody city was what she seemed to be. That much he had learned long ago.

Bain sat ruminating. Beneath him, Colt stood quietly, paying no heed to the bevy of elegant mounts that pranced and strutted about him. Seventeen hands at the withers, he was built more like a draft animal than a riding hack, but he had served Bain well for more than a decade . Too well to trade him for some posh Thoroughbred with more pedigree than practicality.

But perhaps these other steeds had not seen the world as Colt had seen it. Perhaps they had not tasted death. Reaching down, Bain absently placed a hand over the roughened scar that bisected his stallion's crest.

Beside them, a flashy chestnut reared, nearly dislodging his rider.

Straightening, Bain swore under his breath and wished for the hundredth time he had never considered such a ludicrous idea. Perhaps Mrs. Nettles *was* an accomplished rider, but perhaps she was not, and he had no wish to be the cause of some disaster. Hardly that, for his intent was to draw as little attention to himself as possible, to find a way to perform his task and leave with no one the wiser, or at least no lives lost. No *additional* lives lost.

He shifted his weight and watched the mob around him. Half the riders already seemed besotted, which was just a damned foolish way to ride. Then again, what did he care? He had come, after all, only to learn what he could. The inebriation of others might help that cause.

Indeed, Connelly had suggested that it might be wise to get wee Faye inebriated. Of course, Connelly was an unmitigated ass. Then again, intoxication could only make a brute like Bain look better in her eyes. It was not his place, after all, to make certain she was safe at the end of the day. He was not her caretaker.

Through the warbled glass of the inn, a small lass looked out at the world. A mobcap sat crooked on her head. A tray of crockery teetered in her hands. Wee Cat would be about that size if she yet lived. But she had succumbed to a fever a few short days after her father's death. Charlotte had told him that much though she had said little else. Bain winced at the memory of his own pleas, his own profession of undying love. He had fought the duel to save her from Winden's cruelty. But Charlotte had turned away, had shut the door, had taught him a lesson of betrayal he would not soon forget. To this day he was unsure whether her stories of abuse at her husband's hands were fabricated or real. Just as he was uncertain of the cause of wee Cat's death. Had the child been taken by a fever as her stepmother had professed or was there something more sinister afoot? The glittering *ton* might yet think Charlotte the epitome of gentility, but he had learned far better. Few people were what they seemed to be. Even Mrs. Nettles could not be as perfect as—

His thoughts crashed to a halt as a flash of blue caught his attention.

Faerie Faye sat very straight on a handsome bay. She wore a black top hat, head held high over squared shoulders, hands just so on the reins.

Her sculpted body was encased in the riding habit of the *bon ton*. Cobalt blue skirt and jacket. Snowy cravat. Austere, he supposed, or some might think it so, but to his simplistic mind it somehow only made her look more delicate, more feminine, and strangely pure. As fragile as a butterfly caught in a windstorm.

He shook his head, trying to rid himself of such daft thoughts. He'd been a fool before and had no intention of riding that path again.

So perhaps he should leave now. Turn tail and run. It wasn't his way to abandon a fight, but there were battles that could not be won, and his gut told him this was one of those skirmishes. Connelly, after all, thought this rendezvous a marvelous idea, which, of course, meant it should be avoided at all costs. Indeed, Bain thought, lucidity returning suddenly, he should never have come. Should never have even considered—

But in that instant he noticed a dapper, red-headed fellow turn toward her. Saw the man straighten with interest, saw his eyebrows rise as he reined his mount toward her. She spotted him as well, and in that instant, in that one fractured prism of a second, Bain thought he saw uncertainty spark her earth-stone eyes.

It was naught but his imagination. He told himself as much, but it was no use, for he had already touched his spurs to Colt's massive barrel.

There was no hesitation. No delay. Colt flexed his powerful neck, and like a gifted dancer shifted his mass from a standstill to a canter in a second's time, cleaving a path through the crowd.

Reining to a halt between Red and the lady, Bain nodded a greeting, but for a moment he could think of nothing to say, for she was spellbinding. Yet it was neither her gilded beauty nor her polished veneer that held him speechless. It was something more vulnerable, something almost hidden but not quite.

The sun had risen only minutes before and shone now with new-world glory in her upturned eyes. They were the hue of river-washed agates, or maybe the color of the very stone he now wore about his neck. Deep russet flecked with shards of black and green and a dozen shades he could neither name nor consider. A palette of wonder no man could paint.

On some, the stiff riding habits of the elite appeared manly, but in the rosy light of dawn, wee Faerie Faye looked as delicate as a spring blossom. Her tawny face was small, her chin peaked above her white stock. Her shoulders were square but narrow, her leather-clad hands small and still, her waist so tiny he could have spanned it with his hands.

"You've come," she said, and there was something about her soft siren's voice that made his heart sing, for it almost seemed as if she was relieved, nay *ecstatic,* to find him there.

They stared at each other as he searched for some witticisms, some repartee. Nothing.

"So you've not changed your mind, then," he said finally, and couldn't help but notice that his voice sounded as if it issued from the very center of the earth, as if it came from a being entirely unassociated with this woman's lofty species.

"Why ever would I?" she asked, and raised a single brow. It was that expression that convinced him he had entirely imagined the fear of only moments before. But that was good. He was no one's protector. History had taught him that much.

"It has always seemed a strange sport," he said. "This foxhunting."

"Strange?" Beneath her, the bay pranced an intricate step. Her body swayed in perfect rhythm. "How so?"

Because the word "sport" implied there was some fairness involved. Some *sport.* "One fox," he said, and scanned the rowdy assembly, the elegant horses, the hounds, just beginning to bay. "A host of well-mounted riders."

She watched him in silence, head high, plump-plump lips pursed as she studied him, then; "Tell me, Mr. McBain, are all men of war so tenderhearted?"

He returned her gaze. She must be joking; his heart had become calloused years before her birth. "I merely spoke of fairness."

"But the fox are vermin. Stealing chickens and the like from poor tenant farmers," she said. "Surely we are doing a service."

Did that opinion make her heartless or simply pragmatic? "You've no qualms about this day then?"

"Perhaps you have mistaken me for some wilting flower," she said. "I assure you, I am not." Glancing down, she fiddled with the hem of her skirt, plumping the ruffled train across the pommel horn where her right leg was hooked in the manner that made him cringe. How the hell did anyone ride perched atop a mount like a flighty tree finch? And why? "Indeed," she continued, but just then a shout went up as two horses rose on their hinds, forelegs pummeling the air as they sparred. One hapless rider tumbled to the cobblestones amid jeers and cheers.

From the right, three more joined the crush, mounts dancing as they turned from the street. The din of the hounds was all but deafening now. The innkeeper raised a pitcher of beer as his boy hustled through the mob, handing out tankards to those who had not yet received one. The fair Faye, he noticed, did not accept one, though she controlled her gelding with one steady hand. So she had ridden some. And there was steel to her spine. That much was obvious, at least to him. Although, if he looked deeply, past her polished veneer, behind her spoken words, he wasn't even sure *she* was aware of the fact. Still, there was a good deal of difference between sitting quietly in a cobbled courtyard and clearing oxers on half a ton of heaving horseflesh.

But he had no wish to offend her by mentioning such a thing. Then again, neither did he care for the idea of returning with her broken body cradled in his arms.

Although the idea of holding her against his chest made his heart feel diabolically traitorous.

God almighty, he was a dolt. Why had he suggested this at the outset? He had things to do. Things to *learn*. He scanned the mob. There were already twoscore riders assembled. Most of them inebriated. All of them dressed to the gills. He himself felt like a damned stuffed monkey. Though he had always worn the required uniform into battle, he was most accustomed to his tartan, comfortable with his plaid and sporran. But Connelly had insisted he conform to the ways of the preening *ton*. It was all foolishness though, for his stock felt starchy, his breeches tight. 'Twas ridiculous to think he would ever belong in this parade of dandies and swells. He was a Highlander.

Suddenly, a gust of wind flared, flapping the lacy tail of a nearby rider's handkerchief. Startled by the motion, Faye's mount shied, and without intent, Bain reached out to grab the bay's bridle. The gelding stilled even as Faye's gaze met Rogan's.

They sat in silence, frozen in time, a thousand thoughts tumbling between them, but what those thoughts were, even McBain wasn't quite sure.

"I could escort you home," he rumbled, still bent from his saddle to restrain the fidgety bay. " 'Twould do me no harm to miss this," he said, and as he loosed the gelding's cheek piece, didn't add that he'd rather be engaged in hand-to-hand combat than here in this ridiculous circus.

"Don't be silly," she said, and smoothed her expression just as easily as she smoothed her skirts. "I'll be—"

But just then a bugle sounded. The whipper-in loosed the hounds amid an ear-shattering racket while a piebald hack began pitching nervously before settling. The hunt-master raised his scarlet-sleeved arm, and they were off, galloping down the cobbled street toward the countryside.

From Colt's sturdy, rolling back, Bain breathlessly watched Faye gallop away, but there was no need for concern; she rode with confidence and panache.

But they were already approaching the twisting River Darent. Here, so near London's south side, the water was only a few feet wide, but the banks were steep and uncertain. The front three horses took it together, gliding over. But the fourth animal refused for an instant, floundered, then reared, nearly dumping its rider before lunging after its mates.

Tension was building like a storm in Bain's gut. "Mayhap we'd best walk them through this first obstacle," he called.

Faye glanced over her shoulder, eyes luminous with excitement, golden hair beginning to blow free from its containment beneath her dark, flat-topped hat. "What's that?"

"It might be wise to slow for the water," he said, though he felt silly now, and a little breathless, for with the light in her bright eyes, she looked for all the world like a pixie just come to earth.

"Very well," she agreed, and managed to slow her mount to a walk, though the animal shook his head and danced a few steps as others passed.

Colt, having seen the world race by on innumerable occasions and knowing it was bound to slow its pace eventually, dropped to a walk of his own accord, allowing them to approach the creek at a more sedate pace. Side by side, the two horses lowered their heads and descended the bank.

"Is there a problem?" Faye asked, eyeing him as they climbed the opposite slope. "With your mount?"

"Nay," he said, and though he knew he should elaborate, there seemed to be no more words in the face of such disastrous beauty.

She nodded, scowling slightly and looking like nothing so much as a piqued faerie. "Your eye," she said. "I am sorry. It must make it difficult to see."

It took him a moment to realize she was searching for a reason for their leisurely pace. And though he had, on more than one occasion, ridden riddled with bullets and near unconscious in the saddle, he would rather she think him a weakling than know he had remained awake half the night fretting over her safety during these moments together.

"It is healing," he said, and realized suddenly that, indeed, it was mending with amazing swiftness. Reaching up, he brushed his thumb across her gift, hidden as it was beneath the traditional hunt garb. A white shirt, a canary waistcoat, and a dark coat, split up the back and nearly reaching his knees. These English huntsmen wore enough clothing to stop a bayonet. "What manner of rock did ye call this?"

"Bloodstone."

He caught her with his eyes, wondering about her. Who was she? The sophisticated widow she portrayed to the world or the fragile ingénue he imagined peeking from her eyes when no one was looking? "And what made you think it might be helpful?"

She stared at him, speechless for a moment, and he continued.

"A polished lady such as yourself," he said. "You seem too modern to believe in the old ways."

"Modern?"

"Aye."

For a fleeting moment her lips quirked up before her face settled back into serious lines. "I fear you are thinking of someone else. I am quite old-fashioned. But what of you, sir? Tell me of yourself."

Why would she take an interest? He was hardly the elegant pink of the *ton* so intriguing to the English elite. Indeed, some had called him a Celtic troll. A few of those clever wits still retained their teeth; he wasn't as sensitive about his size as he had been in his younger days. "There is little to tell."

"Judging by your accent, I would guess you were not born here in London."

"You would be wrong." His voice sounded gruff

and unrefined, making him immediately regret his foolish truthfulness. He had no wish for her to learn the truth about him. Far better that she think of him as an interesting oddity. It had gained him entrance to the ton's most prestigious venues after all. "My mother did indeed birth me in London, but I did not stay long," he admitted.

"She traveled?"

"She died," he said, then all but rolled his eyes at the bluntness of his own words. Why not tell her how it had felt to hold his uncle's dying body in his bloodied arms while he was at it?

"I am sorry," she said.

"Nay." He tried to negate his words, but implying his mother's death did not matter hardly made him sound any more the prince. "I remember naught of her."

"Nothing?"

"Only that I was the one what—" he began, and stopped himself. She had died moments after his birth, and though his father had never blamed Rogan for her death, that did not mean he could not blame himself. He was, after all, a troll. At least by some estimations. "Only that she had summer eyes."

"What?" She was watching him closely, and he realized suddenly that he had said the words with too much feeling, when in truth he did not recall her eyes a'tall, but only had others' words to remember her by.

She blinked at him. "Summer—"

"Blue," he said gruffly and wished to hell he hadn't started down that path. "They were naught but blue."

"I don't understand how summer—" she began, but he interrupted again.

"Like the sky. In the warmth of the summer when the wildflowers. . . ." He stopped himself abruptly. Good God, he sounded like a raving lunatic. "What of you? Your mother is alive and well?"

"She died shortly after my father. Of a broken heart," she said, then touched the tips of her fingers to her brow as though it pained her.

And it was that pain, that scrunching of her fair forehead that troubled him.

"Tell me they were with you," he said.

She watched him in silence.

"When you lost your husband," he said. "You were not alone."

She stared at him for an elongated, breathless moment, then lifted her attention quickly away. "I believe I heard the field-master's horn," she said, and, touching her crop to her dark gelding's flank, eased into a canter.

They did naught but ride then, Bain behind, her ahead. And though he knew far better, he could not help but admire her. Her balance, her grace, the gentle way she guided her mount.

She glanced back once as if to speak, then the hounds went to full cry, and the run began in earnest.

Colt lengthened his strides, eating up the turf,

taking the stone fences as a matter of course, and always ahead of them, Faye rode like a wood sprite, as light as a leaf on the wind, soaring over downed logs, racing through the woods.

Ahead, the hounds were milling. Perhaps the fox had gone to ground, but in an instant a bay split the air again, and the pack was off, with the horsemen racing behind, crashing through the underbrush like demons, galloping into the open.

Cresting a hill, Bain saw the rolling countryside spread out before them. An open field lay ahead, and there, just past the tricolored pack, he saw the fox. It was racing flat out, twenty couples of hounds behind. More woods lay just beyond.

Horses lathered and blew. The whippers-in urged the dogs on. They shortened the distance on the flagging vixen, and then the first cur leaped. The fox rolled beneath its fangs, and in a moment the others were on it.

There was a cry from the fox, a cheer from the riders. Faye pulled up her mount even as Colt galloped past. Slowing him gradually, Bain pulled him around in a circle only to find the faerielike Mrs. Nettles sitting perfectly still upon her restive gelding.

"Is something amiss?" he asked, heading back. Her face was flushed, her eyes bright, but it took her a moment to speak.

"No," she said finally. A pair of ladies rode past, laughing as they went. She didn't glance their way. "All is well."

He scowled. "Are you certain?"

"Of course." She brushed back a wayward strand of golden hair. "What could be amiss?"

He nodded, glanced behind them. The houndsmen were already beginning to restrain the dogs. Several riders had dismounted to perform their bloody rituals. "I believe they intend to lunch here. Would you care to join them?" he asked, but when he turned back he saw her jerk her knuckles from her cheek.

"Mrs.—"

"If you'll excuse me," she said, and, turning her mount away, urged him back toward the woods behind them. "I need a few minutes of privacy."

Bain watched her ride away. Indeed, he was determined to leave her be, for he had no desire to embarrass her, but it was easy to get turned about in the woods. Thus he followed at a distance.

By the time he entered the copse, her gelding stood alone, buckled reins looped over a nearby branch.

He gazed around, but the lass was nowhere to be seen. And then he heard it. Muffled crying. Sobbing, actually. Inconsolable and incessant, coming from behind a fallen log and tearing at the fabric of his heart.

Chapter 6

Faye's stomach convulsed, her throat felt raw. What had she been thinking? A foxhunt! It had sounded so cultured. So posh. The perfect venue for proving she belonged among London's refined society.

Wrapping her arms about her legs, Faye tucked her feet under the sturdy fabric of her skirt and rocked mindlessly to and fro, wanting to curl up inside herself. Wanting to forget the flaring panic she had seen in the fox's eyes. Wanting with all her might to be unable so completely to empathize with the hunted animal's fear. Communing with beasts was not her gift, yet she could feel the creature's terror throb beneath her own skin. Could hear the footfalls of the hunters in the beat of her own frantic heart and knew she would be caught. Would be—

"Where have you gone?"

Faye's breath rasped in her throat. She jerked her gaze toward the trail. They were coming for her. Tracking her just as they'd tracked the fox.

Hunting. Without mercy. And they'd find her. They always did.

"Mrs. Nettles."

She crouched lower behind the sheltering log, barely breathing.

"Are you in here?"

No. She squeezed her eyes closed, pretending she *wasn't* there. Pretending if they couldn't see her, she'd be gone. Disappeared. Like a wisp of smoke blown aloft by the fitful breeze. But her gifts didn't work that way. Her gifts dealt with pain. With betrayal.

"Are ye well, lass?" The voice rumbled through the woods from some unknown location. But the tone was low and quiet and seemed to have no edge of evil teasing. No threat of retribution. She drew a breath and exhaled shakily, remembering. She was no longer a child. No longer a pawn. She was Mrs. Nettles, polished, educated, powerful.

Lifting an unsteady hand, she swiped her gloved fingers across her cheek, but she could yet see the fox's wide eyes, could taste its acrid terror. And with that painful memory her stomach roiled again. She gritted her teeth, fighting for control.

"Lass?" came the voice again. She jerked her gaze to the right, and he was there. Rogan McBain. Not thirty feet separated them.

"You should not ride out alone, lass," he said.

She straightened her back carefully. "Why ever not?" she asked, and hoped to God he wouldn't notice that her cheeks were wet, her hands atremble.

" 'Tis not safe," he said, and studied her face, as if she might disappear at any moment.

"Well . . ." Her nose was runny, and she wished that for once she had remembered a handkerchief. Wished she could act her age, or her supposed station, or at least her *species*. A fox had died. An animal! "As you can see, I am perfectly fine," she said.

He shuffled his feet in the underbrush. They were clad in black leather boots that rose nearly to his powerful, tightly clad thighs. "All is well then?"

Touching the back of her knuckles to her nose, she hoped to God he would not realize her shuddering sorrow. "Of course. Why would it not be?"

Silence again, deep and pulsing, and when he finally spoke, he canted his head the slightest degree as if to judge her reaction. "You were correct, 'twas naught but vermin," he said.

And yet there seemed almost to be a strange regret in his solemn tone, as if he, too, had felt the animal's fear as his own. Could that be the case? But the sight of him towering above her dashed such foolish notions, for he was strength itself. Dressed in a charcoal, knee-length coat, his shoulders looked as wide as the horizon, as strong as the oaks that towered above him. A man such as he would have no concept of fear. Therefore, this strange tone of his must be some kind of ploy. A game she had not yet deciphered. They oft liked to play games. She stifled a shiver.

"Surely you do not think me upset by the plight of the fox," she said, and steeling herself, raised her eyes to his.

Their gazes met, and for one sterling moment she almost won the battle, almost played the part, but try as she might, she had never been good at this sport. One tear, hot and fat, swelled in the corner of her eye and slipped traitorously down her cheek.

He watched her in silence, his face like granite, his expression etched in solemnity. But there was something indefinable in his stormy eyes. "If not for the fox, then what?" he asked. His voice was level, but strangely soft.

"I simply . . ." Sobs shivered at her throat, but she held them back, held them in. "I twisted my ankle," she said.

"Your ankle?" He sounded dubious, but she hardly noticed, for her head had already begun to tick with that insistent ache she knew so well.

She put her hand to her brow.

"Did ye injure your head as well?"

"Perhaps when I . . ." she began, but she could not challenge another fabrication. "No. 'Tis but a headache. I am certain it will be relieved once I reach home." Home. She wanted nothing more than to be in the safe confines of Lavender House. To hide forever in its darkened recesses.

"I shall help you to your steed then," he said, and stepped toward her, but she jerked involuntarily, ready to scramble away, and he froze. She almost closed her eyes to her own lunacy. How the hell had she ever thought she would fool anyone into believing she was refined? On the best of days she could barely manage sane.

And he was scowling at her. "You're right," he said finally. "You should not rise," There was something odd in his voice. Probably something that suggested she was madder than a caged monkey. "Not until we've assessed the damage."

"I'm fine," she said, but he was close now. Too close to rise to her feet without touching him. So she remained where she was, staring up at him, fear crowding the misery.

"Very well," he said, and, bending at the waist, handed her a handkerchief. She took it with some misgivings. It was white and unadorned but for an embroidered image of the brooch he wore even now on his coat. She scrunched it in her gloved fist, and he stepped away, allowing her to breathe again as he lowered himself to sit with his back against a broad horse chestnut. "But 'twill do no harm to wait a few minutes. The horses should have a few minutes rest, regardless."

Kindness? Compassion? Or was this yet another game? One to keep her here alone? To wait until the others took their bloody trophies and left their prey's tattered corpse behind.

Tears burned her eyes again. She lowered them and wished to God she had been born male. That she was strong and confident and heartless.

"All things die," he said softly.

"But not in terror. Not in—" She stopped herself. He was playing with her mind, trying to draw out the real her. The *weak* her. But she pushed the raw images from her head, remembering her assumed persona. "Might you think I am unaware of that fact?"

The woods went silent. "My apologies," he said. "I had forgotten your loss."

Her loss? she wondered.

"Were you wed long?"

Of course. Her supposed marriage. She closed her eyes and tried to think of a way not to lie. "No."

"I am sorry."

She nodded.

"And there were no children to soften the blow?"

"No."

He was quiet for a moment. "Did he want young ones? Your husband?"

Was he intentionally digging into her past? Did he suspect she was not what she was said to be? Lifting her gaze, she caught him with her eyes, but his face was still impassive.

"Most do," she said.

He watched her a moment, then nodded, but said nothing.

She knew better than to be intrigued, but the

question came just the same. "And what of you? Do you hope for children?"

"I fear I am not the fatherly type," he said, and though his tone was level, there was something in his eyes, some hint of emotion that went unvoiced.

"Why do you say so?" she asked.

His gaze was flat and steady. "Look at me," he said.

And she did. He sat before her, heavy legs spread with his arms resting atop his knees. His hands were wide and open, his shoulders endless, his jaw hard and dark with stubble. But it was his eyes that always snagged her. His eyes, low-browed and silver gilded with a thousand memories hidden behind them.

"Do I look to be the image of the tender sire?" he asked.

No. He looked like an ancient warrior come to life. Powerful and ruthless. Except for that something in his quicksilver eyes, he looked to be the perfect killer. Or the perfect lover. The thought struck her suddenly, shocking her with its unwarranted arrival.

"Not everyone is what he appears to be," she said, and tore her gaze away.

"Not all," he agreed solemnly. "Though I am."

The perfect lover? She wondered and chided herself, for her face was already hot, flushed with the odd twist of emotions that warred inside her. Dread and hope. The stab of fear, the spark of desire. "Are you certain?" she asked, and flitted her gaze up through her lashes at him.

"Do you see me as a troll?"

"No!" She started at his words, for although he had seemed to be the Devil incarnate just days before, new images were beginning to creep into her subconscious. Shadowy, uncertain images of him abed, sheets tangled, eyes at half-mast.

"What then?" he asked.

"I just . . . I . . ." The obscure images were burning holes in her mind, but she yanked her thoughts back on track. "Perhaps your standards of fatherhood are too lofty." Or maybe her own were too low. Anyone who didn't sell his kin to the highest bidder seemed all but saintly.

He watched her in silence, then shook his head. Dark hair waved against his collar. "Fathers should . . ." He paused. His lips were pursed in a stern line, the antithesis of the droll Regency buck. But there was something about the honesty of his expression that touched her. There was no artifice here that she could discern. No pretenses, and somehow that made his rugged features strangely alluring.

"What?" she asked, and the single word sounded breathless, for if the truth be told, she had no idea what a father should do or be. "Fathers should what?"

He scowled. His dark coat was gathered slightly at the shoulders, making them look broad beyond reason. Yet they appeared to have the weight of the world upon them, and for one irrational moment, she wanted nothing more than to touch his face, to feel the coarse stubble that darkened his cheeks. To etch the scar that creased his upper lip.

"Yours was a fine da, aye?" he asked, and now his tone seemed almost hopeful, as if he needed to hear there was some good in the world.

She watched his lips move. He sat very still, his haunting eyes solemn. Upon his powerful knees, his wrists looked sun-browned and broad, sprinkled with sable hair, crossed with pulsing veins. But his hands were not meaty or coarse, and there was something about the way his fingers curled that made it seem that they would be the perfect instruments for writing sonnets or coaxing music from a mandolin.

"Lass?"

She started from her reverie. "Yes. Of course. Until . . ." Her head throbbed again. "He died. In July of 1809." A pulse throbbed in her left eye. "Mother succumbed shortly after . . . of a broken heart," she added, then chided herself, sure she'd said as much before. But if he noticed her freakish need to spill the information she'd so painstakingly memorized, he did not mention it.

"You were cherished then," he said. "As a wee one ought to be?"

Her throat constricted. Her head pounded. She refrained from spewing more lies like a well-versed crow. "Weren't *you*?"

"Cherished?" His lips quirked up again. "In a manner of speaking perhaps."

Memories crowded in. Loneliness, guilt, fear so thick it all but drowned her. "Who bought you?" she whispered, lost for a moment, hopeless.

His brows dropped. "What?" he asked, and she caught her breath, jerking back to reality.

Dear God, she couldn't afford to be mad. She'd made a promise to be sane. A promise she would keep.

"Who *brought* you . . ." she breathed. " . . . to the Highlands? After your mother's death? Was it your father?"

"Nay," he said, but there was still a question in his eyes, as if he'd glimpsed a hint of madness and would wait to see it again. "My father, too, died when I was yet young, but I had uncles."

"*Real* uncles?" Her question made him scowl again, and she caught herself. "I mean, blood kin?" she asked, and though she tried to imbue the words with mere curiosity, her tone sounded almost reverent to her own ears, for despite everything she knew of men, despite everything she had experienced, the thought of true kinship still resonated like waves in her shivering soul.

"Three of them," he said.

"Three." The word came out raspy, for in her wildest imaginings she could not fathom it. Could not see having three blood relatives to care for her. "How wonderful."

"That I didn't have five?"

She scowled.

He dropped his head back against the tree behind him. He wore no hat, and his dark hair was curling with the cool humidity. "Four might well have been the death of me."

Her heart lurched. She'd misread things completely. "They were cruel," she whispered, but he was already shaking his head.

"Nay, lass. Nay, not cruel, just . . ." He was staring at her, thinking. His feet were large, planted well apart, his powerful arms at rest atop them. "Just . . . men," he said.

Cruel then, she thought, but managed not to voice the words as she glanced at the forest bed and felt the memories creep in like evil spirits.

"Perhaps ye should remove your boot," he said.

She glanced up, scared, but he made no move to approach her.

"To alleviate the pressure on your ankle."

She shook her head, finally remembering her lie, and he scowled.

"*I* once left me boot on too long," he said.

She should probably speak now, she realized. A witty tale of footwear perhaps. But nothing immediately sprang to mind.

"After an injury," he explained. " 'Twas not a wise decision."

"No?" It was the best she could do.

"They were forced to cut through the leather. The boot was ruined."

"I meant . . ." She searched for normal, but it was elusive. "How were you injured?"

He didn't answer.

"Did you twist your ankle?" she asked.

"No," he said, and shifted to his knees as if to approach. "You'd best remove that if—"

She yanked her feet back under her skirt.

Silence marched in, lonely and thoughtful. He was staring at her, as if he knew things. As if he sensed things.

"I'll not touch you," he said, words slow, voice quiet. "If that be your wish."

She said nothing. Could think of nothing.

"You've no need to fear."

"Fear?" The word came out rushed. She tried to cover it with laughter, but the sound was coarse and ugly. "I'm not fearful," she said, and felt her head pound.

"Fear is not a shameful thing," he said.

His dark-fringed eyes were thoughtful, filled with his soul. But why? Who was he? What did he know?

"Surely you don't," she said.

He watched her. Somewhere far above a jay scolded the world at large.

"Fear," she explained, and he breathed a sound that might have been a chuckle.

Amusement lit his sea-storm eyes, casting rays of laughter at their corners. "You jest," he said.

"But you're so . . ." She lifted a hand, indicating his size, his strength, his sheer raw power.

"Troll-like?"

"Strong," she breathed.

If he was flattered, he didn't show it. "There is always someone stronger, lass."

She remained silent, taking in the massive breadth of his chest, the amazing width of his leather-clad calves.

"Or quicker. Or smarter. Or better armed."

Their gazes melded silently.

"In truth, I have spent most of my days in the darkness of fear."

She was watching him, reading him, nearly believing, but suddenly she realized the jest was at her expense and almost laughed at her naïveté. "You lie," she said.

He drew a deep breath, then glanced to the right, thoughtful, quiet. "Lies have rarely been my friend."

Or hers. And yet she told them. Told them until her head throbbed. But . . . it did not, she realized suddenly. The pain was gone. She touched her fingers to her brow.

"Does your head yet ache?"

"No," she said, and marveled at the truth. But she would not belabor the point. Stranger things had happened, and there was something to learn here. To understand. "What happened?" she asked.

He shrugged, an economical lift of power. "Did you fall when you twisted your ankle? Mayhap you hit your head. Sometimes it but takes a bit of time for the pain to—"

"I meant your foot," she said. "What happened to your foot? Before they belatedly removed your boot."

" 'Tis not a tale for the likes of you," he said.

"The likes of me?"

"The fairer folk," he said.

She raised her brows. "You think me a . . . pixie?"

Did his face redden the slightest degree? "The fair *sex*," he corrected, and she nearly laughed.

"Perhaps you could tell me nevertheless."

He paused for a moment, thinking, and finally spoke. "I was in Boxtel," he said. "In the Netherlands."

"Why?"

"Because that is what I do." His expression was exceptionally somber again. "What I *did*." He caught her gaze, as if it was difficult to do so and therefore must be done. "I was a Tommy."

She scowled.

"A soldier for the Thirty-third Regiment of Foot. I was young . . . and foolish. My company had been routed." His face was blank as he turned to look through the woods to the open fields beyond. "Outnumbered."

"You were running," she said, and winced. "Like the fox."

Surprise showed on his face, but he nodded. "Like the fox," he said. "Scared out of my wits. But *we* had no place to run. The French were ahead and behind."

The woods were silent.

"What happened?"

"My horse . . ." He paused, almost winced, then shored up his emotions as if they never were. "My mount was shot. He was not so big as Colt, but when he fell, I was broken. And he was dead."

There was no expression on his face, and yet there was something in his voice, something that almost suggested the death of his mount was worse than the pain he'd endured.

"How did you escape?"

"I am not above crawling," he said, voice rough.

She waited, heart beating slowly in the close constraints of her chest.

"I was able to drag myself into the woods. To hide like a cur in a hole."

Her throat felt tight. Her skin itchy. "There's nothing wrong with hiding."

His eyes struck her, flint on steel. She felt breathless, mourning.

"Is there?" she whispered.

He didn't answer. Their gazes melded.

"Please tell me there is not," she murmured, though she knew she gave too much away, knew she exposed too much of herself.

"There is nothing wrong with hiding," he rumbled finally. "If there is a purpose to seeing another day."

She scowled, not knowing what that meant. "Would that the fox had hidden."

He watched her for a moment. "Nay," he said, and drew a deep breath, making his chest rise, making his eyes go sad and dark. "For she had a purpose."

"To save herself," she said, but he shook his head.

Raindrops were just beginning to fall, soft as mist from the darkening sky.

" 'Twas a choice she made," he said. "Herself or her young."

"I—" she began, then stopped abruptly, feeling sick in the pit of her stomach.

"She had kits." Her voice was wooden. It was the best she could do.

He opened his mouth to speak, but perhaps there was something in her expression that stopped him.

"Perhaps I am wrong," he said.

"Where?"

He looked uncomfortable now. "Lass, I may be entirely—"

"Where do you think they are? In the woods ahead?"

He scowled. "Why do you wish to know?"

Her heart felt tight. She could barely breathe past the pain in her throat, but she forced herself to speak, to remember her persona, too long forgotten. "I am but curious. Perhaps you could find them."

"For what purpose?"

"They're vermin." She felt sick again and hoped

to God she wouldn't vomit. "Surely it would be best if we informed the landowner."

"So he can kill them?"

She swallowed painfully. "Yes."

"There's no need," he said, and though his tone was hard, his eyes were something else. Something inexplicable. "They'll perish in a few days' time. We've done our part to ensure that."

She felt the pain in her gut like an open wound, and though she knew she was foolish, she spoke again. "Find them."

He rose to his feet. " 'Tis time to be home," he said.

She shook her head, feeling desperate, feeling lost, and his scowl deepened.

"I cannot leave you alone, wounded in the woods while I rid the world of a few harmless fox pups," he said, and looked down at her as though seeing her with new eyes. "Even *I* am not so barbaric."

Chapter 7

"**G**od help me!" Rogan growled, and hunched his shoulders against the rain. It was darker than Hades and just as damned cold. Although, biblically, the underworld was thought to be hot. Indeed, the ancient Greeks and Christians seemed to be in agreement on that point. But what the hell did they know about hell, he wondered, and almost laughed at his own irony.

But laughing aloud in the rain and the dark would make him seem even madder than he apparently was.

Beneath him, Colt trotted on, impervious to the conditions. Colt should have been the goddamn soldier. *He* should have been the one with medals and commendations and pensions.

Unlike his owner, Bain thought, and just that easily, old memories jostled in, searing his mind. But he shoved them aside. Fatigue always made him melancholy. And he was fatigued. God only knew why he wasn't in bed. It was well past time to sleep, but he was back in the woods where he had ridden with Mrs. Nettles just hours before. The woods where they had spoken. The woods where she had wept.

And there lay the crux of the problem.

Her tears.

He ground his teeth against the memory, for he knew far better than to be moved by a woman's emotions. They could cry on command. Charlotte Winden had cried when she'd told him of her husband's hideous abuses. She had also cried when he'd died by Rogan's bullet. In retrospect, Rogan realized she'd been a veritable virtuoso. Indeed, by all indications, she was a master still, able to dupe any number of people into believing she was something she was not with a few careful tears. Unlike himself, who was nothing but what he appeared to be. Indeed, for as long as he could recall, he had not shed a single tear. Was that something he should celebrate or something he should mourn? These English seemed ungodly comfortable with their emotions, crying over anything from lost buttons to lost lives.

But what of the ethereal wee Faye? She didn't seem the sort to wail over every small disappointment. And yet she *had* cried. Why? Because she was overcome with pain? With sadness? Or was it to gain her own ends? And if that was the case, what might those ends have been? To find the kits so they could be destroyed?

Hunching a little deeper into his coat, he glared

into the darkness and saw her face. Small, oval in shape, golden skin haloed by golden hair, eyes so big they swallowed her face. But it was the emotion in those eyes that had stopped his heart dead in his chest. Because there was misery in those eyes. Empathy. Fear, forgiveness, laughter, tragedy. Hope and . . .

Dammit! He was being an idiot. Because chances were good that he was entirely wrong. What did he know of women? Nothing. Less than nothing. History had proven that. Perhaps she was simply playing him for a fool. Perhaps she merely wanted to *seem* empathetic and fearful and tragic and . . .

But if that was the case, why would she suggest she intended to see the kits destroyed?

That question had been preying on his mind for the past four hours. Longer, since she had been absolutely silent on their return to London, letting his mind rove, making him wonder what she was thinking. She'd looked sad. So much more than sad, in fact.

But why? For the fox? She'd said herself that they were vermin, and even if her words were not to be believed, the fact that she was willing to ride to the hounds certainly must mean—

Colt halted. Bain glanced about. There was nothing to see. It was as dark as a tomb. But he knew a few things about hunting. And if the truth be told, he knew more still about being hunted.

Cursing himself, he tugged the collar up on his coat. Feeling icy rainwater runnel down his back, he left Colt in a protected copse and tramped into the woods afoot.

It was just past dawn when Bain creaked the door shut behind him. He was wet. His chest ached where furrows had been plowed through his skin, and he was, very probably, as daft as a peahen. But at least no one had yet discovered his lunacy. For that he could be thankful, he thought, and kicking off his boots in the small hardwood entry, padded stocking foot into the kitchen. A pot of steaming tea would go a long way to warming him, but first—

"Bain!"

He glanced over his shoulder at the sound of his name, only to find Connelly standing in the kitchen doorway, face perplexed as they stared at each other.

"Where the devil have you—" he began, then opened his sky blue eyes wide and let his jaw drop. Mischievous joy shone on his face. "Are you only now returning home?"

Damn, Bain thought and wished to God he'd never met an Irishman. Remaining mute, he removed the cover from the teapot with his left hand. Why did they insist on making these kettles so ridiculously small.

"You are!" Connelly crowed, and took two celebratory strides into the kitchen. "You've not been home for hours. And you know what that suggests."

Bain couldn't think of a reason to respond.

"It means you owe me a great debt of gratitude, my hulking Highland friend. It means that because of me, you were finally able to—"

Bain turned toward him with malevolent slowness, stopping Connelly's words in his throat and raising his eyebrows well toward his hairline.

"I was about to inquire about our charming Mrs. Nettles, but I . . ." Connelly winced, studying the scarlet scratches that ran downward from Bain's clavicle. *Damn fox.* "I see now that she's a feisty one. Feistier even than the maid I met at Haymarket. Remember her? The plump lass with the big . . ." He motioned toward his chest, then stopped, gaze dropping to the flour bag Bain carried in his right hand. The bag that was moving. The bag that now housed three undersized balls of fury. "What the devil is that?"

Dammit to hell. "Nothing to concern yourself with," Bain rumbled.

Connelly raised his brows even higher, already happier than Bain ever wished him to be. "Since when has 'nothing to concern yourself with' been carried about in a bag? A flour bag. A flour bag that smells like wet hounds or . . . No. Not hounds. Wet . . ." He paused, narrowed his eyes, and sniffed in a show of great, deliberate thought. Bain almost scoffed out loud at the idea. "Last I saw you, were you not about to embark on a foxhunt?"

God help him. Bain pressed past Connelly on

the way to the pantry. There was no hope now. "Where's the damned tea?" he rumbled.

"I'm not certain."

Bain's mood, never good when cold, wet, and scratched to ribbons by fox pups, was deteriorating rapidly. "Why the devil not?"

"A fair question," Connelly said, and tilted his head. Damned bastard. "But an even better one might be . . . why are you wet if you spent the night in the fair widow's—"

"Don't be daft," Bain said, and, rummaging about in the sparsely furnished cupboard, luckily came up with a tin of tea. Unluckily, he was now reminded that he'd dumped the flour into a wooden keg that overflowed onto the upper shelf.

"Perhaps she had a mind to bathe while fully clothed. An odd concept, true enough. But I must say, she seemed a unique sort, and not one I would have thought likely to be thrilled by the idea of sacrificing a fox for a bit of frivolous . . ." Connelly began, but his words stopped abruptly, then he laughed, throwing his head back like a damned lunatic as he flopped into the chair behind him, cravat undone, hair messed after a night of certain debauchery. "Don't tell me."

Bain was going to have to find a lid for the flour keg. And, of course, he was, very probably, also going to have to beat the stuffing out of Connelly. But just the thought of it made him hungry.

"The stunning Mrs. Nettles . . ." Connelly

paused, trying to catch his breath. "Was upset because . . ." More laughter. Perhaps the time had come to start that stuffing beating thing. "The fox . . . which . . ." He'd been reduced to chuckles. "By the by . . . you were hunting . . . was killed."

Bain didn't even like Irishmen. Never had.

"So upset, in fact, that *you* . . ." Connelly's shoulders were bumping up and down with the rhythm of his humor.

In general, he also didn't like men.

"You decided to save the pups."

"Why would I do something so daft?" Bain asked, but the little hellions took that precise moment to wriggle wildly, setting the bag alive.

"Very well then."

Bain had never seen Connelly happier. He gritted his teeth against the other's jocularity.

"Let me guess again. Might you have . . ." He made an elegant motion toward the bag. For a damned mercenary, he was as polished as a pedigreed prince. Bain had always resented that about him. "Salmon? In the bag?"

"Isn't there some woman's husband you could be cuckolding?" Bain rumbled, but his words only set the other to guffawing again before he returned to his ludicrous guessing.

"House cats? Baby dragons?" A kit whimpered, drawing both their attention. "Werewolves?"

"Go to bed, Irish."

"Honest to God, I wish I could," Connelly said, cheerful as sunrise. "But I'm just so . . ." He shook his head. "So demmed fascinated. I keep asking myself what kind of magic does the tiny Mrs. Nettles have that would cause a big Scottish lug like you to . . ." He paused. His jaw dropped again and a look of ethereal joy overcame his foolish features. "Don't tell me," he said.

God help them all.

"She cried," Connelly deduced with resounding finality.

"Find me something to eat or get out of the damned kitchen," Bain ordered.

"I'm right, am I not? I can see it now. The pixie-bright little widow, weeping as if her heart were broken. You're lucky she didn't ask you to kill anybody."

McBain gritted his teeth, but thankfully Connelly was far too dense to realize what he'd said.

"She didn't, did she?" Connelly asked.

"I am not so fortunate," Bain rumbled, and gave Connelly a baleful glare, but the other only laughed.

"You can't kill *me*. I'm the one who made it possible for you to spend the night . . . chasing fox pups." He was grinning like an intoxicated dolt. Bain ignored him as best he could as he attempted to pour tea leaves into the strainer.

"Here," said the Irishman finally. "Let me take your young ones since, by the look of things, they're likely to be the only offspring you'll ever sire."

Bain relinquished the bag, allowing Connelly to undo the top and glance inside.

"Look at that," he said. "They're rather adorable. Considering the sire."

"If you weren't so damned amusing, I'd kick your arse out the door."

He laughed. "So, what are you going to do with the deadly little darlings?" he asked, glancing up, and McBain finally smiled.

"I'm going to give them to *you*," he said.

Chapter 8

"**W**hat did you learn?" Lord Gallo's voice was as even as slate, perfectly modulated, and decidedly cool.

"Very little," Faye said, and refrained from fidgeting like a guilty schoolgirl. The events of the previous day still made her feel raw and uncertain.

"Do you believe your amulet is taking hold?"

Faye scowled, remembering Rogan McBain's disturbing presence, the low rumble of his voice, the mesmerizing cast of his eyes. "I sensed no lies." Which was true yet oddly confusing. "At least, not from him."

Madeline nodded. They were, once again, sitting in the parlor of Lavender House.

"So your own untruths are still causing you troubles?"

"Some," she said cautiously, and remembered that strangely, her headaches seemed to disappear when McBain was near.

"Then the pain is no longer debilitating?" Maddy asked, and watched her closely. It was a known fact that in the past, the headaches associated with lies had left her all but incapacitated.

Faye shook her head. "They were not unmanageable."

"Even if you speak of Mrs. Nettles's past?"

The story, which was entirely different from reality. Entirely more palatable.

"Even then," she said. "But I almost wished to tell him—" she paused, realized what she had nearly admitted, and glanced rapidly toward Lord Gallo.

"Tell him what?" Madeline asked, and Faye forced a shrug.

" 'Tis simply that he seems so . . ."

They waited in silent tandem.

"Truthful," she said, and finally allowed her fingers to fiddle for a moment with a fold in her beribboned skirt.

"You presented him your truth amulet, is that correct?"

"Yes."

"But you don't believe that's the cause of his honesty?"

"I—"

"I don't believe it either," Shaleena said, and sauntered into the room. It seemed she was ever about these days, rarely leaving the house since Joseph's arrival. Why was that? She cherished the gardens as much as any witch, and Joseph seemed decent enough, for a man. Broad-shouldered and hard-muscled, he always conducted himself with somber decorum. He spent much of his time in the stable, polishing brass and oiling harness leather. When he spoke, which was rare, there was a subtle hint of an unknown accent. Something smooth and rolling that conjured up images of the dark Carpathian Mountains and the legends they evoked. Intriguing, even to someone of Faye's skittish nature, so why was Shaleena, an inveterate flirt, so intent on avoiding him?

"Although they might slow him down a bit," she added.

For a moment, Faye almost thought she saw Lord Gallo grit his teeth. Indeed, a flash of annoyance seemed to strike his eyes, and in that instant she found that she almost liked him, almost trusted him. Though in her head she knew it was foolish not to, for he had saved her life just as surely as she had almost ended his. Sometimes fear made her actions a bit unpredictable.

"The amulets," Shaleena explained, and raised a carefully groomed eyebrow. "They are, after all, little more than rocks." Lifting a book from the narrow table near the door, she glanced at the title and dropped it back. "Indeed, I don't know why the child is allowed here at Lavender House."

"I *am*—" Faye began, but the other cut her off.

"What? What are you? A foolish girl hiding from shadows? A danger to this coven?"

"Shaleena," Madeline warned, voice low, but the other turned toward her contemporary and continued.

"I warned you not to trust her with this mission. Unless you've no qualms about someone dying. But you have always seemed so touchy about death."

"I've done nothing amiss," Faye said, and felt her temper flare. Not fear. Not shame. But anger. It was such a rare event. So foreign that she almost didn't recognize the feel of it. "Indeed—"

"Nothing amiss?" Shaleena said and laughed. "Then I must have been misinformed. I thought I heard that you had blackened the eye of the very man you intended to lure."

Embarrassment smote her, but she kept her chin high. "I had no wish to *lure* him. I—"

" 'Tis just as well, then," Shaleena said, and tossed her hair over one shoulder. Her breasts were ridiculously large. "For there would be little hope. 'Tis best to send a woman to do a woman's job."

"I agree," Lord Gallo said.

Faye skittered her gaze hopelessly to his, but his expression was bland once again, his attention directed at Shaleena.

"That is why I meant to ask you to do some tutoring today."

"Tutoring?" Her tone had gone suddenly coy. Her lips curved. "Might I hope you would be my student, Jasper?"

Faye glanced at Madeline, but if his wife felt threatened, she showed no sign.

"No," Gallo said.

Shaleena smiled and slid her crafty gaze sideways. "I would be happy to help your bride hone *her* skills if you feel she needs—"

"The lesson is for Cur," he said, interrupting smoothly.

Shaleena turned with a jerk. "You jest."

"I believe, if I am not mistaken, that he is arriving even as we speak."

Shaleena's eyes narrowed dangerously. "Why the devil do you insist on inviting these odd outsiders into our midst?"

" 'Outsiders'?"

"You would be a fool to trust them with our secrets."

"I assume you are including Joseph in your distrust?" Madeline asked.

"He *can't* be trusted," Shaleena hissed, taking Madeline aback with her vehemence.

"Why do you believe this?"

For a moment something almost primitive passed through Shaleena's eyes, but she lifted her head and leveled her gaze, expression cool and condescending once again. "He's a man, is he not?"

"I believe so, but I've not noticed in the past that you dislike men by gender alone," she said, and glanced at her long-suffering husband with an arched brow.

"Why do you allow them to come here?" Shaleena hissed, and took a step toward Madeline, but at that moment, Lord Gallo rose. He was not a tall man, not a broad man, but in that moment there was something about him that spoke of power just barely leashed.

"They come because I ask them to. Because they are of assistance to us."

"Assistance!" She spat the word. "What can they do that I cannot?"

"Cur seems to have an uncanny ability to find people," Madeline said. "Indeed, he found *us*."

"Why?" Shaleena asked, teeth gritted.

"I have been meaning to ask *you* that," said Gallo.

"Me! Why would you think to question me? I'm nothing to him. Less than nothing." Her voice sounded frantic. "I've not seen him . . ." She stopped, gaze snapping about the room, fists tightening and relaxing. "I had not met him before his arrival here. I'm certain I had not."

A twinge of pain stabbed Faye's head, and Shaleena twisted toward her.

"I do not lie," she hissed "And I've not got the witch's madness."

"No one suggested you were mad," Gallo said, tone level, but at the mere mention of the words, Faye's skin prickled. More than a few of the most gifted were locked away. More still had taken their own lives. "All we ask is that you—"

But at the moment, there was the slightest suggestion of noise from the front of the house.

"I believe that may be he now," Gallo said.

Something shone in Shaleena's eyes, something

almost akin to fear. Then she left, breezing from the room and up the stairs to her own private chambers.

The room went quiet, pulsing with uncertainty. Lord Gallo spoke first.

"Cur," he said though the doorway was still empty. "We've been expecting you."

A young man stepped into view. He was tall and narrow, with sharp, dark eyes that spoke of wit and caution and foreign bearing.

"How do you do that?" he asked.

"I heard you coming."

"I might have been another."

"But you're not," Gallo said.

This ability to feel the powers of the gifted was his one talent. Or so he said. But Faye suspected there was a great deal he did not say. A great deal she did not understand about how he had found her. How he had found the others. Had understood their oddities, had honed their crafts.

"Are you?" Gallo asked.

"Not yet," Cur said, just hinting at that oddness Shaleena had spoken of. And Gallo smiled with his eyes, a rare show of good humor.

"Perhaps you should wait a bit. Shaleena is a mite upset," Madeline said.

And now it was Cur's turn to smile, showing sharp canines and a predatory bent. "I believe I have waited long enough," he said, and, bowing shallowly, evidenced a strange, regal grace. "Worry not, she'll do me no real harm," he said, and left them, following the other's trail silently up the stairs.

Moments ticked quietly away. Madeline scowled. "Some might think it foolhardy to throw two such powers together," she said, voice soft.

"*Three* powers," Gallo mused.

Maddy turned toward him. "I thought Joseph was not particularly gifted."

"I don't believe he is. Which causes me to wonder what brought him here. The one man who seems to raise her ire more than her interest."

Madeline's scowl deepened. "You don't suppose . . ."

Gallo merely glanced at her.

"I'll speak to my sister," Maddy said, and her husband nodded slightly before turning to Faye.

"My apologies. We called you here to hear progress of your mission," he said, but she shook her head.

"No." She tried to keep from fidgeting. "Perhaps she's right."

"Shaleena."

"Yes. Perhaps I am not the one for the job."

"If not you, then who?" Madeline asked.

No one spoke.

"The committee has used the conventional methods to learn what it could about Brendier's death, but little was discovered. The truth now must be drawn out by other means."

Faye felt her heart knock restlessly against her ribs.

"We've no murder weapons for Ella to lay hands on to discern the killer. No ashes for Rosemond to sift through. Though Cur studied the scene, the scents were too old to firmly discern one from the other. There were no witnesses. No clues. Drawing the truth from those most likely to be the culprits is our only hope." She paused, smiled. "And you are the truth seeker, Faerie Faye."

But I am weak, Faye thought.

"If we fail, the committee may no longer be willing to fund us. It is conceivable that Les Chausettes will have to disband," she said. "But if you feel you cannot—"

"No," Faye said, and felt her stomach twist. "No. I'll not fail."

"You'll see to the task set before you?"

"Yes."

"Very well," Madeline said. "Then I think you should attend the annual fete at Inver Heights. We shall obtain an invitation in your name."

Faye almost winced. "But why?"

"Inver Heights is Lord Lindale's estate."

"Lord Lindale," Faye said. "Brendier's cousin." The English peerage was as inbred as lapdogs.

"And debtor," Madeline added.

"Lindale was in debt to his cousin? I thought he was quite well-fixed."

"That seems to be the common belief, but there are rumors suggesting otherwise. We have reason to believe the debt was considerable, and there are

few things that make enemies faster than unre-
turned coin."

"You think Lindale might be Brendier's
killer?"

Madeline rose smoothly to her feet. "That is for
you to discover."

Jasper rose with her, placing a gentle hand to
the small of her back, as if he only needed to touch
her to feel whole.

Faye watched the movement, felt the feelings.

"Oh, and, Faerie Faye," Madeline said, turning
back.

"Yes?"

"You are stronger than you think."

"I fear you might be—"

"We all fear," Madeline said. "That does not
make us weak. It only makes us wise."

"Then I am practically a genius."

Madeline laughed, looking surprised. "Wiser
than most," she said, and sobered. "And stronger
than Shaleena."

Faye felt the compliment in her gut. "I'm sure
you're wrong."

"So is Shaleena," Madeline said. "Won't you
both be surprised when you realize the truth?"

Chapter 9

Lord Lindale was wealthy, refined, and respected. At least that is how he portrayed himself to the world. And this lavish fete certainly made it seem so. Though Faye knew as well as any that appearances were often an illusion. After all, she herself looked quite refined in the mint green gown that flowed, lightly pleated, to her satin dancing slippers.

She glanced about. The food was plentiful. The trappings expensive. The company . . . Well, the company was the same, making her feel out of place, like a flea-bitten cur in a diamond collar.

From the front of their elegant home, perfectly centered in the arched doorway, the lord and lady greeted their guests. They were dressed in French designs that might have just stepped off the fashionable pages of *Le Bon Ton* or *Corriere delle Dame*, she in a white satin ball gown embellished with gold metal embroidery, he in a blue tailcoat and white pantaloons. But though his erect stance hinted of a corset hidden beneath his silver-shot waistcoat, neither his age nor his belly was completely disguised. They were a well-aged couple, neither particularly arresting. But there was obvious affection between them, evidenced by the way she touched his arm and leaned in as she spoke.

Faye watched the exchange and felt a little barb of jealousy twist in her heart even as an ache twitched in her brow. She was grateful for her life at Lavender House, and yet she hungered for something she did not quite understand but knew she would never have. Uncle Max had made certain of that much. She would not love. Would not trust.

The morose emotions flared through her, but she tamped them down, for she was being silly. She had Les Chausettes, and she would not fail them.

"Mrs. Nettles," said someone. She turned, keeping her movements fluid, only to find Lord Rennet at her elbow. He bowed. She managed, with some pride, to refrain from bolting toward the nearest exit. "We meet again."

"Yes." Memories of their last encounter loomed large and dark in her mind, but she kept her hands steady. Naught would happen here amongst the gentry, she told herself. But even as the thought crossed her mind, she knew it untrue. London was ever a place of danger, for while its jaded denizens glittered with hard gems and dry wit, they were as likely to bet on the outcome of an altercation as to interfere with one. Especially if the threatened party was not one of their own, and she had never felt the chasm between herself and the *bon ton* more strongly than she did that night.

Still, she was not alone here. Indeed, Lord and Lady Gallo had accompanied her. Shaleena, too, had intended to come, until she realized Joseph would be at the ribbons. Joseph, who carried himself like royalty but lived like a stableboy, refusing to take a room in Lavender House.

"You look quite as devastating as you did last we spoke."

"And you look . . ." She arched a brow at him. "More upright," she said, and did her best to maintain her breathing, to control both her emotions and her bearing, as she'd been taught. There would be no flying flowerpots this night.

"Yes." He smiled at her jest, but there was the hint of anger in his eyes.

Her stomach churned.

"Someone planted a facer on me. Had I not been on the cut, however, I'm certain I would have bested the bloody bastard. Demmed low of him to strike when I was drunk as a wheelbarrow."

"Those barrows are indeed tipsy. Now if you'll excuse me, I fear I must away," she said, and turned with regal aplomb; but he grabbed her arm, fingers hard just where her full glove ended near her lace-edged cap sleeve.

She froze. He smiled and pulled his hand away, lifting it high as if to show that he meant no harm. "I had no wish to vent my spleen. Indeed, I intended to apologize for my conduct."

It was all she could do to remain as she was.

"I did not mean to be so . . . zealous," he said, and leaned close. Perhaps his grin was meant to be boyish and amiable. But to her skittish mind it looked malicious and sly. Stray thoughts of flying potted palms splashed through her mind, but she banished the notion, locking it carefully away. "I fear your loveliness overcame my good sense. Indeed, I only meant to tell you how comely you looked in the moonlight, but I fear I had had a bit much to drink. Believe me when I say that I would have done you no harm."

Her head was beginning to ache from his lies. "My apologies," she said, "but I promised . . ." For a moment she could not think of a decent fabrication. ". . . . my friend that I would save this dance for him."

"Your friend?" His lips twisted into a smile, but there was malice in his eyes. She was certain of it. "Tell me, Mrs. Nettles, is your friend the beast that interrupted my friendly overtures at Mrs. Tell's?" His tone was wry, his handsome face cynical as he took a sip of port from a crystal cup, pinky raised just so. And suddenly the difference between him and McBain shone sharp as a beacon in her mind.

"Tell me, Lord Rennet," she said, emotions stirring slowly in her mind. "Do you call him a beast to his face?"

"I surely would if he were so bold as to show himself again," he said and smiled.

She raised a dubious brow, and his face colored peevishly.

"Some think it somewhat unwise to strike a peer of the realm," he said.

Emotion flared inside her, but she could not quite recognize it, for it felt more like anger than fear. "Perhaps he mistook you for a drunken molester," she said.

He stared at her a moment, then smiled and bowed.

"Just so long as you did not make the same mistake. I could not bear to frighten someone as lovely as you."

"I didn't say I was frightened."

"No. You don't look the type to frighten easily. Indeed, you appear ever so . . ." He let his gaze slip over her, and with his attention, she felt her breath come faster. "So cool. So controlled. But then, I suppose it is a simple enough thing to remain calm when you have a beast at your beck and call."

Behind her, laughter burst out, frazzling her nerves.

"That would indeed be convenient," she said, and turned away.

But he snagged her arm once more.

"You'd best warn him not to try something so foolish again." Anger drifted off him.

She dipped her gaze to his hand and raised her brows as she met his gaze. "Warn him?"

"He might be interested to know that I've

danced with the likes of Salvage Shelton and Tommy Cribb."

She shook her head, hoping she looked haughty; but fear was mingling with a dozen confusing emotions, causing her hands to shake, her heart to stutter. She knew the singsong lyrics of the *ton's* mercurial cant. Indeed, she oft tried to speak it herself, to meld with the *flash morts* and *swell coves* of the rarefied upper crust, but just now she was unable to decipher the jargon.

"Boxing," he explained. "I can hold my own in—"

"Lass," rumbled a voice.

Faye jerked her gaze from her captor.

Rogan McBain stood only inches away. Towering over both her and Rennet, his dark brows were lowered over stormy-sea eyes, his endless shoulders tense as he found her with his gaze.

"Is aught amiss?"

Relief slouched through her, but she forced herself to glance coolly at her abductor, to push out a steady rejoinder. "I was just about to . . ." What? Blather like a fainthearted idiot? Pray for a savior? She tugged at her arm, keeping the movement casual, though panic had seized her in its gigantic fist, squeezing her heart. Still, Rennet did not relinquish his hold. " . . . fetch some refreshment," she said, and though she tried to resist, tried to be strong, her gaze turned hopelessly back to the Highlander's.

Truth stormed between them. His eyes burned

hers, and when he spoke he did not look away.

"Release her."

Rennet tightened his hold, but against her skin, his hand felt stiff with fear.

"Perhaps you do not realize who I am, Scotsman."

McBain turned his attention slowly from her face. The movement was steady, utterly controlled, but something in the very air around them seemed to change, to shift. "I believe you're something of a pugilist," he said, words little more than a growl.

" 'Tis good to know my reputation—"

"Is that not a sport better played at with two hands?"

The atmosphere hung like a stormy cloud around them, charged with electricity, humming with expectation, then; "Are you threatening me, Beast?" Rennet hissed.

Bain's expression changed not a whit. Neither did he speak, and yet his intentions reverberated through the room. Rennet held on a moment longer, then released his hold, backed away, and bowed. "There will be repercussions. Believe that," he said, mouth twisted as he turned away.

They watched him go, but finally McBain shifted his gaze back to hers. "My apologies," he said.

She felt breathless, all but dizzy with relief. Too winded to voice her appreciation.

"If I misinterpreted the situation," he added.

"What?" Her voice sounded raspy.

He inhaled, expanding his boundless chest,

then clenched one hand seemingly subconsciously into a fist. "Perhaps you were enjoying the gentleman's company."

"Do you jest?"

He scowled down at her. "Rarely."

"You think I might have wanted him pawing . . ." She stopped herself, realizing with sudden lightheadedness that she had lost even the semblance of her arrogant demeanor. "You think I welcomed his attentions?"

He searched her face for several seconds, then lifted his solemn gaze and glanced away, scanning the glistening assemblage. "I will be the first to admit the ways of the nobility are oft a mystery to me," he said.

"I am not nobility."

"You oft seem too refined for this company."

"Now you *are* jesting." She knew better than to say such things, but the words came unbidden. It was, it seemed, almost impossible to spew ridiculous untruths in his presence.

His gaze was piercing, hard and steady and earnest, a bit of sanity juxtaposed against the tittering laughter that wafted up from behind her.

"Yet you *look* to be the epitome of this society."

"Epitome?" she asked, and almost smiled at the strangeness of such a vocabulary coming from a man who seemed to embody the very essence of the ancient warrior.

He shuffled his feet. "I am a Tommy, not a beast . . ." He glanced into the crowd again. If there was anger in his eyes, she could not tell, but there certainly was not happiness. "As some would think."

"A foot soldier," she said, though she knew enough of his reputation to realize he was so much more. A lieutenant at the very least, though he didn't claim the title. "Why are they called Tommies?"

He paused for a moment, watching her, then, "Thomas Atkins was a good lad." He seemed to be far away suddenly.

She shook her head, at a loss and surprised that she cared. "Thomas . . ."

"He died at Boxtel." There was something in his eyes. Sadness maybe, but more. "Without remorse or blame. Or so Arthur said."

"Arthur?"

He scowled at her as if just remembering her presence. "If you'll tell me your preferences I shall fetch your refreshments."

But she would not be waylaid. "Arthur who?"

Regret seemed to twitch the corner of his mouth, but he answered. "Wellesley."

It took her a moment to realize whom he spoke of. She raised her brows in surprise. "The Marquess of Wellington."

He nodded once, but even that seemed regretful.

"You refer to the Marquess of Wellington by his given name."

He glanced away again. "The trifles look . . ."

His brows lowered a scant degree. " . . . tiny."

"Who are you?" she asked.

He shook his head. "Naught but a High-lander."

It was a lie. That much she knew. And yet it did not feel like a lie.

"And what do you think I am?" she asked.

"You are a lady."

"As I said, I am not nobility."

"I believe such a thing is not defined by blood."

She felt a little breathless, a little light-headed. "What then?"

"Character. Courage. Goodness."

Something crunched in her heart, for she possessed none of those lofty qualities, but she would play the game. "It's the gown," she said, and lifted the pleated confection. "Everyone looks good in mint."

"It is you," he said, and the solemnity of his tone bored through her careful artifice.

"Perhaps you misjudge me," she said.

He studied her. "Perhaps you misjudge yourself."

Music played in the background. A lively number.

"Perhaps I hope others will do the same," she murmured though she knew she shouldn't. Knew she should guard the truth with every precious breath.

"Do you mean to say you are not what you

seem?" he asked, and she wanted, quite desperately, to tell him the truth. That she was terrified. Had been terrified her whole life. That she was weak and guilty and cruel. But before the truth could spill from her lips like essence of banewort, she caught herself.

"Not at all," she said. "I was but jesting. I am exactly—"

"Mrs. Nettles."

She turned to the right, remembering to keep her expression placid, to keep from bolting, to *act*. "Mr. Cunningham."

"How nice to see you again. I believe we met some months ago. At Lady Branton's garden party."

She remembered the day. It had ended with an innocent oboist being catapulted into a percussionist to escape Cunningham's less-than-reputable hands. And though perhaps most did not realize the ensuing clatter was her fault, the memory brewed a squalling tempest in her soul.

"I was hoping I might have the dance you promised me then," he said.

She knew she should speak. Indeed, she should be witty and gay, or at least conscious.

"I fear that will not be possible," McBain said.

The aging lord turned toward him. Faye did the same, all the while believing that Rogan McBain feared nothing.

"Mrs. Nettles and I were just about to take to the floor."

"Oh. I see. Very well," Cunningham said, and bowed graciously toward the twirling couples that thronged the ballroom. "Be my guest then."

There was a moment of strained stillness before McBain turned to her.

Their gazes met. Moments passed like bullets. Finally, he offered his arm, and when she took it, it felt as stiff and solid as an oaken bough.

They walked in breathless tandem toward the dance floor.

"My apologies again," he rumbled.

She didn't look at him, couldn't; her gratitude was too deep. "Whatever for?"

"Perhaps you wished to dance with him."

She didn't respond. The poor oboist had suffered a broken arm. This was so much simpler.

"I can return you to him if you like," he said, and glanced down. She could feel his gaze on her. "If I misinterpreted your feelings."

She knew she should lie, but a lingering ache in her head insisted on the truth. "No," she said. "You did not."

They had reached the dance floor and turned now toward each other.

"Then I must apologize for something else," he said.

She raised her gaze to his, felt the hard thrust of his earnestness. "What's that?"

"I do not know the reel," he said.

They stood facing each other near the gleaming expanse of the marble dance floor. He had saved her . . . again. And yet he looked chagrined. Almost guilty.

"But this is a quadrille."

His scowl darkened. "I also cannot distinguish one dance from the next," he rumbled, and she almost laughed, for he said the words the way another might have confessed to murder.

"Then come," she said, and turned away, but he failed to follow. Turning back, she caught his gaze with her own. "Come," she repeated, and, reaching out, took his hand.

His skin was warm, his palm broad with strength and calluses. Breath left her throat. No posh dandy, he, but a man filled with power and life. With triumphs and regrets and anguish. They froze in place, staring at each other, doing nothing, but in a moment she realized her foolishness. She was Mrs. Nettles. Sophisticated. Worldly.

"Come," she repeated, and finally he did so, following her through the crowd, past the arched, open doors, and into the fragrant expanse of the garden. Every witch's refuge.

She turned toward him. A half dozen hanging lanterns lit the expansive, sweet-smelling grounds. Diffused light softly illuminated the foliage, the burbling fountain topped with laughing cherubs, the strong lines of McBain's face, the dark sweep of his hair. And here, in the tender grip of nature, he did not look so much like a devil as an avenging angel.

Their gazes met and lingered with something

like breathless anticipation. She still held his hand, and from that simple touch, a thousand feelings stormed the bastions of her heart.

"Lass," he rumbled, and something tightened low in her gut at the low sound of his voice.

"Yes?"

"You should not be here."

She knew what he meant. And he was right, of course. She should not be alone with him, a veritable giant, a foreigner, a stranger, but her heart was racing with anticipation. Though in the past, she would never have *wished* to be alone with such a man. Indeed, with *any* man. "But I love gardens," she breathed. Every witch did. She managed not to add that.

"Men cannot be trusted."

She let the seconds tick away. "Even you?" she whispered, and forgot to breathe as she waited for his answer.

"Especially me," he said, and she felt her heart pick up the pace.

"Are you so dangerous then?"

"Aye," he said.

"But surely I would survive a few minutes, even with the surly likes of you."

His expression was dark, but there was a quizzical quality to it. "Why would you wish to?"

Why indeed? What was wrong with her? "I owe you a dance."

"As I said, I do not know how—"

"Then I shall teach you," she said, and slanted

a glance at him through her lashes, feeling light-headed. Feeling *flirtatious*. Good heavens, was she bewitched? "You did not think I brought you here for another purpose did you?"

"Lass . . ." he warned, and she laughed.

The sound wafted merrily through the garden, light and happy, almost as if it had come from some other source. As if she were normal, happy, unfettered by the detritus of her past, and the enormity of that realization rocked her to her very roots.

And they were still staring.

She cleared her throat and pulled her gaze from his but could not quite divine where to look, for every part of him seemed to hold a strange sizzling magnetism she had never felt before.

"I do not *feel* unsafe," she said finally, and when he did not respond immediately, she glanced up, only to find that his gaze had not ventured from her face.

"Neither did . . ." he began, and stopped.

She felt the breath clog in her throat. "Who?"

He shook his head. "I do not think I am the sort," he said.

"For dancing?"

"For . . ." His eyes were soulful, turbulent, haunted. And if she hadn't known better, if she hadn't realized he was the very embodiment of power and courage, she would have sworn they were also fearful. "You," he said finally.

"Am I so hideous?" she asked. It was meant as a poor attempt at a jest, but in the depths of her being she knew the answer, for though her face might be fair enough, her soul was not. And he was a man to see past the surface. Indeed, even now it felt as if he was peering into the very core of her.

In the lengthening silence, her heartbeat was surely as loud as a gong, then; "If I could but find a fault," he said.

She stared at him, lost, broken, floundering in the silence. "You think me flawless?" she breathed.

"If I am mistaken, I would know now, before it is too late," he murmured. "I've no fondness for lies."

She shook her head, wanting, nay, *needing* to speak the truth. And yet she would not. Not today. Not ever. "Too late?"

"For me heart," he said and, even though she knew far better, even though she realized with every atom of her being that she risked all, she reached up to caress his stubbled cheek.

His world-weary eyes fell closed as though her touch injured him. Scorched him. Cut him to the core. And with that expression there was nothing she could do but kiss him.

Chapter 10

Her lips touched his, firm yet cautious. And with that tentative touch a thousand warring emotions stormed through her whirling system. Excitement, lust, fear. But she could not stop. Could not help herself. He might well be the enemy. The very embodiment of the Lucifer that had bedeviled her childhood. She knew that, but it hardly seemed to matter, for she was a fool. A weak, trembling coward. Had always been. Had always needed a savior, a protector.

And as he slipped his hand down to her waist, she knew she was in over her head, deep and going deeper. Falling as she had never before, with nothing to break her rush to—

"Mrs. Nettles, are you here?"

Faye jerked away, heart pounding as her mind fluttered to place the voice. A woman's. A . . . Madeline! Here. By the fountain. About to find her kissing the very man they suspected of murder!

"Mrs. Nettles . . . Ah, there you are," said Madeline, and seemed to materialize almost instantly from the darkness surrounding them. "I thought I saw you venture this way."

"Lady Gallo," Faye rasped, and felt her face flame with a dozen uncertain emotions. "You were looking for me?"

"Indeed I was. You left the ballroom so quickly. I wanted to make certain you hadn't taken ill."

"Oh. No." Panic and shame filled her. What had she been thinking? She had made a vow to find a killer, yet here she was, all but breathless with a man she'd only just met. "I am quite well."

Madeline raised a dark brow. "I see that you are," she said, and paused expectantly.

Silence settled in.

"Oh," Faye breathed, and knew there were social obligations to be met. "Let me introduce Mr. . . ." And the name was gone.

Madeline waited in silence, but Faye was out of control, out of her depth, out of her *mind*. Thus the other finally turned toward the Scot with regal aplomb.

"Rogan McBain," he rumbled, as he pulled his deep gaze from Faye to Madeline. "Though most call me naught but Bain."

"Bain," Madeline said.

"Aye."

"What an unusual—" Madeline began, but Faye could not tolerate another moment of this blistering civility.

"My apologies," she said, and, lifting her skirts,

prepared to flee. "I just now remembered I must speak to the lady of the house."

Bain watched her graceful exit through the moon-shadowed garden, like a pixie among the nodding roses, like an angel among men.

Lady Gallo cleared her throat, drawing his attention back to her. She was a comely woman, he supposed. But she was neither angelic nor—

"And how do you know Mrs. Nettles?" she asked.

He was a fool. He knew that. A fool who would not learn. There was no such thing as angels. And yet wee Faye had, for a moment, seemed so innocent. So lost and small regardless of the steely bravado she shared with the world. "We were acquainted some days past."

"Ahh." The lady's dark gaze sharpened. "And what were your intentions escorting her out of doors?"

He scowled, remembering the fear that had momentarily sparked in little Faye's eyes upon the lady's entrance into the garden. Or had he only imagined that emotion? "Why is it you ask?"

She looked mildly surprised by his question. "I ask because she is my friend, Mr. McBain, and I am not one to forgive easily."

He said nothing but watched her, assessing.

"Do you understand my meaning?" she asked, emotion bright as shooting stars in her eyes. But what emotion was it exactly?

"I am not certain I do," he said.

"I am saying that if something amiss happens to her, I shall not take it lightly."

It was not often that people surprised him. Not after all these years, and yet he *was* surprised. He was quite certain he weighed a good eight stone more than his challenger. "Are you threatening me, my lady?"

She stood absolutely still for a moment, then straightened marginally. The top of her head almost reached his chin. "Yes," she said.

He stared at her, looking past the well-groomed features and the steady eyes to the woman beyond. But she did not falter, and finally he nodded once, satisfied.

"I shall hold you to that," he said, and turned, leaving her to stare after him as he returned to the ball.

"Why are you here?" The voice was quiet, little more than a murmur of darkness, but Cur heard it clearly and turned with a start. A figure stood among the shadows. The lights of the noble estate did not reach the spot where Cur crouched among the greenery. They rarely did. Yet Joseph had found him.

"I would ask the same of you," Cur said, rising as he eyed the other's livery, "but I can see you've become their servant."

"Every man is another's servant. No matter the circumstances."

"Ahh, words of wisdom. Just what I've needed all my wayward life. I shall cherish them always," Cur said, and moved to slip farther into the darkness, but the older man caught his arm. Despite his unassuming manner, his grip was firm.

"Revenge does not spawn happiness, *fiu*. That I can promise."

They stared at each other in the darkness, thoughts tumbling like eagles in flight, dark gazes clashing.

"If you think I seek revenge, you would be wise to watch your own back," Cur snarled, and, jerking from the other's grasp, disappeared into the darkness.

What the devil had she been thinking? Faye's head felt overheated, her hands clammy. She'd kissed him. *Kissed* him! Like a twittering schoolgirl. Like an undisciplined demirep. And if that wasn't bad enough, she had been caught at it. What kind of witch was she? She was here on a mission. She was here to find a killer. A killer who might very well be in this very house.

The idea seemed logical. Despite Lindale's seeming affluence, Madeline had suggested the opposite might be true. Perhaps Brendier *had* held his cousin's dun, and perhaps that debt was now null and void. Of course, it had not been Lindale who had challenged Brendier to a duel at the outset. That unfortunate was dead, as was Brendier himself. Why, if his affliction had only been a minor one?

And why this merrymaking? Though Faye knew little of family, it seemed that Lindale should be mourning his cousin's death rather than hosting his annual fete. Then again, more than two decades separated them in age. And she had no way of knowing how emotionally attached they had been.

Searching the ballroom, Faye found Lord Lindale in the corner of the room. He was laughing with a young woman, seeming oblivious to any guilt, to any pain. She concentrated on him, trying to sense the honesty in him, but the distance between them was too great.

And then she felt it. Just a niggle of something unknown.

She turned. The feelings grew in strength. Truth. She could feel it like a tangible object. It was calling to her, pulling at her. She looked up the winding staircase. No one was there, and yet she felt a tug like a cord about her heart.

She moved toward it, legs numb. Beneath her fingers, the newel post felt cold, the banister as smooth as glass as she ascended the carpeted stairs.

Up ahead a door was closed to her, but it mattered little, for inside that room she would find answers to questions still unasked.

She turned the knob like one in a trance only to see rows upon rows of leather-bound volumes spread beneath an azure blue ceiling. Faye gazed upward. Bulbous clouds dappled the summery expanse, and standing beneath the imaginary sky was a statue of an angel, wings spread as he welcomed her into his library. Faye almost smiled as she stepped inside. Redemption was here. A journal that would explain Brendier's death, perhaps. Or—

"Can I help you?"

Faye turned, startled by the revelation that the room was occupied. Lady Lindale stood only a few yards away, just to the left of a six-panel door. Her brows rose, as did those of the young man beside her.

"Mrs. Nettles?" Lady Lindale's soft, ivory cheeks matched her ball gown to near perfection.

"Oh." It was as if Faye were being snatched back to reality by sharp talons Confusion curled like smoke in her head. "No. I—"

"Are you feeling unwell?" asked the matron, hurrying toward her. "You look quite pale."

"No. I'm fine," she said, but nerves or something like it made her reach for the wall to steady herself.

"Mots, dear boy, might you get poor Mrs. Nettles a bit to drink?" asked the lady. Faye scowled, trying to straighten out the rambling facts in her mind, but Lady Lindale glanced at the retreating man's back, then shook her head. "My husband's nephew," she said, and took Faye's arm in a gentle grip, steadying her. "I fear I was taking him to task. It's time that he married, but these young bucks these days . . ." She shook her head with a tolerant smile that bordered on maternal. "So unprepared to settle down, even if the woman in question is most acceptable.

"Here then, let me help you to the settee," she said, and assisted Faye to the powder blue lounge beside the benevolent angel. "You sit. Mots will return in a moment with a nip of sherry."

Faye sat, mind churning. She should speak. Should make some sort of explanation for her presence there. The moneyed *ton* took the marriages of their kin extremely seriously, and she had interrupted these two while they were discussing the future of their coffers. "Please forgive my intrusion. I was told of your lovely library and was hoping to get a glimpse of it." Pain sparked in her cranium for the lies, but they could hardly be avoided.

"How kind of you," said her hostess, glancing about. "I do so enjoy it. Often libraries are such stuffy old things. Especially in these ancient estates. Inver Heights has been in Henry's family for years out of mind. While I was reared in Cheapside. An actress. Lady Macbeth, Kate, even Juliet. Our union caused quite a scandal." She laughed, clasping her hands before her and glancing about. "How I loved this old house from the moment I saw it. Perhaps it was bold of me to insist on refurbishing this chamber, but I did so want a library."

Faye felt misty, disembodied. Why had she ventured here, wandering up the stairs like one entranced? Truth didn't call to people. Not *sane* people. But neither did lies throb in their heads like a smithy's driving hammer. Had the madness finally found her, or were her gifts yet evolving, changing? 'Twas said a witch's powers could grow and shift until her last breath was drawn. "Lord Lindale doesn't enjoy the written word?" she asked.

"Not so much as he enjoys a good port and a nap by the fire. Though lately . . ." Her eyes looked troubled.

"Is something amiss?"

"He's not been sleeping well, and sometimes he complains of pains in his chest. He worries so . . ." she added, and glanced toward the doorway.

"Worries?"

"That horrible duel," said Lady Lindale, and shuddered.

"Oh yes." The effects of the strange truth trance were fading. And she found, to her surprise, that she could play this game, could speak the necessary lies despite the pinpricks in her head. "Poor Lord Brendier."

The lady nodded, setting the loose skin beneath her skin to jiggling. "He wasn't a bad person. But he did have a short temper. That's what precipitated the duel at the outset."

"But I thought he sustained only a flesh wound."

"As did we. My husband . . ." She winced. "They were blood kin, you know. He so hoped Richard would recover. That they could be friends again."

"Was there trouble between them?"

"Trouble?" She looked startled. "No. They had argued. You know how it is when men drink." She shook her head. "I told Henry to make amends before it was too late but . . ." She shook her head, eyes troubled, and in that moment Faye saw the beauty she must have been as a maid.

"I'm sorry," Faye said. "I shouldn't make you talk about it."

"No." She drew a sharp breath. They were facing each other on the settee, knees turned in as women do. "There are so few people I can confide in, but I feel I can talk to you."

It was often true of decent people. But it was decent people she had hurt with the secrets she had ferreted out for Tenning. The secrets she had learned using gifts that should have been employed for naught but good. The thought made her head throb dully. "Your husband must feel dreadful," she said.

"You can't imagine the guilt."

"Why guilt? Surely he had nothing to do with Brendier's death."

"The truth is, Henry thought a duel might knock some sense into the boy. Make him more cautious. Less arrogant. As you know, duels are rarely fatal. And there was a surgeon standing by. He assured us all would be well."

"What do you think might have gone wrong?"

She shook her head. "'Tis said the wound became septic without anyone the wiser. It all happened so quickly. He had no children to mourn his passing. But his poor young bride. My heart is breaking for—"

"Brendier," said Mots, stepping into the room with a glass of sherry. "What a terrible waste."

"Devastating," said Lady Lindale. "But what am I thinking? Here you were feeling unwell, and I burden you with my tale of woe."

"It's no trouble," Faye said.

"Are you much improved?" Mots stepped closer. He was tall, fair, elegant in his slim-fitting cutaway coat and gray breeches.

Faye managed a smile. "Perhaps I but needed to sit for a moment."

"Yes," Lady Lindale agreed, and patting Faye's hand, rose to her feet. "You stay here as long as you like. But I'd best get back to my other guests or dearest Henry will worry."

And leave her alone with the looming Mots? Faye felt her throat tighten.

"Perhaps I should stay," said the nephew, "make certain you are well?"

Faye felt fear flash in her soul.

Lady Lindale looked into her eyes, then smiling kindly, slipped her plump arm through his in a motherly fashion.

"I believe the fair Mrs. Nettles needs some time to herself," she said, and, ushering him from the room, stopped in the doorway. "I'll make certain no one disturbs you. Unless you would have me send someone up."

"No. My thanks, but I'll be fine in a moment, I'm sure of it."

"Very well then," she said, and, taking Mots with her, closed the door behind them.

Faye sat in silence. Her head was spinning with information. Perhaps that was why it throbbed dully. Or had a lie caused the pain? And if so, was the lie her own or another's?

Glancing about, she remembered the surreal allure that had brought her here. What had caused that unusual phenomenon? Rising to her feet, she turned, and in that moment the light flickered off, shutting darkness into the room.

Chapter 11

Fear turned Faye's legs to lead, her throat to marble. She tried to push out a question, but she couldn't speak. Foolish. She was safe, after all, surrounded by others.

But was she? She realized suddenly that she couldn't hear a single noise from below, for the walls were thick, the doors the same. The room was simply, inexplicably dark. She turned, searching the interior, then she saw it. A hunched shadow.

"Who's there?" Her voice trembled, barely audible to her own ears. Fear quivered up her limbs, trembled in her soul. Lucifer had found her at last. Just as Tenning had said he would. Had found her and would punish her for her lies. For her disloyalty and . . .

But no. All that was behind her.

"Who's there?" Her voice was stronger now, and she managed to step toward the door.

But suddenly the shadow was there, looming in front of her.

She tried to scream, but a hand shot out, covering her mouth, freezing her breath.

"So you've come." His voice was a whisper from hell as he pressed up against her.

Panic suffocated her, freezing her limbs, her mind.

"I hope I didn't keep you waiting too long."

She shook her head, trying to drive away the nightmare. But he remained. She was pressed into a corner, her spine cutting into the books behind her.

His free hand groped her breasts. She tried to scream, but he leaned closer still, breath hot against her ear.

"Quiet now. Quiet so we can enjoy this the more."

She sobbed something inarticulate.

"Do you understand me?"

She jerked a spasmodic nod.

"Good. Good," he said, and yanked up her skirts.

Memories flooded in, dark and terrible. Her mind scurried for cover, for hiding as it always had. She couldn't breathe, couldn't fight back.

"Such a sweet little piece. So delicate. So fragile," he hissed, but it was a lie. She knew it suddenly. Knew it in her head, in her core. She lurched forward, throwing every ounce of her weight against him, making him stumble back a pace. Hope made her strong. Anger made her wild. She flew at him, clawing like a feral beast, but he caught her hands.

Something struck the side of her head. She wobbled to the right. Consciousness wavered. Her knees buckled.

But fury still roared in her mind like a maelstrom, and suddenly the ceramic angel flew forward. There was a resounding crash. Her attacker crumbled. She bolted past him, but even as she did so, he reached up, snagging her skirt.

"Come back, witch!" His voice was guttural as he tried to yank her back, but she had reached the door and snagged the handle. His fingers slipped, and she was through. Safe, slamming against the far wall of the hallway, twisting about, staring wide-eyed at the yawning rectangle of the doorway. Standing outside of hell, the light all but blinded her.

"Faye!"

She turned with a jolt to find Madeline just a few yards away, worry stamped on her face.

"What happened?" Shaleena appeared, holding her skirts with both hands as she rushed up the stairs.

"In there," Faye whispered, and tried to point, but her arm was too shaky, her body too weak.

"Where? What?"

"The Devil!" Faye rasped.

Shaleena met Maddy's worried gaze for an instant, then the latter stepped inside.

"No!" Faye forced herself to take one wooden step forward, to try to save the woman who had saved her. But Madeline was already inside, and try as she might, Faye could not find the courage to go farther.

A diffused shaft of light fell from the hallway at an oblique angle, slanting through the library's doorway. From where Faye stood, the room looked empty, innocuous. She shook her head, waiting desperately for Madeline to return.

And then light sprang into the room. Madeline strode back into view. Unscathed but somber.

"Are you certain someone was there?" she asked.

Madness stalked Faye like an ogre. She shifted her gaze from Madeline to the library.

"Are you certain?" she asked again.

It took all of Faye's faltering nerve to step toward the room, all of her flagging strength to enter it; except for the trappings of the rich, the room was empty. Only the angel was displaced, facedown on the plush carpet, arms outstretched, the tiniest scrap of mint fabric caught on the tip of its wing.

Faye scanned the room once and again, then shook her head. "I'm not mad," she whispered. "I'm not," she said, but even she was uncertain whether her words were true.

Madeline was staring at her, brows furrowed. "Perhaps he escaped through the window," she said.

With one glance, Shaleena strode past them to the far wall and tugged at the heavy wood that encased the thick pane. "Locked," she said, "from the inside."

Faye skittered her gaze to Madeline, and in the shadow of her eyes, Faerie Faye saw doubt.

"Let's get you home," Maddy said. Wrapping her shawl around Faye's shoulders, she glanced at Shaleena.

"I'll find him if he's here," said the other.

Madeline nodded. They stepped together into the hallway.

"Is something amiss?" Lady Lindale asked, hurrying toward them. "I heard a noise."

"Mrs. Nettles is feeling unwell," Madeline said. "Might you have someone fetch my husband? I think it best if we see her home."

Hailing the nearest servant, Lady Lindale gave instructions before turning back. "Whatever could be wrong?" Her worried gaze skipped to Faye.

"He was there," Faye whispered.

"I'm not exactly certain," Madeline said. "If you'll excuse us—"

"He came for me," Faye whispered.

"Is she well?" Lord Gallo was there suddenly, eyes dark with intensity.

Faye jerked back, feeling invaded, feeling struck, but he turned his gaze from her, settled it on his wife.

"Yes. Certainly," Madeline said, "Just overtired."

"He was there," Faye murmured, voice low as she searched Maddy's eyes. There was worry there. And uncertainty.

"Who was there?" asked Lady Lindale, face paler than ever.

"The Devil."

"Most likely a dream," Gallo said. "My wife tells me Mrs. Nettles is prone to fitful nights."

"Of course," Maddy said. "That must be it. She was feeling a bit unwell. Might you have fallen asleep, Mrs. Nettles?"

They were treating her like a child. Or worse, as if she were mad. But there was entreaty in Madeline's eyes, forcing Faye to nod, to play along, to hope they were wrong, that she wasn't crazy.

"I was resting on the . . . on the lounge. Perhaps I nodded off without knowing," she said, and felt her head begin to throb in earnest with the force of her lie.

"We'll get you home straightaway," Madeline said, then to Lord Gallo, "Could you have Joseph bring the carriage round?"

He nodded and disappeared.

Madeline tightened her arm about Faye's shoulders and eased her forward. They didn't allow madwomen to remain without chaperones.

At the bottom of the stairs, the crowd seemed to surge toward her, lies pounding at her brain, but Madeline steered her through the mob.

The night air felt cool and soothing as Lord Gallo ushered them inside the dark landau.

The springs creaked beneath them as they bent to enter. Madeline sat close to her side. In a moment, they were alone. In another, they were moving.

Faye tried to remain quiet. Tried to pretend,

but she could no longer do so. Not to Madeline. "I was not dreaming," she whispered.

"I know."

Faye caught Madeline in a fleeting, hopeful glance.

"You believe me?"

"You are the truth finder, Faerie love. Why would you lie?"

"I would not. Not to you. Not intentionally," she whispered, then winced, remembering a thousand childhood memories: a hulking shape watching from her window. Scratching at her door. In trembling whispers she had mentioned her fears to Cassie, but the scullery maid had scoffed. Lucifer did not walk among them. There were no giants at Bettington. "But maybe Shaleena is right. Maybe I am mad."

"She didn't say that," Madeline said.

"She thought it."

"Reading minds is not your gift," Madeline said, and smiled gently before drawing a careful breath. "What happened?"

She wanted to answer, wanted to spew forth the truth, but the painful events were stuck in her soul. She glanced to the left. "What of Shaleena?"

"She'll not ride with Joseph at the ribbons."

Faye fidgeted. "And Lord Gallo?"

"He stayed behind as well."

She felt restive suddenly, jumpy. "He should be with us."

Madeline's gaze narrowed thoughtfully. "Even though he's male?"

"It was not he."

"No," Madeline said, and if she thought Faye insane, she did not show it. "But who was it? Were you able to see his face?"

Faye managed to shake her head.

"But it was a man."

She nodded. It was always a man.

"Did you recognize his voice?"

"It was low. And quiet. Whispered." Like the Devil himself. She stifled a shiver.

"What else do you recall?" Maddy asked, and hugged her closer.

Warmth flowed through her at Madeline's touch, granting her a modicum of strength. "He was big," she whispered, and felt a tear slip down her cheek.

"Tall or broad?"

She controlled a wince. "Both, I think."

"Taller than Jasper."

She swallowed, closed her eyes, managed a nod.

"Taller than Ella's husband?"

"I . . . It was dark and I was—" Words failed her.

"You were scared," Madeline said. "There is no shame in that."

And suddenly Faye remembered similar words. Remembered and felt herself go pale.

It couldn't have been McBain. It couldn't. But he had warned her not to lie to him. And she had sinned.

Chapter 12

Jasper stood beside Madeline in the doorway of Faye's bedchamber.

She was curled tight beneath the covers, knees drawn up, face nearly hidden. All that was visible was one smooth cheek and a halo of sun-bright hair.

"What did you give her?" Jasper asked.

"Motherwort and goat weed."

"She'll sleep till morning?"

"I'm not certain. She's distraught. I wish Ella were here."

"Then she will be soon," he said, and, closing the door softly, turned toward her. "This is not your fault."

Torment crossed her beloved face. "I was the one who said she was ready."

Reaching out, he took her hand and led her down the hall to their own chambers.

"Who is to say she's not?" he asked.

"Ready?" she said and huffed a harsh laugh. "Look at her, she's—" She winced, then collapsed into the winged upholstered chair near the window and drew her knees to her chest as if she could block out the world.

"What is she?" he asked.

She shook her head, miserable. "She's scared out of her . . ." She stopped, expression breaking.

And he could no longer bear the distance between them. Crossing the room, he knelt beside her chair.

"So the fact that she's scared means that she's unready?" he asked, and took her hand in his.

She shook her head. "No. It's the fact that she is . . ." She paused.

"What?"

She squeezed her eyes shut.

"Hallucinating," he said.

"I told her I believed her."

"And for that you feel guilty."

"Truth means everything to her. It took all the power that's in me to make her believe. What will happen if she realizes I lied?"

"Esperanza," he said softly. It was the name he had called her in his mind for all the years he had held her in his heart but could not hold her in his arms. "It is your *caring* that means everything to her. Your support."

Her eyes were haunted. "There was no one in that room, Jasper."

"No one you saw," he corrected.

She let her feet slip rapidly to the floor, eyes sud-

denly alight. But that was her way. Ever the opti-
mist. "You found something."

He shook his head, untied her slippers, the right,
then the left, before tossing them aside. "No."

"But you felt something," she said, and let him
urge her to her feet.

"I am no witch," he reminded her, and, turning
her back to him, unlaced her gown, then pressed
a kiss to that favorite spot at the base of her neck.
The spot that called to him even in the midst of a
crowd.

"But you can feel—"

"Shh," he said.

She turned toward him, ready to protest, but he
pressed a finger to her lips. "Do you remember her
last conversation with Shaleena?" he asked.

She scowled. She was so beautiful when she
scowled. Almost as beautiful as when she slept or
smiled or laughed. He tugged the gown from her
shoulders. They were perfect. He kissed the right
one.

"She defended herself," she said.

"For the first time since her arrival at this
house."

She opened her mouth again, but he kissed the
corner of it, shushing her.

"Because of you. Because of your faith in her,"
he said. "There are worse things than lies, my
love. And indeed, sometimes lies are truths yet
unseen."

She lifted her gaze to his, soul on fire. "Why are you so good?" she whispered.

"Because I have you," he said, and kissed her again.

Outside Lavender House, Shaleena sat in dark silence. She could not sleep. Rarely slept, in fact. Tonight was no different. Thus, she had slipped outside to gather strength from the waxing essence of the garden around her. The purity of thyme. The peace of loosestrife. The magic of wolfsbane. The experience would have been better, fuller, if she were sky-clad, but the boy named Cur was often slinking about, and he made her feel . . . naked.

But this night it was thoughts of another that disturbed her solitude. Someone unseen. Someone . . .

Joseph!

Anger surged through her. Why was he here? Pretending he was another. It was insulting enough that he had fooled the others into believing he could be trusted. But to make her uncertain of her own thoughts, to make her imagine things that were untrue . . . that was unforgivable. Madness did not suit her. She was not the type to take her own life. Even less so to spend her days in an institution gabbling at the walls.

Swiping moisture from her cheek, she rose to her feet. None would see her cry. None had. Not for years. Not since she had realized she was alone.

A serving girl in a foreign land, carrying her master's grandchild.

So much for love, for devotion, for all the sweet delusions he had whispered in the pulsing heat of the darkness. She had learned much that winter: Men lie. Hearts break. Babies die. Life continues, even when you hope it will not.

But perhaps the most important lesson learned was that she was strong. Stronger than any impostor. Not that this Joseph professed to know her. He merely watched her, but there was something in his eyes . . . Something that said they had shared hope, passion, dreams. But it could not be. Mariano was dead. She had seen to that herself. And this intruder would meet the same fate if he was careless.

But in the end it wasn't Joseph she found beneath the ancient rowans.

"Why are you here?" She asked the question from inches behind the giant intruder and waited for him to gasp, to start. But he did neither of those things. Instead, he turned slowly toward her. And it was in that instant that she felt another's presence. So, the pretender, too, had felt the Celt's presence and come out of hiding. Good.

"Might this be the house where Mrs. Nettles lives?" His voice was little more than a growl.

She raised an impervious brow at the sound of it. "You must be the Scotsman?"

He paused, his brows lowered. "I am *a* Scotsman."

She studied him, circling. So what she had heard of him was true. He was strong. Yet his power was not attributed to his size alone. "Why have you come?"

"I was told the lady was . . ." He paused. She could sense some emotion in him. Frustration perhaps, or worry barely restrained. "I heard there was trouble at the fete this night."

"Oh? And what fete might that be?"

Impatience ticked in him. "Is she well?"

"Tell me, Scotsman, did you come all this long way . . ." She glanced about, but if he had a mount nearby, she could not see it. " . . . on foot, in the dark of night just to pose that question?"

He stared at her.

She smiled. "I believe you came for other reasons," she said, and, reaching up, touched his chest, just below his loosed cravat.

He stood, unmoving but for the massive muscles that twitched heavily beneath her hand.

"Is she well?" he asked again.

She shrugged. "That is a matter of some discussion," she said, and flicked open the top two buttons of his shirt. It was a gift of hers, this ability to undress men so neatly.

"Discuss it now," he said.

"Physically, I believe she is well enough," she said, and circled him, skimming her gaze down his length. The man called Joseph was behind her and to the right some forty strides, unseen in a copse of horse chestnuts.

"Well enough?" asked the Celt, and turned his head to watch her over his shoulder. His neck was broad and corded.

"Unharmed so far as I know," she said. "But mentally . . ." She shook her head and trailed her fingers across his back. Even there she could feel the shift of his muscles. "She is not terribly strong."

"I think you're mistaken."

She laughed as she faced him again. "So, are you her champion then?" she asked, and, reaching up, flicked open two more buttons.

He caught her wrist and her gaze, grip unyielding as a vise.

"What are you to her?" he asked, but she barely heard the question, for her attention had dropped back to his chest.

"Tell me, Scotsman," she said, attention welded to the dark furrows that scraped his skin. "How did you come by those scratches?"

He lowered his gaze to his own chest, but at that moment, there was a rustle of sound.

"Leave him be," Joseph said.

She jerked toward him, temper flaring as she pulled her wrist from the Scotsman's grasp. "Who are you to tell me what to do? Who are you at all?"

Silence filled the darkness, then, "You know me."

"You lie!" She hissed the words.

"Not to you, Becca."

A sob tore from her throat. "I know no one by that name."

"That is unfortunate. She was everything to me once," he said, and stepped toward her.

"Everything!" she spat, and choked a laugh. "You left . . ." She caught herself, fighting off the madness of hope. "I am not this weak-kneed maid you speak of."

"You loved—" he began, still approaching, but she jerked her hands up, palms out, mind burning with power, throwing him back a half a pace, where he remained, frozen.

"Love is for cowards!" she hissed.

"Then a coward I am," he said, and, wresting free of her spell, took a broken step forward.

"What goes on here?" rumbled the Scotsman, and she remembered, just barely, that they were not alone.

She lifted her chin. "This man is attempting to molest me, giant. You were once a soldier. 'Tis your duty to protect and defend."

He watched them both, eyes shadowed. "And I would do so if only I knew which needed me protection the more."

"Protect *her*," Joseph said, and with his words, illogical anger flared in Shaleena's soul yet again.

"I don't require your help. I don't need any man's help."

"Require it? No," Joseph agreed, and suddenly his tone was filled with such tender agony that she felt the very fabric of her heart rend. "For you are strength itself," he said. "But love, it can never come too—"

"I do not love!" she hissed, and, gritting her teeth against hope, raced back into the shadowy refuge of Lavender House.

Chapter 13

Les Chausettes were gathered in the parlor when Faye made her way down the stairs. It was yet some hours before dawn, but she could hear their voices rising and falling in a soothing cadence. Darla, quiet but firm. Francine, perceptive but wary. Beatrice and Heddy and Ivy. All different. All powerful. They would be sitting in a rough circle, Shaleena on the elegant divan beside the well-dressed hat stand, Madeline near the door. Lord Gallo present but mostly silent, tending the teapot on the sideboard.

"And what of you, Rosemond?" he asked now. "Were you able to discern anything in the ashes?"

"A bit," she said, "but I shall need more time to consider the—"

Her words stopped abruptly as Faye entered the room.

"Faerie Faye," Madeline breathed, and stood, expression troubled, gilded fire crackling behind her as she set her teacup aside. "I thought you would sleep for some hours yet."

Faye glanced about the room at the sisters of her heart. Ella had returned to Lavender House, leaving her family behind in the small hours of the morning.

"Are you well?" she asked now, and Faye nodded, unsurprised that they had all gathered here at such short notice. It was their way.

"Physically at least," she said, and smiled, hoping to emulate others. Others who were not so damaged, who were not such cowards. She drew a careful breath. This was her time. Her time to protect, to *do*. She would not let her coven sisters solve her problems and in so doing risk themselves. It was, after all, entirely possible that whoever had attacked her had done so because he knew of her powers.

"*Come back, witch.*"

The words were singed into her soul. She would find the culprit and, if she deemed him a danger to the others, she would rid the world of him. No matter his identity.

Madeline glided across the room to take her hands in her own. "And have you any idea who might have attacked you?" she asked, brows lowered.

Fear stalked her. Uncertainty haunted her. "No," she said, and felt the first niggle of a headache strike her brow. "Indeed, I think . . ." She swallowed her terror, straightened her spine. "I believe an apology is in order."

"An apology?"

"It is because of your kindness that I am . . ." She paused and skimmed her gaze from one face to the next, lighting on each for just a moment and feeling the impact of their presence in her life. ". . . that I am alive. It is because of your tolerance that I am a Chausette," she said, and felt a strange twist of pride at the word. "Because of that . . . because of your faith in me, I will become more than I am." She forced a smile. It felt watery, but she drew strength from it. "Surely I can withstand far worse than a fright." She let her attention drift to Ella, for of them all, she had endured the most. "For each of you has."

Tears shone in Ella's eyes, but there was something besides sadness in her expression. It might have been pride. But seeing it was too difficult, for it might well be misplaced. Faye shifted her gaze to the others, knowing that each was stronger than she.

"What are you saying?" Maddy asked.

"Perhaps Shaleena was right," she said, and carefully avoided looking at the redheaded member of their coven, though she was, for once, fully clothed. "Perhaps I was mistaken."

"So you think you were dreaming?" Ella asked.

"Yes," she said, and finally turned toward Shaleena, but the other was atypically silent. Indeed, she looked nothing but weary, her eyes redrimmed, her brow troubled.

"What of the bruise on your cheek, then?" Madeline asked.

Faye refrained from touching the tender spot, refrained from remembering the all-encompassing fear. "I was . . . After some thought I believe you were right, Madeline. I think I did fall asleep. And when I awoke I was disoriented. I thought the angel was an interloper. 'Tis a silly thing to place an angel in the library. A foolish—"

"The Scotsman was in the garden." Shaleena's voice fell into the room like droplets of undiluted hemlock.

Every eye in the room turned to her, but she was not gloating. Indeed, a scowl marred her smooth, alabaster features.

"The Scotsman?" Faye whispered.

"*Our* garden?" Ella asked, and rose to her feet, ever graceful.

"When did this occur?" Lord Gallo asked. His tone was level, but there was the suggestion of tension in his tone.

"Near to midnight perhaps," Shaleena said.

"And?" Madeline's tone was curt, waiting for more information. At some unknown time she had become the heart of the coven. None could say quite when.

"He said he had come . . ." Shaleena paused, still thoughtful. "He inquired about the girl's health."

"Faerie's?" Ella asked.

"Why?" Faye's voice was breathy to her own ears.

Shaleena shook her head as if to dispel some unwanted thoughts. "He had heard there was trouble." She turned her eyes to Faye, her own still solemn, unlaced with their usual caustic gaiety. "Or so he said."

"Is there reason to believe he was lying?" Maddy asked.

Shaleena turned her attention to Madeline. "He is a man."

But she had always seemed to appreciate men. Or at least appreciate using them.

"Did you question him further?" Lord Gallo asked.

Shaleena turned toward him and blinked as if drawing herself from a trance. "No," she said simply.

"That's unlike you," Madeline said. It was an understatement of astronomical proportions. Generally, if someone appeared uninvited on Lavender property, Shaleena made the Spanish Inquisitors appear congenial by comparison.

"There was . . . another distraction."

Maddy exchanged a glance with her husband. "In our garden?" she asked.

Shaleena shrugged. Perhaps the motion was meant to seem dismissive. It did not. "I sensed something."

"Is this something still alive?" Ella asked.

Silence reigned for a moment, then, "It turned out I was wrong. It was no one of import."

"You were *what*?" Ella asked.

Shaleena raised her chin, jaw tensing. "I have admitted before that I was wrong."

If that was true, it was not in Faye's recollection.

"So you investigated the other noise?" Madeline asked.

"Yes."

"And you found nothing?"

"That is what I said." Shaleena's tone was becoming terse, crisp with anger.

"No. It is not. You said—" Ella began, but Lord Gallo interrupted.

"And what of the Scotsman?" he asked.

"He left."

"You let him get away?" Ella asked, and the last of Shaleena's unexpected patience erupted in a black explosion of rage.

"Why are you here?" Jerking from the elegant divan, she faced Ella across the room. "Do you not have a husband awaiting your return? A child! Some would die for—" She paused, unspoken words trembling on her lips.

Stunned silence dropped into the room, but Lord Gallo rose smoothly in the echoing quiet. "Let us all relax a bit," he said. "There is no need for agitation. Faerie Faye is safe. We are all safe." He glanced at the others, letting his gaze linger on his wife for a moment as if to make certain he was correct. And for the first time Faye fully realized the truth: He was neither coolly aloof nor quietly scheming. He was passionate. For her . . . his wife.

Indeed, he would die for her. Would give his life without a second's hesitation. Strangely, it made her want to cry, but she stifled the emotion, clasping her hands carefully together.

"I am perfectly well," she agreed. "And given my tumultuous past . . ." She tried to smile at the understatement. "I think it likely that my mind simply fabricated—"

"There were scratches on his chest," Shaleena said.

Faye's heart lurched in the abrupt silence.

"What?" she whispered.

Shaleena turned toward her. But again the glee was notably absent. Though Faye could sense no other emotion on her. "Did you not fight him?" she asked. "The man in the library, did you not try to escape his grasp?"

"In . . . in my dreams," Faye said, but the battle was already lost. Her greatest fear was coming to life yet again. The one man she thought she could trust. The one man she *needed* to believe in had betrayed her.

"You are making a serious accusation, Shaleena," Lord Gallo warned.

"You truly believe the Scotsman—" Ella began, but Faye stopped them with a raised hand. The room had gone breathless.

"I did not mean to bring him to this door. To cause you trouble."

"We have no proof that he *will* cause trouble," Madeline said. "No reason to assume he is anything other than what he proclaims himself to be."

"And what is that exactly?" Gallo asked.

Madeline shrugged. "A soldier, decorated yes, but a simple man of—"

"He is not simple," Faye said, and knew she was right. He was more than he appeared. Much more. And he was interested in her. Why? It was not unheard of for powerful men to sense the gifts that her kind embodied. It was also not unheard of for them to wish to usurp those gifts. It had happened before, just months ago within her own coven, in fact. Had caused the death of a gifted young woman, had driven Ella from Lavender House.

Faye would not let that happen again.

"I will not allow him to harm you," she said, and though she felt weakness like a cancer inside her, she also felt the strength, growing like a wind-blown fire.

"Let us not do anything hasty," Lord Gallo said.

"Not hasty," Faye agreed, "but final."

"What are you saying?" Madeline asked. She was scowling. Faye knew that without looking.

"You have protected me long enough," she said.

"Shaleena could well be mistaken," Ella said. "About the scratches. About everything. After all, it was, I presume, dark in the garden last—"

"There were scratches!" Shaleena snarled. "On his chest."

"And how do you know that?" Ella challenged.

"*Why* do you notice the Scotsman when there's another who would give all for your—"

"Elegance," Gallo warned quietly.

But Shaleena's eyes had already narrowed. "What have you done?" she hissed.

"You have steeped us in your bitter guilt long enough," Ella said.

"What have you done?" shrieked Shaleena and jerked her hand upward. A sphere of fire shot from the hearth and into her palm. She heaved it at Ella, but it was devoured in an instant, engulfed in a burst of flame that roared past Shaleena to consume the hat stand in a fountain of gold.

The redhead turned to stare, eyes wide and sparking as she raised her fist again, but Faye could tolerate no more.

"Enough!" she rasped, and in that instant the teapot hurtled through the air, emptying its contents on the crackling chapeaus.

The fire fizzled out. Not a murmur of noise interrupted the sudden silence as every breath was held, every eye turned to her.

"Enough," Faye whispered, and, turning, left the room.

Chapter 14

He was dead.
    Rogan stood amid the swirling mists, looking down at the scene below him. Down at himself and the man who lay sprawled at his feet. Gregor Winden. Dead. Shot through the heart, though pistols were not Rogan's weapon of choice. The muzzle smoked as he dropped it beside his thigh.

He felt no remorse. There was little reason to pretend otherwise. Winden had hurt Charlotte. Charlotte the beautiful. Charlotte the kindly. The bastard had bruised her, and therefore deserved to die. It was as simple as that, and he was a simple man. When he set his mind, he carried through. It was what he had been taught.

But sometimes things were not as they seemed.

Memories roiled in, painful, disorienting. The images below him stirred and shifted. A comely woman looked down at him. But something was askew, off kilter, for there was glee in her bonny eyes, malice in the twist of her lips as she turned toward Winden's tiny child.

Rogan awoke with a start. He sat upright, muscles aching with tension. The dreams had found him as they so often did before battle. Nights of insomnia oft brought hours of deep unconsciousness; but he dare not sleep so soundly, for he could not count on his strange premonitions to warn him of trouble. More than a few good Tommies had been found in their bedrolls with their throats slit. It had happened to a score of his comrades. Indeed, he should make certain his men were safe before . . .

But one glance at the embers glowing in the grate reminded him there was no army massed against him. No need for the keening worry that nagged at his soul. Indeed, no need for him to sleep in naught but his plaid. But the blankets had seemed stifling. Confining. He needed his right hand free in case the attack came . . .

He drew a heavy breath. Reality eased in a few sparse inches. He was not in some corpse-strewn Dutch province. He was in London, had arrived here to do his uncle's bidding. But once again he had failed, he thought, and turned miserably toward the window.

It was in that instant that he saw her. She stood not ten feet from his bed, golden hair loose about her pale shoulders, falling like a gilded waterfall across her ivory-clad breasts.

And suddenly three years slipped away and

once again he was in the throes of love so intense he could barely breathe.

"I trusted you," she whispered, and though her face was barely visible in the moon-stained darkness, her hands looked demure and pale, clasped as they were against the soft sweep of her graceful gown.

But he would not be duped by her innocence. Not again.

"Mild as Mullen!" he rasped, rage spewing through him. "What have you done with the child?" Jerking back his plaid, he lurched to his feet.

It was then that the apparition gasped.

Reality settled uncertainly into place. He peered through the shadows.

"Who are you?" he rumbled, half-afraid to hear the answer, to know the truth.

"Why did you do it?" she asked, and in that instant he recognized the lyrical music of her voice.

Ripping a shred from the paper on his bedstead, he gave it a quick twist and thrust it in the embers in the hearth.

Light flared as he straightened, then sparked across ethereal, pixie features.

"What the devil," he rumbled and froze. What was she doing there? In the flesh. In his room. But no. He shook his head. She was just one more in a long line of apparitions. Still, there was something about her eyes that showed a depth and substance that no artist could—

But suddenly she reached out and struck the twist of paper from his hand. It tumbled to the floor, where she snuffed it out beneath her slipper.

". . . thinking?" she gasped.

He raised his gaze from the charred paper to her face.

She was scowling as if she were the one surprised by this odd turn of events. As if *he* were the intruder. "Are you trying to set yourself—" She began and motioned to his body before turning her face abruptly away.

He glanced down. It wasn't until that moment that he remembered he was naked.

Reaching out, he yanked his plaid from his bed and dragged it in front of him. He was almost beginning to believe she wasn't yet another dream, another ragged hallucination. Or if she was she was a potent one, for his fingers were beginning to sting as if burnt.

Wrapping the long woolen about his waist, he placed another log on the grate and waited for light to flare across the room. But it failed to chase away the dream.

She stood perfectly still, watching him.

He glanced at the door, then at his bed, trying to retrace where the world had gone mad.

"Did you hurt your . . ." She glanced at his hand and froze.

Looking down, he realized he'd not bunched the fabric properly over himself. He also realized the thought of her affected him rather noticeably. Readjusting his plaid, he hoped his first assessment had been correct, that she was naught but a misty shard of his imagination.

She averted her eyes, slightly flushed, and he scowled.

His dreams were often sad. Sometimes bawdy. But never shy.

"What are you doing here?" he asked, and even to his own ears the tone sounded frightening.

Her eyes flickered closed for a moment, but determination bunched in her jaw. She raised her chin and stepped toward him.

"I've come for the truth," she said.

He was almost tempted to step back, though he'd been taught early and often that retreat was the role of cowards. "You shouldn't be here."

"Why?" she asked.

He glanced toward the bed again and was half-surprised to find that he wasn't there, sprawled across the heavy duvet left by the owners. What did that mean? That he was as mad as a sequestered monk?

"Is it because you do not trust yourself?" she asked.

He froze. His chest burned with an odd heat, but her eyes were entrancing, distracting him from that quandary. "I trust myself a good deal, lass," he said. "It does not mean you should do the same."

"I should not trust you?"

Others had. It had been a mistake. "How did you arrive here?"

"That hardly matters." She took another step toward him. He felt her presence like a tangible force. Felt his heart thump in anticipation.

"Why would you do it?" she asked.

He scowled, fighting the confusion, the disorientation. It was still entirely possible that he was dreaming. He'd seen her here before, after all. But usually she wore fewer garments. Beneath his plaid the woolen felt itchy to his growing desire. "I do not know what you mean," he said.

"Despite everything, I found you rather allur—" She stopped herself. "Force was not—" Her eyes spoke of a sorrow deeper than time. "Power should not attack weakness."

He was trying to follow her thoughts, but he had not slept well for some time, and insomnia was not a boon to clearheaded thought. "You think me . . ." What? What exactly. "Powerful?" It was the only attribute he would allow himself to believe.

She scowled a little, like an irritated pixie. "Your size alone should suggest as much."

"Some are not what they seem."

"No." She was within reach now and still her eyes looked tortured. Everything in him ached to touch her, but he would not. He would hold steady. Hold back. "But that does not mean we deserve to be hurt."

Something twisted in his gut. "What is it you're trying to say?"

Doubt flickered through her bottomless eyes. "You were at Lord Lindale's estate some hours before, were you not?" Her voice was as dulcet as a rock dove's.

"Aye. You know well enough that I was."

She seemed to be holding her breath as she took one more abbreviated step toward him. "In his library," she intoned.

It was as if a fist gripped his heart as he gathered her meaning. "That I was not," he said.

She scowled, gritted her teeth, then, taking the final step that separated them, she reached out and curled her fingers around the amulet that lay against his chest. The coolness of her skin met the heat of the stone in a sudden clash of feeling.

"We . . ." She seemed to be struggling to speak, to remain as she was, looking up at him, eyes as wide as forever. "We kissed in the garden." Her voice was nothing more than an entrancing whisper.

He managed a nod, though it was difficult to do even that much.

"But you wished to do more."

"Aye." There was little point in denying the truth. Little point in even trying.

"But we were interrupted."

He could do nothing but stare. She was bewitching, intoxicating.

"You are not a man accustomed to disappointment," she whispered, and suddenly her mouth twitched as if she could no longer contain the sadness.

He curled his hands to fists, but kept them carefully at his sides, lest he touch her and burst into flames.

"There you are wrong, lass," he murmured. "Disappointment is oft my companion."

A flicker of confusion shadowed her face for an instant, but she continued.

"You followed me into the library."

So the rumors were true. She had been accosted in Lindale's house. Anger roared through him, but he held it at bay. Great pain had taught him to do that much. And pain visited him now, for he knew the truth. She believed him to be her attacker. Shame smote him, shame melded with anger and guilt and hurt. The need to defend himself warred with the self-sustaining desire to prove that he did not care. He longed to walk away, to play the disdainful rogue he would never be, but he could not. Her gaze was all-consuming. "Had I known you were destined for the library, I might well have done so." For it had taken all his willpower to let her leave him. "But I did not."

"You preceded me there then." Her tone had gone sharp. It twanged something inside of him, drawing at the truth.

Pain sharpened in his chest, but he had no intention of explaining himself. "I am a mercenary," he said. "Surely I look more the sort to burn libraries than occupy them."

Her gaze never wavered, and again that something twanged in his chest.

"I *can* read," he admitted finally.

She stared at him, pulling at his soul.

"Well into the night if circumstances permit," he admitted. "But I prefer to sketch." His uncles had found it disconcerting to find him bent over the nub of a pencil on the eve of a battle, but there was something soothing about the stroke of each solid line. Something hopeful. Something sustaining.

"Sketch?" She looked confused, as if the question was not the one she wished to pose.

He gritted his teeth, but nodded reluctantly toward his bedstead. The drawing lay angled across the smooth wood, the bottom torn away.

She scowled down at it . . . a picture of a dove perched atop a saddle, and he hoped with all his might that she would not see the resemblance, would not know he had seen her face with each careful stroke. Had remembered the way she held her head, the way her lashes brushed upward just so.

Surely she would not realize his obsession, for no man could capture her essence.

But her eyes fluttered to his. "It looks like . . ." She paused. He held his breath. "The eyes almost look . . . human."

His face felt hot. " 'Tis merely something I do to pass the time."

"Were you thinking of . . ." She began and stopped herself again, but in that moment she stepped forward and put her fist against his chest. "You were in the library," she said. "Admit it."

The world ached, but he was not surprised. There was no reason she should trust him. Indeed, he had told her as much, but the truth was too seductive, too alluring. "I was not," he admitted, and slowly her fingers opened to spill softly against his skin.

Her face was as gilded as a waxing moon. And even as he knew he should draw away, he wanted most desperately to reach out, to take her in his arms, to propel her to the bed behind her. But he remained, though she trilled her fingers across his chest. Feelings smote him like an axe, driving toward his heart, tearing his flesh asunder.

He let his eyes fall closed against the rocking sensations, gritted his teeth against the agony as she pressed her palm to the inferno of his skin.

"Where did you come by these?" Her musical voice seemed to echo inside his own skull, but for the life of him he could not quite decipher her meaning, for with the touch of her skin, it almost seemed that he could feel a sliver of *her* emotions. Fear, perhaps, yet naught but confidence shone in her eyes.

"The wounds," she said.

It took every ounce of his strength to pull his gaze from her eyes, to lower it to his own chest. Four furrows had been scratched into his skin, plowing bloody tracks from clavicle to nipple.

He shook his head. The injury was already healing. Almost gone in fact, and he had no intention of sharing the shameful truth. Far better, far *safer*, that she believe the worst of him.

"Where?" she asked again, and let her eyes fall closed. Against his naked chest, he felt her intensity burn brighter.

Heat seared him like a torch, but he could not draw away. Neither could he lie.

"The foxes," he said, though the words were little more than a murmur between gritted teeth.

She opened her eyes with a snap. "What?"

He tried to keep his mouth closed. "They were more spritely than anticipated," he admitted, and at that precise moment a yip echoed from the bowels of his rented home. It sounded far away and muffled, yet he was quite certain she had heard it. He almost swore, but she was already reaching for the twist of paper on the floor. In a second the wick on the nearby lamp flared, but she was already turning away. For one fractured moment Rogan contemplated grabbing his breeches, making himself decent, but Connelly might have returned, and God knew the Irishman was anything but.

By the time he reached her side she had already opened the door to the alcove beside Connelly's bedchamber. A fire red tail was just disappearing into an overturned wooden crate spread with a blanket. Then, for just an instant, it was replaced by a pointy nose.

She stared, silent, absorbed.

He scowled, absently rubbing his chest. *Damn fox.*

"You found them," she said.

He gritted his teeth against the sensations caused by her nearness and forced out a denial. It was like pushing a brick through his pupil. "These English think it good sport to chase them," he said. "In time the young ones will be of some value."

She narrowed her eyes. Somehow, he felt the movement in his throat. "Are you saying you plan to sell them to the hunters?"

"What else?" he asked, but even that was almost too much to manage.

"So you did not intend to save them?"

He forced a laugh, but in that instant, she reached out and pressed her hand to his wounds.

He clenched his jaw, trying to hold back the truth, but the words came nevertheless. " 'Twas a foolish notion. The wee beasties fight like cornered Frenchmen. But when I set my mind to a thing, 'tis all but certain I will do . . ." He paused, feeling doltish.

"You went into the woods, through the rain just because you believed me to be distressed by their plight?"

He tried to lie, but nodded nevertheless.

"Well, you were wrong," she said, and pulled her hand away. "As I told you before, they are naught but vermin."

He stared at her, drinking her in, doing his best to read her. "I am not certain if you are so poor at acting that you cannot hide the truth, or such a fine thespian you only seem to wish to," he admitted.

"Whatever are you talking about?"

There was depth to her, depth and light and strength. He was sure of it. But he had been sure before. Had been sure and forfeited his soul. "You try to hide the sadness," he said.

Surprise shone on her ethereal face like light on magic. "What would I have to be sad about?"

He waited, watching her, knowing he should turn away before it was too late. "There was trouble at Inver Heights," he said.

"Trouble?" She seemed to pale. Was that something a woman could contrive? "No." She shook her head. "No trouble. Silly me. I but had a fright and thought—"

"Did he hurt you?"

"Who?" Her voice was breathy.

"The man you believed to be me. Who was it? Rennet? Was it he?" The thought roiled like poison through his system. But she shook her head. "A servant then? Lindale?"

"No." She denied all, gaze held fast on his. "I am well, Rogan."

It was the first time his name had brushed her lips, and the feel of it wafted through him, lighting his thoughts like wayward moonbeams.

"Did he touch you?" he asked, and slowly, ever so slowly, she reached up to caress his cheek.

Feeling flowed through him. Hope and fear and forgiveness, as sharp as shards. And though he knew he should pull away, he could not. Indeed, he seemed to be drawing closer, pulled under her spell, nearing her lips.

"So how are our wee bloodthirsty—"

Bain jerked away from her touch. Sanity rolled in almost immediately, followed by a forsaken sense of abstract loneliness.

But Connelly, never in tune with subtle nuances, spoke again, and when Bain glanced his way, the Irishman was grinning like a monkey in a sugar cabinet.

"And to think I had all but given up on you, McBain."

Chapter 15

She had tried to think, had tried to sleep. But was successful at neither. Thus she had enlisted Joseph to drive the landau early through the streets of London. She could have had Sultan saddled instead, of course, but the idea of riding alone in the darkened confines of a closed carriage, unseen and unjudged, was too appealing. There was something about the rhythmic movement of a pair of beautiful steppers that helped to sort her thoughts. And think she must, for her mind was all a-muddle.

She had gone to wrest the truth from McBain. To ferret out the facts, not only about the terror in the library but about Brendier's death. Indeed, she had used the most potent weapons in her arsenal, had held her amulet against his skin. But when that failed to produce the desired effects, she had gone so far as to touch him. It was then that all coherent thought had flown from her mind. That she had been flooded with nothing but incoherent feelings: a need to believe him, to hear her name on his lips, to caress the aging scar she'd seen slashed across his hard-packed abdomen.

How could this happen to her? She didn't trust men. Didn't like them. Certainly did not *desire* them.

Yet she had believed his every rumbled word though God knew she had learned far better. Worse still, she had given him a glimpse of herself. Her *true* self.

She closed her eyes against such idiocy.

Following that point, she had not even *attempted* to draw out the truth. She had been far too absorbed with the blizzard of emotions that had stormed through her to try to sift honesty from lies.

And who could say? Perhaps he had been truthful the whole while. Perhaps he had not been in Lindale's library. God knew his eyes spoke of integrity and sadness. Of beauty and pain and a thousand . . .

Bringing her thoughts back to the here and now, she focused for a moment on the staccato clip of the team's rhythmic trot before reminding herself of her vow. A vow more sacred than blood. A vow that she would reach past her fears, would learn the truth, would be strong.

She was not the fragile urchin Tenning had proclaimed her to be. True, he had weakened her with his toxic lies, frightened her with his threats, wounded her with his cruelty, but he had not broken her.

She was a white witch, and witches stood alone against the atrocities of the world. Therefore, she would do what she must. She would confront McBain again. Would tear the truth from him, even if it meant forfeiting his very soul.

And yet, at that very moment, she was traveling in the opposite direction, willing even to return to Inver Heights rather than challenge his charms yet again.

He had saved the foxes. The wee beasties, as he called them.

The memory of his voice as he'd gazed down at the faux lair sent gooseflesh skittering across her arms while the thought of his chest . . .

She jerked her mind back to reality.

It was all foolishness. He had implied that he had taken the kits for coin. But regardless of her amulet and her own waxing powers of truth persuasion, she had not believed him. What was true and what was false? What she wished to believe or the portion she *must* believe?

It was time to learn the truth. That much she knew, and yet she did not have the strength to return to him. What if he was yet abed? What if his chest was bare, one bulging arm bent alluringly above his head? What if the unyielding muscles of his chest roiled beneath the tempting sheet of his skin like a tide that could not be stemmed? Like a magical . . .

Good heavens, it would be all but a relief to reach Inver Heights, regardless of the terror she had experienced there. But who had caused it? And was it mere coincidence that she should be attacked while searching for clues to Brendier's death? Perhaps the Devil had intended more than rape.

Perhaps he planned to kill her. To prevent her from learning the truth. But how could he know she searched for clues unless he knew of her powers. Unless he knew of her coven. The thought set her hands atremble, but she controlled them with an effort.

By the time Joseph opened the landau's narrow door, she was once again in control of her emotions. He bowed, regal and solemn. She nodded, ducking her head and refusing to glance up at the manse's looming height.

A black cabriolet with a folding top stood beside the curb, its chestnut cob content to rest a hip and doze in the morning sun. Faye only wished she could appear so relaxed. But her hands were trembling as she approached the looming door. Her neck was perspiring, making her realize she had, once again, forgotten a handkerchief to . . .

The door swung open. Her breath hitched as an elderly man stepped through, gray mustache drooping. Nodding solemnly to the portly woman in the foyer, he turned away, then started when he saw her.

"Can I help you?" His voice was raspy with age. He carried a small black bag in his right hand.

Faye gathered her courage. Who knew there

were so many men in the world? "I've come to pay a visit to Lady Lindale," she said.

His brows drew together. "I fear you must return at a later date."

Confusion melded with fear inside her, but she fought them both, struggling for poise. "Is the lady not home? I only wished to thank her for her lovely—"

"There has been a death."

"A—" Her heart recoiled in her chest.

"Perhaps you could return in a few days' time," he said, and descended, stiff-legged, onto her level.

Premonition weighed like a stone boat on her chest. "Whose death?"

He scrutinized her. "Might I ask your name?"

"Whose death?" she asked again, voice barely audible over the hard beat of her heart.

His scowl deepened. "I fear Lord Lindale has been taken from us."

A half a dozen emotions smoked through her. "Are you certain?"

He drew himself up, narrow and lean. "I am a physician, miss. I assure you, I am quite certain. He has passed."

She stumbled a little, but Joseph came up from behind, steadying her so gently that she forgot to move away.

"How?" she asked.

"Are you unwell?" asked the doctor.

"I saw him just last night."

His deep, bushy brows had been low over his eyes, but they rose now as if perception had just dawned on him. "Lady Lindale is a good woman. Another shock would all but kill her now."

Faye shook her head in bemusement. But he ignored her.

"I have administered laudanum to help her sleep." He glared at her. "I might suggest that you get some rest yourself," he said, and, brushing stiffly past her, headed toward his dark carriage.

But she caught his sleeve. "How did he die?"

He glanced down at his jacket, bunched in her frozen grip. "His heart simply gave—" he began, but in that desperate moment she curled her free hand around his scrawny biceps. Even through the layers of fabric, she could feel the truth seep regretfully from him.

His brows lowered dramatically, but he did not try to lie. "Debauchery has killed younger men with stronger hearts. This was not the first time he drank himself to unconsciousness," he said. "It was merely the first time he died of it."

Her hand dropped away. "Intemperance killed him?"

He drew a breath as if relieved to do so. "When they first wed, it was thought that he chose unwisely, her being a woman of the stage. But as it turns out, he did not deserve the lady he took to wife." He eyed her up and down. "Perhaps he did not even deserve you," he said, and brushed past.

The journey back to the landau seemed misty

and surreal. She didn't even flinch as Joseph helped her inside.

"You are well?" he asked.

"He's dead." And what did that mean?

"Was it he who attacked you?"

She glanced up abruptly, finding his dark, cleanly etched features. "How do you know—" She stopped herself, looked away and shook her head. "'Twas but a dream."

"Becca would not have searched the grounds for a dream."

She turned back toward him. "Becca?"

The glimmer of a smile lit his dark eyes but did nothing to his quiet features. "Not all are what they seem."

"Shaleena," she said. "How do you know her?"

"Were we not speaking of you, madam?"

"I hope not," she breathed, and stifled a shiver.

"Was it he?" he asked.

She considered denying all knowledge of the subject, but she was too tired, too confused. When had she last enjoyed a full night's sleep? "I don't know. I thought . . . It seemed so real, but when the light came on . . ." It was so reminiscent of old days, like a ghost from her past. But the ghosts had been planted. The past manipulated. "He was gone."

"Do not some old houses have *rejtett* . . ." He paused, searching for the proper words. " . . . secret ways?"

She looked at him anew, for he was right of

course. Ancient estates had often been built with hidden passages, Lavender House being no exception.

"Someone in the household, then. Perhaps a member of the staff," she said, but he shook his head.

"The *mester* of such an estate would not inform his servants of these things." His expression was wry. "On this you can trust me."

"Lindale himself, then? But how did he die?"

"You do not believe in fate?"

She shook her head.

"What of vengeance?"

Her throat knotted. "No one knew of the attack."

"No one?" he asked, and in her mind, she saw Rogan McBain. His eyes were flat and hard, filled with an emotion she could not quite read.

"Did he touch you?" The low rumble of his voice echoed through her mind.

Lindale had never been mentioned, but if Joseph had come to such a conclusion, there was no reason to believe Rogan would not do the same. There had been something in the Highlander's dark demeanor that insisted on revenge.

And perhaps, if she were honest with herself, she wanted the same.

Chapter 16

"**M**r. Connelly," Faye said, injecting her voice with surprise and straightening abruptly from her perusal of a mind-dizzying array of whips. It was, for her, an acting feat worthy of a Parisian stage; she felt immediately light-headed with the effects of the lie. She had traveled to Bond Street with the express purpose of finding the Irishman there. Indeed, she had spent near an hour trying to look intrigued by the day's carica-tures posted in the window of the Repository of the Arts, all the while hoping Connelly would eventually arrive at the shop, which purportedly fascinated him.

The questions that nagged her could no longer be ignored. No longer could she wait to learn the truth about Rogan McBain; neither could she trust herself to keep her head in his presence for he had some kind of power she could not explain. She distrusted men, feared them, had for the entirety of her life. But now she wondered if, perhaps, in the deepest recesses of her being, she had also felt a need to be aligned with them, to be protected by them. Perhaps that was why she found McBain appealing, for certainly if ever there was a man who could protect if he so chose, it was he. But was he protective or was he deadly? Or was one the price you paid for the other? Questions raced through her brain like red squirrels until she was exhausted with the chaotic turnings of her mind and found herself on Bond Street.

Connelly turned toward her now, delight showing on his elegant features. "Mrs. Nettles, I cannot tell you how thrilled I am that you have finally decided to stalk me," he said, and reached for her hand.

For a moment she was tempted to turn and run. For longer still she teetered on the verge of disagreeing, of blathering denials and lies and long-winded explanations, for his accusation was, in fact, entirely correct. But something in her, a feminine instinct that could not be entirely extinguished, perhaps, told her that he was doing nothing more harmful than flirting.

"Well, certainly no mere woman could be expected to resist you a moment longer, could she?" she asked, and feeling her throat close up, pulled her hand cautiously from his.

"I certainly hope not," he said, and smiled.

"Are you here alone?" she asked, and he lifted one eyebrow as she glanced about, and it was not until that moment that she herself realized that even though she had come to speak privately with Connelly, some small part of her hoped that McBain would be there too. Just so she could catch a momentary glimpse of his solemn, silver eyes, his rough-hewn features.

And all the while the entire episode made her long, rather desperately, to hide behind the display counter that housed yet another dozen whips.

"Are you looking for someone in particular?"

She jerked her attention back to the Irishman, even as she felt herself flush. Felt heat rush to her extremities.

"Please tell me, beautiful lady, that you are *not* searching for someone large and socially inept when I am at your disposal."

She forced herself to meet his eyes, to raise her own brows in challenge. "If you are suggesting I am looking for Mr. McBain, I assure you that an effort would hardly be necessary."

"Oh?"

"He is, after all, not an easy man to miss."

He laughed. "You'd think not," he said. "Though several have managed. I always recommend a flintlock at close range. Unreliable at times, but deadly as an adder."

She furrowed her brow. "I beg your pardon?"

He stared at her thoughtfully for a moment, then, "Might I buy you an ice, Mrs. Nettles? It's rather warm today. "

Every screaming instinct in her demanded that she run, but her instincts had been honed by a man who was the personification of deceit. She knew that now. Had learned it through years of pain. Thus she forced herself to face her demons, to move her lips, to tug a handkerchief from her reticule. "Perhaps you could do me a favor, Mr. Connelly."

He bowed, bending gracefully from the waist. "It would be my greatest honor."

"I have been carrying this about for some days. I believe it is Mr. McBain's. Might you return it to him?"

He looked down at it. "Bain carried a handkerchief."

Her legs felt wooden. "Yes."

"One not made from wool?"

"I believe he did. Indeed, he loaned it to me during the hunt."

"When you were distressed about the fox," he said, and took the proffered linen.

"Will you return it to him for me?"

"Certainly," he said, and bowed again, handkerchief flopping from one long-fingered hand. "If you will agree to join me for an ice."

Again she wanted to flee, but there was little purpose in getting him to agree to take the carefully imbued handkerchief if she did not question him while he held it. It was not like the amulet she had given Bain, after all. Fabric did not have nearly the stored power of minerals, but it would do for a while.

In a moment they were seated at a small round

table in an establishment called Timber and Danes, which sold confections of every conceivable sort.

Connelly had tucked the handkerchief inside the sleeve of his cutaway coat, letting the embroidered end dangle out. Leaning back in his chair, he watched her, eyes alight with an emotion that might have been pleasure, but might just as well have been some feeling she did not understand.

"So, besides my charming personality and exceptional good looks, what brings you to Bond Street on this fine day?" he asked, hooking a lanky arm across the back of his chair.

She watched him for an instant. Perhaps he *was* good-looking. Indeed, perhaps he was charming, and maybe that was why she felt twitchy in his presence. Charm, in her opinion, was often false and enormously overrated. Unlike sobriety, earnestness, and a chest as broad as a stallion's.

"Mrs. Nettles?"

She cleared her throat and her mind. "I was searching, rather fruitlessly, I fear, for a gift for a friend," she lied, and braced herself for the consequences, a twinge of pain in the center of her temple.

"Not a friend of the male persuasion, I hope," he said. And though she had studiously prepared herself for this meeting, she found that she could not prepare herself for someone of Thayer Connelly's odd humor.

It made her want to question every word, dissect

each innuendo. Instead, she raised one haughty brow and prayed. "I *am* allowed to have male acquaintances, am I not?" she asked.

"I imagine you are," he said, and, tasting his ice, shook his head sadly. "It seems rather silly, however, knowing your infatuation with me."

"Ahh well, there is that," she said, and calmed her heart as she sampled her own refreshment.

"And too," he added. "I might well be quite jealous. The sort who flies into a vengeful rage at the slightest provocation."

"You're not," she said, and, sweeping a twirl into her ice, cautiously caught his gaze with hers. She could read his expression. It was one of surprise. "Men with such astounding egos as yours rarely make time for jealousy."

He furrowed his brow. "I'm quite certain you're wrong," he said.

"About the fact that you've an ego the size of Gibraltar or that you're not the jealous sort?"

"About the jealously issue."

"So I'm correct about your ego."

"Of course," he said, flipping a palm upward. "I'm as vain as a cockerel, but who wouldn't be . . . if he were I?"

"Tell me . . ." She forced herself to take another bite, though her stomach felt traitorous. "Are all Irishmen so narcissistic as you?"

He cocked his head at her.

"Vain," she explained, and found it hopelessly intriguing that this man with the elegant manners and witty ways lacked the vocabulary of a man some called "Beast." But perhaps each of them had his means of coping.

"Oh," said Connelly. "Only those who have reason to be."

"And what of the Scots?" she mused. "Are they known for their vanity or their jealousy?"

"Mercy," he said, and spread his long fingers dramatically across his chest as if her interest in another had wounded him sorely.

Drawing herself from her reverie, she gave him a look for the affectations while mentally chiding herself for rushing things. She was not meant for these games, but neither could she wait forever for her magic to take effect. "Are you ill, Mr. Connelly?"

"I may well be if you intend to tell me you are honestly interested in that hulking Scot."

"Might you be speaking of Rogan McBain?"

"Do you know another hulking Scot?"

She tried a smile, but for the life of her, she could think of no pithy rejoinders. "Is *he* the vengeful sort?" she asked, her tone far more serious than she had intended. Breathless, in fact.

Something passed across his expression, an odd flicker between amusement and curiosity, perhaps. Or perhaps not. What did she know of men? "Vengeful? No. Not particularly. But deadly . . ." He canted his head, watching her.

She felt no lie in the statement. *What the devil did that mean?* she wondered, and realized in that instant that the moments were slipping into silence. It was a situation tantamount to high treason in the elegant world of the chattering *ton*. "It's simply that wrath . . . Well, it is one of the deadly sins, is it not? And I would hate . . ." She was floundering, searching for footing in murky waters. "It is simply that I've no wish to see him bear more hardships than he's already endured."

"You think Bain has endured hardships?"

"Well, there's the scar on his . . ." she began and caught herself, face burning as she remembered the mark that stretched across his furrowed abdomen to sink beneath the length of plaid he'd snatched around his waist.

"The scar on his what?" Connelly asked, brows raised slightly.

She pursed her lips. "He came to London on business with Lord Brendier, did he not?" she asked, fishing carefully.

He watched her, half-smiling. "Is that what he told you?"

Her every fiber was taut with impatience. Against the silver handle of the spoon, her knuckles ached with tension. "Is it an untruth?"

Did his expression sober slightly or was she merely imagining? "So far as I know, lass, Bain is incapable of lying. Or perhaps he has yet to find a compelling reason."

She resisted scowling and forged on. "I assume Lord Brendier's death made his business dealings more difficult."

He stretched out his legs, watching her, eyes slightly narrowed, mouth still quirked up the faintest degree. "Considering Bain had come to London with the express purpose of meeting the lad, yes, I suspect his death did put a bit of a crimp in the works."

The scowl was too much to resist. "Why did McBain wish to meet Brendier?"

"I believe it was a favor to his uncle."

Faye shook her head.

"I know," Connelly said, grinning. "Difficult to believe the lug has kin, is it not? When first we met, I was not entirely certain he was human."

"What else would he be?" she asked, and refused to remember she had once thought him the Devil.

"I would guess he failed to tell you of Boxtel."

"I believe he said he lost his mount there."

Connelly laughed. "Did he tell you that Wellington's horse also fell and that the marquess, just a lieutenant colonel at the time, was able to make it to safety because Bain covered his retreat?

"Wellington gifted him with a new steed. Three days later. After they could find him amongst the corpses."

She felt a little sick. "What?"

"He stayed behind to defend the damaged animal against the French. Hence the scar you saw near his . . ." He nodded downward.

She refused to blanch. "Why would he—" she began.

"Listen," he said, leaning forward abruptly. "Are you certain you wouldn't rather speak of me? Perhaps you've yet to notice my dimples." He dimpled. She ignored them.

"Why?" she asked again, and he sighed.

" 'Tis impossible to guess Bain's mind," he said, and stared into the middle distance as if seeing things that were not there. "One day he is mad in love with a maid, the next he won't speak her name."

"What maid?" She hadn't meant to ask that question, but surely she should learn all she could.

"Charlotte." He rallied a little, but his grin was wan, her magic strengthening. "Spoken in hushed and reverent tones."

"What was her surname?"

"He never said. And indeed, he'll not say now. Since that day he has all but shut himself off from life. Though it's not as if he was the giddy sort before. Still, he's all but transparent compared to his uncle."

"Tell me of him."

"His mother's brother. Scotch to the very root of his being. Distinctly different from Gerald."

"Gerald?"

"His father. An Englishman. And rather refined by all accounts." His eyes were going somber, his features somewhat slack. "A far cry from Bain's uncle." He nodded to himself. "The old man died some months ago. A bayonet to the gut. In truth, I was fair surprised he could be killed."

"And here I assumed he was human also," she said, and wondered dismally if she sounded witty or just dense.

"There was some doubt," he said, and found a smile again. "Most of his friends called him Stone."

"And his enemies?"

"His enemies will be silent for a very long while."

She watched him.

He fiddled with his ice, but seemed far away. "I was never actually certain Bain had feelings . . . until recently. First old Stone's death, and now . . ." He paused, finding her with his azure eyes.

She felt strangely breathless, wanting more than anything for him to continue with his line of thought. But she had not come here on some schoolgirlish whim. She straightened her back and remembered her mission.

"And what of Brendier? Did Mr. McBain feel badly about his passing?"

"So far as I know, the baron was virtually unknown to Bain."

Did that mean the giant Celt would feel no need to avenge Brendier's death? And what of herself? If Rogan had, in fact, believed Lord Lindale was her aggressor, would he have felt compelled to do him bodily harm?

"And something of an ass," Connelly added.

"Why then did Stone wish for Rogan to meet him?"

"Perhaps old Stone knew the lad was about to find trouble and hoped Bain would protect him. 'Tis my best guess."

"Why Rogan?"

"If Bain wants someone alive . . ." His tone was pensive. He bent his neck as if flexing a half-forgotten wound. ". . . he generally stays that way for some time."

"And what if he wants a person dead?"

"Then his target tends to cease to breathe in fairly short order. But enough about the lug. Let us . . ." he began, and in that moment she leaned forward, tugging the handkerchief from his sleeve and squeezing it between his hand and hers.

"Mr. Connelly," she said. "Did Rogan kill Brendier?"

There was a pause, then, "I wouldn't think so."

"What of Lord Lindale? Did the Scotsman kill him?"

His features had become increasingly slack, his eyes all but sleepy. "Lindale of Inver Heights?"

"Yes."

"He died?"

She scowled. "Sometime during the night. Do you think Rogan might have had a hand in his death?"

"Did Lindale do you some harm?"

"I'm not certain."

"Then neither am I."

"Are you saying Bain is not above avenging me if he thought me damaged?"

"He protects those he cares for."

"And he . . . he cares for me?"

"Yes."

"As a . . . as a sister do you think or—" she began, then stopped, angry at herself. "So you believe he would be capable of killing Lindale."

"There is little McBain is incapable of," he said. "There is none in all of Europe to best him. Be it weapons, strategies, or bare knuckles."

She held her breath and leaned forward, desperate to know if she truly had him entranced. "So he is your superior?" she asked.

One corner of his mouth twitched up lazily. "I'm a child by comparison."

"If he killed Lindale, how would he have done so?"

"By any method he desired," he said.

"Poison?"

He scowled. "I don't believe—" he began, but in that instant the door opened. For a moment the light of day was blocked, then Rogan McBain stepped inside.

His gaze fell on her immediately. Their eyes clashed like lightning bolts before his attention dropped to the hand she had laid on Connelly's. Something shone in his eyes as he pulled his attention back to her face. She tugged her fingers away and stood.

"McBain," Connelly said, voice returned to its normal jocularity. "We were just talking about . . ."

Faye jerked toward him, breath held, willing

the Irishman to refrain from spilling the truth, but there was no need to worry. Her powers had not failed her.

"Something . . ." he said. "Happily, I'm quite certain it was not you. Which, by the by, makes me curious. What are you doing here?"

"We agreed to meet."

"Did we? When was that exactly?"

If Bain heard him speak, he made no response. Instead, his gaze remained absolutely steady on Faye. Emotions stormed between them in waves she failed to identify.

"Are ye well?" he rumbled.

"Yes," she said, the word tinny.

He stared at her a moment longer, shifted his gaze to Connelly, then nodded once and turned away. In a second he was gone.

The little shop went quiet, and Connelly laughed.

"Well," he said, "that went quite well, didn't it?"

She turned breathlessly toward him. "What the devil are you talking about? He looked extremely . . ." *What?* "Cross?"

He rubbed his hands together. "He did rather didn't he?" he said, and, stepping up beside her, peered out the window to watch McBain stride away. His broad back was stiff, his big, artist's hands clenched to fists. The sight seemed to bring Connelly nothing but glee. "Well, I believe my work here is done." He smiled down at her. "Unless you wish to risk my life further."

"I believe you to be quite mad," she said. "And I know a bit about lunacy."

He grinned. "A single kiss between us might well put him over the edge." He was standing very close, his sky blue gaze locked on hers. "No? 'Tis probably just as well, for one kiss might also put me in the grave. Until later, then," he said, and, bowing, hurried merrily from the shop.

Chapter 17

"**M**cBain," Connelly called, but Bain ignored the noise just as he would the buzz of a bothersome insect. Instead, he rolled the tension out of his shoulders and kept walking.

"McBain, slow your ungodly long strides," Connelly called, and ran up to his side. "My apologies, I entirely forgot we were to meet. But what a serendipitous bit of good fortune that Mrs. Nettles showed up, aye?"

Anger stormed through him, but he kept it carefully at bay. He had no wish to knock the Irishman unconscious. Perhaps.

"She looked fit, didn't she?" Connelly asked. "A little . . ." He flapped his hand in front of his chest. "A little scrawny perhaps, but bonny enough in a frail sort of way."

Some kind of noise escaped Bain's throat. Even he wasn't sure what it was.

"Still, the lady *is* unattached," Connelly continued, "and far be it from me to turn aside a fair damsel's interest in myself. She is a widow, after all. And as you may or may not know widows are known to long for a man's . . ." He tilted his head as if searching for the proper word. "Attention."

Rage began to boil in earnest. Bain gritted his teeth and lengthened his strides.

"And though I prefer a lass with a bit more . . . substance, I would feel amiss if I made her feel she were less than appealing. After all, I've certainly bedded women with fewer charms and would be happy to—"

Upon later consideration, Bain never remembered turning. Never recalled drawing back his fist, but suddenly Irish was stretched out on the cobblestones. He remained there a while, looking stunned before he tested his jaw, then grinned like a drunken longshoreman.

Bain stared at him for an instant, then turned away, but Connelly stopped him with a question.

"You don't mind if I accompany her to the opera then, do you?"

It was well past dusk. Midnight was approaching relentlessly. Not the time to pay visits, of course, yet Rogan made his way down the dark streets toward Lavender House. It stood silent atop its lone hill, towering above the others and seeming to glower down at the world at large. For a moment, Rogan glowered back, but finally he lifted a heavy leg over Colt's croup, stepped from the saddle, and strode resolutely up the curved, cobbled walkway.

It had been a devilishly long day. After seeing Mrs. Nettles with Connelly, he had ridden to Inver Heights in an effort to determine who might have intended her harm, only to find that the very man he'd suspected had mysteriously died during the night.

Questions simmered like bad stew in his soul. Questions that would be answered. Questions that would ease his mind, would allow him to forget her. After all, he could understand why she preferred Connelly. He could understand and accept. Indeed, 'twas for the best. After all, McBain himself was hardly the sort to make a life with a lady of such breathtaking—

"So you return."

The voice from the darkness startled him from his rancid thoughts. He stopped, glared into the shadows, and exhaled carefully.

The red-haired maid was once again in the garden. He swept his gaze to the left, though in truth, every instinct in him suggested that he back away and do so slowly. He found the average woman frightfully beyond his ken. How much less did he understand the ladies who lived in this glowering house on the hill.

"I would see Mrs. Nettles," he intoned to the night.

"Surely even hulking Scotsmen realize it is long past the hour of proper visits."

Despite his best intentions, he snorted quietly. The last time he had stood in this garden, she had been engaged in some strange, inexplicable altercation with another.

"Are you suggesting I am less than proper?" she asked, and stepped from the shadows.

"I am saying I will see the lady," he said simply.

She smiled as if thrilled by the bite of challenge he let infuse his tone. " 'Tis my task to make certain you do not bother those who have no wish to be bothered."

"Your task," he said, and scowled.

She shrugged. "Our Cur oft runs off, leaving me to defend the ladies within."

This was a strange place with strange people. There was an eerie feel to the house, even to the garden in which he stood. It made the hair stand up on the back of his neck. And he did not like that. He was an uncomplicated man, comfortable with more conventional conflicts, and yet he was here. What did that say of him? "And who are these ladies who have no wish to be bothered?"

She smiled again, teeth bright in the shimmer of moonlight. "The ladies of Lavender House are simple womenfolk, widows mostly, gathered together to discuss politics and share the joys and woes of life."

And I am a turnip. "What do you know of Lord Lindale?" he asked.

For a moment, he thought she would refuse to answer, but she did not. "I know that he is dead."

"How did it happen?"

"Not by my hand."

Perhaps her unconventional answer should have surprised him, but it did not. "Who are you?"

"No one to trifle with," she warned, and took a step forward.

He refrained from retreating, though it was a close thing. "I've no intention of trifling, lass. I only wish to speak to Mrs. Nettles."

"Then you'll return in the morning," she said, and stepped more directly into his path.

"Perhaps that is so, but I will see her this night also," he rumbled. "Thus I ask that you move aside."

"I cannot do that, Scotsman."

"Because 'tis your duty to guard the house," he said, tone dry.

She raised a brow in a sort of agreeable challenge.

Taking a deep breath, he stepped forward, but in that moment a rustle of sound issued from the rowans to the left. They turned in tandem as a dark silhouette stepped from the shadows.

Absolute silence lay on the tension-soaked garden, but in a moment she spoke, her voice low with anger.

"You dare disturb me again?"

The man's voice was quiet with warning and deep confidence, though he did not address the woman. "The lady is right, Scotsman. 'Tis not the proper time for this."

God almighty this was a strange place. Did no

one ever sleep? "And who might you be?" Bain, too, kept his voice deep and gruff, but if the truth be told, he was thrilled near to tears by this new challenge. Better to face a fully armed regiment of battle-scarred soldiers than tangle with a woman who held a grudge.

"I'm of no concern to you," he said, "unless you harm the lady."

"I'll not harm—" he began.

"I do not want your help," she said, tone pitched high in sudden, overt rage.

McBain glanced at her, but her attention was on the man near the far wall.

"And yet I give it," he said.

"Go away," she hissed.

"I did that once." Silence echoed in the wake of his admission. "I'll not do so again."

"You will leave me be," she snarled, "or—"

"I've no wish to interfere," Bain said, and thought that a truer word had never been spoken. Nevertheless, he made a move to step around her, but she turned toward him with a snap, eyes blazing in the darkness.

"You may not pass, you hulking—" she began, but the threat was never completed.

"Why have you come?" asked a quiet voice.

Bain lifted his gaze toward the front door. A dark shape stood there, indistinguishable in the overhead shadows. And yet he recognized her in the melodic glory of her voice. Could feel her goodness like a blade to his heart.

"Faerie lass," he breathed, and, though he told himself to stay away, he could not do so. He moved toward her. In a vague corner of his mind, he was aware that Shaleena raised her hand in anger, but the man spoke from the shadows.

"This battle is not for you, Becca."

"Get out of my life," she hissed.

"And spend another decade in search of you?"

"You've not been searching. You're dead. I made certain of that."

"So it *was* you who asked of me in Leiria. I thought I felt your magic there. 'Twas what first made me suspect the lies of my father."

"It's *you* who lie!" she railed.

"I do not. That you know," he said, and, bowing, disappeared into the darkness.

Shaleena stood for a moment, fists clenched, then lunged after him. "You are dead. You're dead!"

McBain watched her race into the deepest shadows, then stepped toward the house, searching blindly for some acceptable salutation. Talk of the weather seemed rather bland.

"Why are you here?" Her eyes were as bright as washed agates in the moonlight.

"Because . . ." He tried for a reason that would not sound doltish. Then searched for a lie. Neither would pass his lips. "Because I could do naught but come."

Thunder rolled off to his left. But the sight of her was all-consuming.

"You are well?" he asked, and knew, absolutely *knew* there were other things he had meant to address.

"Yes."

He nodded, unable to move closer. Unable to move away. "I worried you might—" He glanced into the distance, remembering the sight of her hand on Connelly's. "I worried."

Lightning flashed behind him, and for a fractured instant he realized the oddness of that; there were no clouds.

"How much?" she asked.

He scowled.

"How much did you worry?"

He had no idea how to answer that. He was a far cry from a wordsmith.

"Lindale is dead," she said, and he nodded.

She stepped toward him, slowly, reluctantly, as if afraid. "Connelly says you are not particularly vengeful. He did not say the same about being deadly."

"Irish is . . ." He felt the muscles bunch in his jaw and remembered the intensity he had seen in her face as she'd stared into Connelly's eyes. Was that intensity passion? Was it love? "He is a good man . . . for the most part."

He could sense her scowl more than see it.

"Is it true?"

"Aye." He forced out the word. "Though he cannot always be trusted with women."

A growl sounded from the street. Bain glanced

back, but there was naught to see but shadows.

"I meant to say, is it true that you are dangerous?" she asked.

"Aye." Regret scourged him, but he kept his
gaze steady. "I have killed."

"Would you kill for me?" she asked.

A thousand thoughts seared his mind, a thousand ideas regarding how he should answer.
Surely he should inquire about the circumstances.
But once again the truth was too alluring. "Aye,"
he said.

They were close now, close enough to touch.

"Did you?" she breathed.

Something tightened in his chest. "Would you
wish me to, lass?"

Her lips moved, as sweet as lavender, but for a
moment no sound could be heard.

"Lass?" he murmured again.

"I am not certain," she said, and there was
something about the truth of it, the agony of it,
that made her irresistible.

He reached up, slowly, against his will, against
his better judgment. Her cheek felt like wild petals
against his fingers. Her eyes were midnight pools,
gazing into his soul, probing his deepest secrets.
And yet she did not turn away at the horrors surely
seen there. Instead, her lips parted, and he was
drawn in, pulled closer. Her kiss scorched him. It
seemed almost that he could smell smoke.

"Move aside," someone snarled.

Faye jerked away as the redhead stormed nearer,

but something sparkled in the darkness as she brushed past.

"Shaleena . . ." Faye began.

"What?" She spun toward them, anger hissing from her lips.

"Is something . . ." She gasped. "Your gown's on fire."

Shaleena glared at her skirts, then, yanking up her hem, swatted out the flame. "And you think sky-clad foolish," she said, and, swearing, disappeared inside.

"There was a time I thought *Connelly* strange," Rogan mused.

Faye blinked. "I think . . . Perhaps I'd best see to her," she said, and turned away.

"Faerie lass," Rogan breathed.

She swiveled back, eyes bright in the darkness.

"Irish would make a fine protector," he said, and forcing himself to step back, left her alone.

Chapter 18

"Why are you here, Irish?" McBain growled. Nearly twenty-four hours had passed since he'd last seen wee Faye. Since he'd touched her, since he'd painfully admitted that Connelly was not entirely a bastard. Rogan's mood hadn't improved much since.

Beneath his considerable weight, Colt's hooves clipped steadily down a rutted side street.

He had spent the day speaking with the family of Edgar Daimmen, but if they planned revenge on Brendier for the duel that took their kinsman's life, he could not tell it.

"I am here," Connelly said, "in an attempt to discern what the deuce you're doing."

McBain watched the street traveling between Colt's ears and wondered what to do next. He had not mourned when he'd learned of Brendier's death, for he had felt no kinship with him. No instant bonding. But he *had* been surprised at the other's passing, for when they'd first met on the previous day, he'd seemed fair jolly on his plush, four-poster bed.

How, then, had he died? And what of Lindale? How was his death connected to the breath-stealing Faerie Faye?

"Although you may not be fully aware I have not yet won Mrs. Nettles's undivided adoration. If you used your head you might yet have some hope."

Rogan glanced at his irritating companion. For there lay the crux of the problem: Rogan *did* have hope. Hope that she might care a small whit about him. Hope that she thought of him in the wee hours of the morning. That she lay sleepless and alone, thinking of none but him. Hope that she was as good, as right, as wonderful as she seemed. Hope. Even though he had seen her clutching the Irishman's hand.

"But you'd best quit mucking about with meaningless drivel if you're to catch her interest," Connelly said.

"Meaningless drivel?" McBain said. "Such as murder?"

"Exactly."

Anger boiled silently in his soul. "And what if the man murdered had threatened Faer—Mrs. Nettles?"

The dawn of understanding shone in Connelly's eyes. "Is that what this is about?"

Rogan said nothing.

"Well that explains a bit of your ridiculous preoccupation, I suspect. But really, the man is dead so it matters little if . . ." He paused. "Tell me it's not true."

Bain remained silent.

Without looking, Bain was certain the other's face would be stamped with disbelief. The Irish bastard had always been as dramatic as a debutante. "Surely you do not think that someone as comely . . . as refined . . . as breathtaking as the scrumptious—"

Rogan gritted his teeth and glared.

Connelly grinned but continued. "Surely you do not think Mrs. Nettles might have caused the man's death."

Rogan remained silent for several seconds as memories wreaked havoc in his head. "Is it your esteemed opinion, then, that those who are beautiful cannot be evil?" Bain asked and turned baleful eyes on the Irishman. He grinned like a toothy serpent.

"So you're not entirely daft. You *do* think her beautiful."

McBain turned forward before the other could see the truth shining in his eyes; of course she was beautiful. She was light and goodness and . . . He swore in silence.

"Go home, Connelly," he ordered.

"Very well," agreed the other. "I will concede that not all beautiful women are innocents. But if you think her the culprit, why do you continue to search for another killer?"

He didn't deign to answer, but Connelly finally grinned. Rogan could hear it in his voice.

"It is because you don't *wish* to believe she's the culprit."

"Shut up, Connelly."

He laughed. "So that's it, then. You're infatuated. Besotted. Smitten. The giant has finally—"

"I've no wish to hurt you, Irish. Well . . ." he corrected, not liking to lie. "I've *some*—"

But Connelly wasn't listening. "Not to worry, old man, because I don't think it's entirely beyond the realm of possibility that she has some interest in you."

Rogan turned toward the other with a snap. "What makes you think—" he began, then stopped himself with abrupt and painful discipline. He was nearly nine and thirty years of age. Too long in the tooth to sound like a love-starved urchin. "It matters not if she is interested in me," he said.

"What's that?" Connelly asked, still grinning.

"For I'll not touch her," he added.

"You jest!" Absolute astonishment sounded in his voice. "I know you think her in love with me, and what woman isn't? But truly, she's all but panting . . ."

Rogan turned toward Connelly again and the man suddenly stopped his chatter. Sometimes that happened when the Scot looked at people a certain way. Sometimes there was also an abrupt scattering of bodies toward the nearest exit. But no one had ever accused Connelly of knowing when enough was too much.

"Don't tell me you have yet to kiss her."

"If you touch her . . ." he began, then calmed himself, remembering; she was in need of a guardian. And despite Connelly's irritating demeanor, there were few better equipped to protect her. "She is not for the likes of me," he finished poorly.

"Who then?"

He glared again. His teeth were beginning to hurt.

"I mean, why in heaven's name—" Connelly began, and then his eyes lit up with monkey-like mischief. "Is it because of the difference in your size? Because I don't think—" Connelly began, then lowered his gaze to Rogan's crotch, seeming to remember. "Tell me, old man, how long has it been since you've been with a woman?"

True ire began to rumble in his soul. "How long has it been since I've rendered you cataleptic?"

"Good Christ!" Connelly crowed. "That long? Well then, it's little wonder you're nervous. But this isn't something you forget readily. In fact. . .

"Look, an inn," he said, interrupting himself. "Let us stop. It'll give me a chance to educate you properly."

"Let us stop conversing so I no longer feel compelled to kill you."

He laughed. "My silence has never guaranteed that outcome in the past."

"I'm feeling charitable."

"Excellent," Connelly said and reined in beneath the inn's bright shingle. "Feel free then to buy me a pint."

Rogan considered arguing, but he disliked wasting that much energy on irritating Irishmen. Thus he stopped Colt beside Connelly's mare.

Inside the inn it was dark and cool. Five tables occupied the public space. Only two were open. A fair-haired maid in a simple blue gown and white apron nodded to them as they pulled out chairs.

Rogan settled in, stretching his legs beneath the oaken table even as the barmaid hurried toward them. "What can I get you, gents?" Her voice was brusque, but when she glanced at Connelly, she paused for just an instant, as if caught unawares.

The Irishman smiled as he always did in the face of an interested woman. Or *any* woman. "I'll have a pint," he said.

"Very good, then. And what will you be having, luv?" she asked Rogan.

"What have you got to sup?" he asked.

"To sup?" Perhaps there was humor in her voice, but there was also kindness and more than a little fatigue, Rogan thought. Enough so she did not linger on Connelly's idiotic smile.

"What my large friend means is, what is your fair establishment offering for the evening meal," Irish explained.

"Ahh, well, you've a choice there between lamb stew and boiled fowl."

"How's the stew?" Rogan asked and she shrugged.

"Fair to middlin' if you've a taste for charred taters and stringy mutton."

"I'll have the fowl and a pint," Rogan said, then, sensing her fatigue, added, "when you've a minute."

For just an instant there was the flicker of something in her eyes and then she turned back to Connelly. "And you, sir. What'll you have to sup?"

He smiled, charming to the death. Bastard. "I'd best have the same so as to know what caused my large friend's demise."

"Oh, the fowl don't kill folk," she said. "Not usually at any rate. It just makes 'em wish to God it had whilst they hurl their guts out behind the privies."

"Marjorie," growled an aging man, scowling from the doorway of the kitchen. "There be meals waiting."

"I was but extolling the quality of those very meals," she said and shifting her gaze wryly toward Bain, bustled away.

At which time Connelly leaned closer. "What of her?" he asked.

Rogan returned his gaze to his so called friend. "What's that?"

"Marjorie, the comely lass just gone. Surely you noticed her . . . charms."

McBain scowled. "She had a pleasing enough smile I suppose."

"*Smile,*" Connelly said and laughed. "Well, aye, I failed to glance that high as of yet, but I suspect she did, and she didn't seem to find you entirely repulsive. So, would you touch *her?*"

Rogan glowered and turned back to perusing the modest establishment. The room where they sat was smallish and dim, lit by little more than the flickering fire. A trio of young swells sat round a table near the far wall. Two aging fellows leaned over their beers by the fireplace, and near the window a seasoned man and a youngish woman sat in silence. He was squat but well groomed, she, as frothy as fresh milk, dressed in a lemon yellow gown that seemed to spout lace at every possible juncture.

"I didn't think her your type," Connelly said. "But if your taste runs toward frippery, it looks as if you're in luck." He leaned forward conspiratorially, but the barmaid was already hustling back, forearms pale but capable beneath the upturned sleeves of her plain gown.

"There you be. Pints for the two of you," she said and swished the beers before them with practiced ease.

Rogan nodded his thanks and tried to ignore his companion. It was no easy task even as they took their first sips.

"So what think you of them?" Connelly asked, tilting his head sideways toward the pair by the window. "Might the lass be the bloke's sister?"

Rogan glanced wearily toward the maid in

frothy yellow. Dear God, she could not have been more than seven and ten years of age. Barely old enough to eat unattended. Surely he had caused enough trouble among the bairns of London.

But Irish was already shaking his head.

"Doubtful. I have a sister. We've not yet been caught in the same room without warfare breaking out. They must be father and daughter." His eyes were lit with some kind of sadistic glee. "Which means this is a fine opportunity for you to introduce yourself."

Rogan settled a little deeper into his chair and took another swig of his beer. It was fair to perfect.

"Tell her you're a friend to the Marquess of Wellington. Dropping a title here and there has proved to lift the skirts of even the most reluctant lass."

Bain took another swig of beer. The cool brew almost made him think he might not have to disable the Irishman after all. "I suppose you've not considered they might well be husband and wife?" he said.

"Husband!" Connelly started, immediately upset. "The old gaffer could easily double her age. Of course . . ." he shrugged and drank, which, blessedly, hid all but a corner of his irritating grin. "So could you."

Rogan ignored the gibe, took another draught and turned his attention to the left.

The barmaid had just brought additional drinks to the trio by the far wall. One of the lads was dark, one smallish. The third wore a black, beaver hat at a rakish angle. She smiled down at the lot of them with animated camaraderie.

"But some women are quite forgiving of aging oafs. At least if the aging oaf in question has a bit of coin."

The smallish lad reached for the barmaid's hand. She seemed momentarily surprised, then she tugged her fingers out of his grip and continued with their conversation.

"Perhaps fair yonder lass be one of them. 'Tis impossible to say until you engage her," Connelly said, and at that moment the lad in the hat stood, blocking Rogan's view of the barmaid.

"The proper thing would be to simply swagger over and ask if she favors lumbering oafs," Connelly continued.

The boy jerked back a sharp pace as if elbowed, but in a moment he was stepping up close to the maid again. By then the other two lads had risen as well, surrounding the girl as they crowded her silently toward the stairs.

Rogan rose with a scowl.

"Deuce it all, McBain—" Connelly began, sputtering beer. "I didn't truly intend you should . . ."

But Rogan ignored the Irishman as he strode toward the far wall.

"What news, lads?" he rumbled, approaching the table.

The boy in the hat turned toward him with a snap, mostly hiding the maid behind him.

"Good Christ," he said, looking Rogan up and down. "Has the carnival come to town?"

His friends snickered obligingly at their leader's razor-sharp wit, but the maid's face was pale, her right arm hidden between her back and the dark lad behind her.

Rage simmered quietly through Rogan's system, but he kept his tone level. "Aye, it has lad," he said. Convivial. He would be naught but genial. No body parts would be loosed this day. "And word has it that they're looking for a simpleton with a jaunty hat at which to throw flaming knives. If you run right along you might yet convince them to appoint the task to you."

His friends chuckled cautiously, and Jaunty glowered, face going ruddy. "This little bit of muslin invited us to her chambers, oaf," he said, stepping forward. "Bad luck to you. Now you'd best sit before we take offense to the interruption."

Rogan shifted his gaze to the maid, quietly assessing. It was possible, after all, that he'd read the situation incorrectly. But her eyes looked wide and dark in the pale oval of her face, and she shook her head once, a short, almost imperceptible jerk.

Rogan lowered his shoulders, spreading his legs the slightest degree. "I was already enjoying me beer, lads," he said, "but a wee tussle would only make the brew that much more gratifying."

"You want to tussle, do you?" The smallish lad shifted, drawing a knife from his handsome tailcoat just as Jaunty grinned and leveled a pistol.

Rogan glanced down at it, then raised his gaze slowly and gave one shake of his head. "'Tis a bad idea, laddie," he warned quietly. "'I've no wish to get blood on your fancy clothes."

"If you want to keep your blood in your freakish large body, you'd best get back to that beer," hissed Jaunty.

Rogan almost smiled at the misunderstanding. "Indeed, I would, but I fear I cannot."

"And here I thought you too foolish to know when to fear," Jaunty said and glanced sideways to enjoy his friends' appreciation of his fine wit, but in that instant Rogan wrenched the muzzle of his pistol sideways. The lad screamed as his fingers were bent backward, but Rogan was already yanking the boy forward as he himself stepped behind. In less than an instant, he had the lad's arm twisted up against his spine.

He hissed in pain, but Rogan was far beyond trying to decipher any possible words.

"Are you well, lass?" he asked, ignoring all but the maid.

She nodded. He did the same, then turned his attention to the dark-haired fellow who still held her captive.

"Loose her," he said quietly.

The boy shot his gaze toward Jaunty, but that one was bent forward at a painful angle and failed to respond.

"Now would be as good a time as any," Rogan added and gave Jaunty's arm an almost imperceptible tug toward his scapula.

There was a squawk of pain that might have been considered an order. The swarthy fellow dropped the girl's arm and stepped away, hands raised.

Rogan turned his attention to the third lad. He swallowed, shifting his weight restlessly as he tightened his grip on the knife.

"You're fair fast for a big bloke," he said.

"It's been said before, lad," Connelly admitted. He'd risen quietly from the table and sauntered now toward the wall to retrieve the felled pistol. "Usually on a dying breath, though, so thus far you're ahead of the game."

"Listen," said the dark lad, hands still held upright. "We're not looking to cause trouble. We heard there was a maid here was willing to bed a gent if the money was right, is all." His eyes darted from one of his companions to the other. "We were going to pay her. Weren't we—"

But in that instant, the fellow with the knife struck at Rogan's exposed arm. And in that same moment, Rogan catapulted his captive sideways, propelling him into the side of the blade. The attacker's arm swung wide, but Rogan caught him by the coat front before he could twist away. Caught him, drew him near, and plowed one battering-ram fist into his nose.

He went down like a spanked child, legs astride,

blubbering incoherently, hands pressed to his face as blood gushed onto his snowy cravat.

Rogan watched him for an abbreviated second, but there was no threat there. He raised his attention to the dark lad; that one was already backing away.

"I told them . . ." His voice was shaking. "I told them I didn't want to get in the suds. But—"

"Get them from my sight," Rogan growled.

"Too much strong drink." The boy was starting to babble. "Father always warned me that too much—"

"Now," Rogan suggested evenly. The boy popped off a nod, rushed toward his downed companion.

"He drew my cork," blubbered the smallest of the three.

"Come along," the lad urged, gaze still on Rogan.

"The bastard broke my—"

"Shut the hell up!" he hissed. Grabbing the other's arm, he dragged him to his feet and propelled him toward the door.

Jaunty was still bent over his ruined hand, face contorted in a bizarre meld of pain and rage.

"You forgot one," Rogan rumbled to the most coherent of the three.

"Presley, for God's sake, come along!" he ordered, and Jaunty left, cradling his arm against his chest as he stumbled out the door.

The inn went absolutely silent. All eyes were on McBain.

He cleared his throat, uncomfortable in the glare of their attention, and turned toward the barmaid.

"Are you certain you are unharmed?"

"Yes." Her voice was still soft, but the color had returned to her face. "I owe you my thanks." She tried a smile. It was weak, but strengthening. "And more," she breathed, "if you've an interest."

He watched her a moment, then nodded succinctly. "I'll have another pint then, if it's no trouble," he said and strode resolutely back to his chair.

Chapter 19

Faye rode alone through the darkening streets of London and tried to think. But everything had gone topsy-turvy. Upside down. Inside out. It had been nearly a full day since she had seen Rogan McBain, since he had assured her Thayer Connelly would be a good protector. What the devil was that about?

Who was this Rogan McBain? And what did he want from her? Each time she resolved to pry the truth from him, he gave it eagerly. Or so it seemed. But was it the truth he spoke, or was he so adept at lying she could not tell the difference?

A quiet side street lined with chestnuts and small shops called to something deep inside her and she reined Sultan to the right, letting her thoughts roam.

What of Shaleena and this Joseph? Did they share some sort of tumultuous past? Or were they merely sharing a tumultuous *present*? Even Faye found it tempting to trust their newly hired servant, but she knew little of the situation. How had he arrived at Lavender House? Who was he, really? And why had Shaleena's gown been smoking? Did Joseph have powers of his own?

It had taken all of Faye's courage to inquire, but Shaleena had shared no information. On the other hand, she had not threatened to turn Faye into a sewer rat, either. Instead, she had fled to her chambers, though everyone knew she rarely slept.

In truth, Faye was not sleeping well herself. It had been a long and harrowing night, fraught with ugly dreams and unsolved mysteries.

By morning, she'd felt more tired and fretful than she had on the previous night. But she dare not let that change her course. She would find Brendier's murderer if there was one to be found, no matter the outcome. Was his death tied to Lindale's? Were they both tied to McBain?

His somber eyes flashed in her mind, piercing her with his caring, with his earnestness.

She gritted her teeth against her thoughts, for she did not know if he was being earnest. She did not know, despite her powers, despite her determination. Or was she simply too frightened to see the truth? Indeed, learning he was as gentle and fine as he seemed might well be as terrifying as learning he was the devil she'd first thought him to be.

But either way, she would learn the truth. To that end, she had visited a maid who had once been in Lindale's employ. The girl spoke furtively of roving hands and illegitimate children, though when questioned, she wasn't certain who those children might be. There were also rumors of spats Lindale had had with his contemporaries. The late Brendier was certainly not the first nobleman with whom he had argued. Apparently he and Rennet had known their share of confrontations. So why had that fair-haired lord been invited to Inver Heights if—

All thoughts stopped abruptly as a strapping chestnut stallion turned his head toward her. Too large and striking to be any other than McBain's Colt, he was tied to an iron post beside Connelly's mare.

But what would McBain be doing in this part of the city? Faye's heart beat erratically in her chest, and suddenly she realized her mount had stopped. With a tap of her quirt against her skirt, she urged the gelding on. She could not possibly explain her presence there without either admitting her conversation with Lindale's maid or allowing Connelly to believe she was, in fact, stalking him. Both possibilities made her head—

Before the thought was complete, the door of the inn slammed open. Three men limped out. One cradled his arm. Another's hand quivered over his blood-spattered face. And the third, though apparently unscathed, looked as pale as death itself.

Mind racing, Faye rode on, but in that instant the man in the top hat glanced at her. The malevolence in his eyes all but stopped her heart, and suddenly, with stunning clarity, she realized Rogan, too, could have been injured.

In a matter of moments, she was beside the two mounts near the inn.

Slipping her foot from the single stirrup, she dropped to the cobblestones. She was no master healer. Far from it, but she had some skills, and she would do what she could to assist Rogan.

Steeling herself, she hurried to the building and opened the door.

It took a moment for her eyes to adjust to the dimness. But in a second, she had found him. Rogan McBain. He sat with his left side toward the door, and though his face was turned away from her, she knew him immediately. Felt his presence like an odd shiver of truth. His back was broad, his body still, and she found she wanted nothing more than to go to him, to touch him. Even as she realized the strangeness of those feelings, she took an involuntary step forward. It was at that moment that she noticed the woman sitting beside him. She was buxom and pretty, with wide eyes and flawless skin. Her hand was on his arm, and his gaze, that intent, unwavering storminess was for the maid alone.

Drawing one uneven breath, Faye froze for just an instant, then wrenching herself from immobility, backed brokenly toward the door. Just then a voice interrupted her retreat.

"Mrs. Nettles!"

Faye jerked her gaze to the right. Thayer Connelly was already hurrying toward her.

"Whatever brings you here?" he asked, but

he couldn't hold her attention, for at that precise moment she felt Rogan turn toward her. Felt his attention strike her like flint on steel. Felt her breath leave her throat in a heavy rush.

"McBain. Look who's just arrived," Connelly said.

Panic or common sense suggested that she turn and run. But it was already too late; Connelly was reaching for her hand, drawing her into the room.

She heard a murmur from the barmaid, saw Rogan turn toward the other for an instant, and in that same amount of time the maid cupped his cheek with her palm and kissed him.

Faye's breath froze in her throat.

"Come in. Come—" Connelly began, then realized her gaze and turned in Rogan's direction. "Ahh that . . ." he breathed as the woman rose to her feet. Her eyes were bright, but for the life of her, Faye could not guess her emotion. Disappointment? Fear? Gratitude? "That is a rather longish tale," he said, as the maid turned and disappeared up the stairs with only a single backward glance.

"What is it?" Faye murmured, and, surprising even herself, turned her attention back to Connelly. His grin was slightly twisted at one corner.

"What's that?"

"What's the tale?" It took all her nerve to voice the question.

"Well . . ." He cleared his throat. "It begins with an oversized Celt born in London but raised in the wilds of the Scottish Highlands just north of . . ." His attention strayed to McBain, and his grin fired up in earnest. "Bain, look who's here. It's the comely Mrs. Nettles."

For a moment, Faye thought the Scot might stay exactly as he was. In the next, she thought he might turn and follow the maid, but finally he gathered himself and rose slowly to his feet. His chair scraped against the rough, wooden floor even as his brow lowered and his expression darkened. She resisted hiding. Resisted even looking away. *She*, after all, was doing nothing wrong.

"Funny thing, this," Connelly was saying. "I did not *truly* think you were stalking me." He winked. "But now I begin to wonder."

Rogan shifted his gaze to Connelly for a brief instant before settling his attention on her again, ignoring him completely.

They stared at each other for a breathless eternity before he spoke, his voice a low rumble of sound.

"Surely you have not come this long way alone, lass."

Terror warred with curiosity and a dozen other fractious emotions, broiling like moon-drenched hensbane in her restricted chest. "I was . . ." She searched for a lie, but it promised vindication. She hedged cautiously. ". . . passing by when I was drawn in this direction," she said, and realized suddenly that it was true. Why had she first turned onto this street? It was not one with which she was familiar, and yet she had felt a comfortable allure. It was not until she had ridden some way that she had spotted the three lads. One angry, one bloodied, all scared. And her only thought had been for a giant Highlander's well-being. "At the sight of the inn, I realized I was somewhat gutfounded." *Gutfounded?* She sounded like some scatterbrained pink of the *ton*.

And she couldn't even tell if he believed her? Did he know her lies better than she knew his?

"So . . ." It was all but impossible to force words past the desert dryness of her throat. "How is the fare here?"

His brows lowered even more. "You've ridden all this way cross town for a meal?"

God help her. "I'm quite famished." That much at least was true. Or perhaps there was another reason her stomach felt as if it had been tied in knots. "I'm in the mood for a steaming hot pigeon pie."

"Could you not get pigeon pie at—"

"Is the food good or not?" she asked, and though she tried to hold her decorum, her tone had slid into exasperation.

He looked naught but confused. Possibly there was some irritation.

"Indeed, we've no way of knowing the quality," Connelly said, attention shifting from one to the other as if he viewed a lively match of tennis. "The maid has yet to deliver our meals . . . Though one can hardly blame her . . ." He was grinning. She could hear it in his tone, though she couldn't quite seem to tear her attention from Rogan's glowering eyes. "She had a bit of a fright, I fear."

At those words, McBain's brows lowered even farther. A muscle seemed to shift restlessly in his jaw.

"A fright?" she asked, but McBain changed the subject.

"I'll see you home if you like," he rumbled. "Or Irish could accompany you if that be your—"

"It seems the three young bucks just here were planning some mischief involving poor Marjorie," Connelly interrupted.

Faye blinked, breathless. "Marjorie?"

"The barmaid. You may have noticed her. She was just now thanking Bain here for his assist," Connelly said, conjuring up the sight of the buxom maid kissing Rogan's lips. And suddenly, despite everything, a dozen scenarios flashed through Faye's befuddled mind. Oddly enough, each of them involved Rogan. Odder still, none of them involved clothing.

"'Tis getting late," Rogan interrupted, and spared an all-but-lethal glare for Connelly before turning back to Faye. "You'll be wanting—"

"The scrappiest of the three was toting a pistol," Connelly said.

Faye snapped her gaze to the Irishman. "No." The word sounded breathless to her own ears.

"Not to worry, though," Connelly said, grinning again. "His second had naught but a blade."

She skimmed Rogan's face. Their gazes fused. Something simmered between them like moon-shadowed magic.

"He's quite unscathed though."

Was he? She scanned his chest, his arms. He looked well enough. But how did she know really? He had scars upon scars on his beautiful body, and she longed to feel his heart beat beneath her hand. To skim her fingers over his lively muscles and know that all was well. To feel safe. The oddness of that thought barely registered in her mind. "Perhaps I'd best check," she murmured.

The room went quiet. Rogan seemed to be leaning toward her like a windblown pine.

"What's that?" Connelly asked.

Reality struck her like an errant shaft of lightning. She drew back abruptly and cleared her throat. Her face felt suddenly hot.

"Perhaps . . . I'd . . . best . . . check . . ." She was about to die. What the devil was wrong with her? "At Lavender House."

The two men waited in silence. Connelly's brows were raised like two ascending caterpillars. Rogan's rested just over his storm-cloud eyes.

"To see if they have pigeon pie," she finished, and only just managed to keep from moaning at her own stupidity.

Rogan scowled. Connelly laughed out loud.

"I'm certain there'll be no need for that, lass," he said. "Here . . ." He swept an elegant hand toward the table recently vacated by Rogan and the moon-eyed maid. "Take my seat. Our meals will arrive shortly, I'm certain. You're free to have mine."

"I can't—"

"Certainly, you can," he said, and prodded her gently toward the table. "It's not pigeon pie, but I heard the boiled fowl is quite . . . edible." He pulled out a chair and nudged her to sit.

She did so. "But what of you?" she asked, glancing up and half-wishing she were somewhere else. Anywhere else. Possibly dead.

"As it happens, that elderly gentleman"—he nodded surreptitiously toward the table to her right where the old man and the frothy girl were just rising to their feet—"is looking for a match for his young ward and thinking a fine fellow like myself might be just the thing."

She scowled.

"Though he may not know it yet." His eyes were shining with mischief. Faye's head felt too light. "I may be a bit late, McBain," he added. "Hence, if you feel a need to . . ." He shrugged. " . . . stay the night, please feel free to do so."

Faye wouldn't have thought it possible for Rogan's brows to lower farther. Had she placed a bet to that effect, she would have lost her coin.

"Until later," Connelly said, and, bowing, strode, long-legging and determined out the door behind the others.

The room fell into silence. Faye glanced toward the window. Rogan shuffled his feet.

"Are—"

They said the word in unison. She caught her breath and refrained from passing out. He glowered.

"My mistake," she said.

"Nay." He shook his head. "Speak."

She refrained from clearing her throat *and* passing out. Good heavens, she was doing shockingly well. "Are you certain you're unhurt?"

"They were but lads."

"Lads with weapons," she corrected.

He shrugged one weighty shoulder.

Which meant, of course, that the *lads* were no longer in possession of said weapons. Which also meant that he had risked his life for another woman, she realized, and soothed the almost unrecognizable barb of jealousy.

"I'm certain she's quite grateful," she said.

He was watching her with an intensity so deep and real that she felt as if she were being consumed.

It should have made her uncomfortable. And perhaps it did on some level, but in a more primeval way, it made her feel as though she could soar. She lowered her eyes, calmed her heart rate. "The maid whom you saved."

He said nothing until she could bear the silence no more, then she shifted her gaze fretfully back to his.

"Was she not?" she asked.

He was slow to answer. "Aye, she seemed to be."

That barb again, deep in her gut. She pursed her lips. "She would probably like to repay you for your help."

"She seems a generous enough maid," he said finally.

"Good-hearted." She nodded weakly and remembered the most generous part of the maid seemed to be propped atop her bodice. "Yes. She did that."

He was still watching her. "Are you feeling quite well, lass? I would escort you home if you've a mind to—"

"Did she offer to bed you?" The words spurted from her lips like spilled venom, stunning her with their arrival. It was impossible to guess which of them was more surprised, and yet she continued. "Did she?" she whispered.

There was a hammering lifetime of silence, then, "I believe she felt somewhat indebted."

"Or perhaps she longed to feel you against her." Oh God. She'd spoken again. She glanced away, hoping to faint. No such luck. "Were you considering her offer?" Her voice was very small, barely audible, and yet she knew he heard her. Could feel it in the frozen stillness of the air.

"This is no place for a lass like yourself to be found so late at—" he began, but she stopped him by grasping his hand.

"Were you?" she whispered.

" 'Tis not for a man like meself to take a wife."

She stared.

"And yet I am, at times . . ." The muscle jumped in his jaw again. "Ofttimes . . ." He closed his eyes for a second as if fighting honestly. "Usually . . ."

She waited.

"Lonely," he said finally, and, wincing at his own feeble choice of words, rose abruptly to his feet. "My apologies," he rumbled. "I fear I must return to me home lest—"

"I can help you." She said the words without thinking, without breathing.

He, too, had ceased to breathe. "What say you?"

She felt as if her heart might explode. "I could help assuage your loneliness," she said. "If you like."

Chapter 20

Rogan stood absolutely still. What had she just said? That she could assuage his loneliness?

Were they talking about what he thought they were talking about? Did she realize that he spent night after night as hard as yonder hitching post, aching with frustration and hope and longing?

"Lass . . ." he said, but she refused to look up.

"Sit down," she said.

But he couldn't. He was too shocked. Too confused. Too deuced *hard*.

"Please," she said, and indicated his chair.

He forced himself to sit, though it felt all but impossible to bend. He stared at her, because he could not help himself, because his body was galvanized, and his mind was buzzing.

She cleared her throat.

"I—"

They spoke in unison again. She closed her eyes, opened them.

"You—" Again they spoke together.

He ground his teeth.

"You've no need to feel embarrassed," she said. She was fiddling distractedly with a fold in her gown. "Everyone feels lonely now and then."

Well he was damned near lonely enough to erupt right where he sat. "Do *you*?" he asked.

"Get lonely?" Had she ceased to breathe?

He managed a slow nod.

"Of course."

He picked his way carefully through the emotional battlefield. "And you would be willing to assist me with . . ." He ran out of words, but she finally spoke, maybe to keep the world from tumbling down on their heads like falling stars.

"I am, after all a . . ." Did she wince the slightest degree? "Widow."

"And widows get lonely?"

"Of course."

He nodded, having no idea what they spoke of. "I would not have you believe that I oft seek . . . friendship . . . from maids I've only just met."

Her gaze flitted to the stairs.

"I'm certain she's . . ." She drew a heavy breath. "Marjorie was it?" she asked.

He nodded though for the life of him, he could not even begin to guess what the woman's name had been. He only knew that even though he was eager enough to explode like a primed cannon, he had turned the maid aside.

"I'm certain Marjorie is a wonderful girl." She said it with some sincerity, which, if he could breathe, might have been amusing, because, in his own estimation the stunning Faerie Faye was considerably younger than the maid, whose name he couldn't recall and would never recall if he lived to be a hundred. "Kindly and surely . . ." Her gaze flittered up and away. "Comely."

The word fell like rain from her kitten-soft lips. Touching those lips with his own had been naught but a breath of heaven. What would it be like to allow himself to do more? To smooth his hands across her shoulders, to kiss her satiny neck?

"You do find her comely, I assume."

He scowled. The maid had been troubled by the boys. He had stepped in. It was as simple as that. There would have been no possible way he could have noticed her appearance. Not with the enchanting, pixielike Faye plaguing his every thought. But she was still sitting there, waiting in silence, and, most probably, thinking he was as daft as a gargoyle.

"She is bonny enough I suppose."

"Bonny enough to . . . befriend?"

He'd give his left stone to know what the devil they were talking about. Well, maybe a kidney. "I suspect so."

"And what of me?" she asked, voice as soft as a dream, as sweet as a song.

His throat felt tight. "You?"

"Am I—"

"You are sunlight and laughter." The words came unbidden, falling from his lips.

She stared at him in silence for a short eternity, eyes bright as polished amber before she shifted them away. "You know very little of me, Mr. McBain."

"Perhaps if we become friends I could learn more."

"Perhaps you would not like what you learn," she said, and glanced toward the stairs where the maid had disappeared, and suddenly a sharp, wayward thought struck him like a blow.

"Have you often . . . assuaged men's loneliness?"

Her brows dipped slightly. "What?"

"I do not mean to imply that I would think less of you. 'Tis simply—"

"No!" she said, then smoothed her features just as she did her skirt. "No," she repeated, quieter now.

He allowed himself to nod, but truth to tell he wasn't certain if he was relieved or disappointed. True, the thought of her touching another made his skin feel too tight for his pulsing body. But perhaps if she had strayed a time or two, if she did not seem so perfect, he could convince himself he had some sort of right to touch her.

"That is to say, there was my husband." A tiny muscle jumped in her cheek. The movement was nearly imperceptible, but it seemed almost that she would not have had to react at all. That he felt the tic himself.

"Of course," he said.

From the kitchen, the proprietor hustled out, carrying two plates boasting boiled fowl. Steam rose from pale parsnips nestled against small, pearly onions. Setting down the plates, he bowed solemnly.

"For this, sir," he said, "there will be no charge."

"I am able to pay my way," Rogan said, but the other was already shaking his head.

"The maid is a bit flirtatious," he said. "But she's mild as Mullen."

Rogan refrained from gritting his teeth. If he could swipe but one phrase from the English language, that would be it.

"And I answer to her father," added the old man.

Rogan managed a nod. The other bobbed in return, then turned and bustled away, leaving them with their meals. Despite the maid's description, it smelled quite delectable, but truth to tell, he'd lost a bit of his appetite. And, too, he was not at all comfortable with the idea of eating in the company of the fairer sex. It had been suggested on more than one occasion that his table manners left a bit to be desired. Irish had stated a preference for dining with starved wolves.

But then, Irish was an ass.

Faerie Faye cleared her throat. "It doesn't seem proper to be eating Mr. Connelly's meal."

Rogan waved dismissively, and suddenly his hand seemed too large for the table. Too large for the room. Certainly too large for the fork that lay beside his plate. "I am certain he has forgotten all about it by now."

"Forgotten his meal?"

"Yes."

She looked perplexed for a moment, but finally a spark of humor shone in her eyes.

"Because of the maid," she said.

Perhaps he was expected to respond, but once again, he was mesmerized, frozen. She was beauty beyond description. Light beyond hope.

"Am I wrong?" she asked finally, and the melodious sound of her voice brought him back to the present.

"You are not," he said, and forced himself to pick up the fork. It wasn't as if he was an ogre, he thought, but he'd cleaned his teeth with bigger utensils.

He could feel her watching him and refrained from squirming. "By now he has probably convinced her of a walk in the moonlight."

"Ahh," she said, and her apple-blossom mouth quirked up in a way that made his own go dry.

Concentrating on his meal, he skewered a parsnip and cut it into a half dozen miniature-sized pieces.

As for the girl, she seemed intent on eating, and since it was all but impossible to watch her without pulling her onto his lap, he cut up the tiny onions before masticating carefully.

By the time he'd consumed his third onion, she had pushed her plate aside.

"Oh," she said glancing up and realizing, apparently for the first time, that he had not yet made it halfway through his meal. "It appears that I was hungrier than I realized. Or you . . ." She paused. "Is the fowl not to your taste?"

He had no idea. So far, all he could taste was lust . . . maybe a little bit of fear. Uncertainty. Frustration. Confusion. Oh hell. He was going to starve to death if he remained in her presence much longer, and, sadly, he was willing to do so.

"There is something amiss with the fowl?" asked the proprietor, rushing out.

Rogan all but ground his teeth. "The fowl is fine," he said. "Very good."

"Then why . . ." began the proprietor, then smacked his brow with the palm of his hand. "You need bread."

"Nay, I—"

"A hero such as you must have bread," he said, and hurried away. In a matter of seconds, he was back with two round loaves the width of his skull.

Dear God, if the ravishing faerie lass continued to watch him, it would take him all night to consume those.

"Better now?" asked the proprietor.

"All is well," Rogan assured him.

"But you are out of beer," said the other, and, retrieving the mug, bustled away again.

Rogan glanced at Faye.

Her smile was almost visible as she pushed back

her chair. "If you'll excuse me for a moment," she said, and, turning elegantly away, left the room.

Rogan felt his shoulders slump, but as the proprietor hurried back in, he realized this was his opportunity to eat in peace.

By the time she returned two minutes later, every dish on the table was empty.

He refrained from shuffling his feet like a recalcitrant lad and hoped she wouldn't mention the speed with which he'd inhaled the meal.

"If you've no objection, I would escort you home, lass," he said, and rose to his feet.

"Are you certain you would not rather take a bed here?" she asked.

And suddenly his heart stopped. The world ceased to turn. Logic failed to exist, for it almost seemed as if she was offering to share a room.

As if magic yet remained among mortal man.

Chapter 21

The reality of what she had just said hit Faye like a spell gone awry.

Good heavens, it was bad enough that she had offered to *befriend* him without sounding as if she was ready to rip off his clothes and have her way with him here and now. Even though . . .

She let her gaze fall to his chest, then yanked her thoughts back to more acceptable regions.

He was staring at her with an expression she dared not try to interpret.

"That is to say . . . I'm certain they would be honored to have you . . ." She almost let her eyes fall closed at her own idiocy. "A great warrior like . . ." She was staring at his chest again. God help her. Snatching her gloves from the table, she straightened her back. "I know my way home," she said, and marched out of the establishment.

In some mortified portion of her blushing mind she quite desperately hoped he would let her go. Would not follow her. But another part of her felt

entirely different. Titillated and shivery and un-
mistakably hopeful.

She loosed Sultan's reins with unsteady fingers,
then glanced up at the pommel, wondering how
the deuce she was going to get aboard without
floundering about like a disoriented duckling.
She'd just offered to bed the man here at the inn.
How would it seem if she now begged for assistance in mounting. Mounting what? Mounting
whom? And when had her mind become such a
wanton wasteland, she wondered frantically, but
in that moment she realized he was behind her.

"Might you need assistance?" he asked.

She didn't really. She could simply wedge her
left foot in the lone stirrup and swing her right
leg over the cantle . . . if she didn't care that all of
London would thereafter be agog by her bold and
improper actions.

"Please," she said instead, and, still facing the
gelding, raised her left foot, ready to step into his
hands.

But suddenly she was lifted from the ground
and set into the saddle like a porcelain vase atop
a mantel. She stared down in amazement. His
hands remained on her waist for a moment,
strong but gentle, before his left dropped to her
thigh. Instincts roared to life inside her, confusing in their ferocity. She could flee, could easily
escape atop Madeline's kindly mount. But other
instincts were present, too. Instincts that sang
like wild larks beneath the weight of his dark-

fingered hand. Instincts that suggested that perhaps he only dared to touch her now when she was afforded height and speed. When she had. But would any woman truly ever have him at a disadvantage? He was power personified, strength well leashed. And perhaps it was that thought, the knowledge that he kept himself in such careful control, that almost made her long to slide into his arms and get on with that ripping and having stuff.

Their gazes met like lightning. Tension steamed between them, seeming to sizzle from his thoughts to hers, to twitter from his fingertips to every tingling part of her.

"Mayhap . . ." he began, and stopped.

"What?"

His tone was deep and low. Hers was breathless.

"Are you lonely now, lass?" he asked, and the world stood still, for she *was*. Despite her wellfounded fear of men, despite the fact that she had a mission . . . a mission that would not keep, she was undeniably lonely.

And she couldn't quite breathe, but he was standing there, gazing up at her, eyes as solemn as sin, waiting.

"Yes," she whispered.

His hand seemed to burn against her thigh. "Lass . . ."

"Yes?"

"I would know your definition of lone—"

"Sir. Good sir."

They turned in tandem as the proprietor came hobbling out, face florid in the waning light. "I've put together a bite to see you on your way."

" 'Tis not necessary," Rogan said.

"It's nothing really. Just a loaf of barley bread and a leg of mutton. A thank you for your bravery."

Rogan nodded once, seeming to want nothing more than to put the entire episode behind him, but the other was not yet done.

"There are not many who would risk himself for those less fortunate these days."

"I assure you, it was no great—"

"It was different when I was a young man. There was honor then. Dignity. Men knew to treat maids with respect."

Rogan lowered his hand slowly from Faye's thigh, and in its wake, she felt strangely bereft.

"You are a lucky woman," said the little proprietor and, with one birdlike nod, scurried back into the inn.

Rogan cleared his throat. Turning away, he mounted in silence, smoothly swinging his broad thigh over Colt's cantle before settling firmly into the deep seat of worn leather.

Connelly's mare whickered flirtatiously as they reined their horses away, unspeaking as they headed toward home. Beside Sultan's snappy cadence, Rogan's stallion sounded steady and slow. But he would need great strength to carry such a master. Great strength to carry great strength.

Faye glanced sideways just as Rogan did the same. Their gazes met for one crackling instant before they turned abruptly back.

Sultan's mane seemed suddenly as mesmerizing as a serpent as Faye studied each strand. Silence stretched between them, taut with anticipation, heavy with embarrassment. Which was mind-boggling, for surely he was not a man who should be embarrassed. He had everything. Strength, intellect, courage. And yet he seemed strangely uncertain where she was concerned. And somehow that spoke to a part of her as no strutting peacock ever would. It pulled at the base of her being, touched a spark to bone-dry tinder.

"You were very brave," she said. The sounds of London seemed muffled and soft around them as the city settled in for the night. "At the inn."

He turned toward her, eyes solemn, then, "You are wrong, lass," he said and no more.

She chanced a glance in his direction, sure he could not mean what he said, but his expression suggested no humor. .

"There were three of them," she reminded him, which was probably silly, for it seemed unlikely that he would forget their number.

A trio of scrawny hounds trotted past, slinky and furtive. Somehow they reminded her of Cur. "Young cubs," he said, voice thoughtful and distant. "Untrained and undisciplined."

"Yet dangerous," she said.

He paused an instant, as if thinking. "Neither training nor strength is required to be dangerous," he said, and looked into the distance, seeming to see something not readily discernible to the rest of the world. "Just the desire to hurt."

"And you have been hurt." She said the words softly.

"Not today," he said, and glanced her way.

"And neither was the maid because you are brave."

"Nay," he said. His lips twitched the slightest degree, and that glimmer of humor lifted her mood more than another's bellowing laughter had ever done. " 'Tis because I am large."

"You are that," she said, then blushed at her own foolish words and hoped he couldn't see her high color in the descending darkness.

He was watching her closely now. She shifted her eyes away but could not ignore him for long.

"Is that troublesome for you, lass?"

"Troublesome?" she said, and raised one brow, hoping to appear haughty rather than discomfited, self-confident rather than self-conscious. "Certainly not. Indeed, I'm certain Marjorie was very grateful for your size."

He was scowling at her. "Marjorie . . ." he said, then seemed to remember. "The maid at the inn."

Had there been so many women he could not remember the one who'd last offered herself to him? Or was he even worse at social interaction than she?

That possibility made her feel strangely warm inside.

"She seemed a good enough maid," he said

With bosoms as big as autumn gourds, she thought. "Yes, she was rather . . . Yes," Faye said, not particularly wishing to discuss another woman's cleavage.

"But she was not perfection come to earth." His tone was low with sincerity, heavy with emotion, and suddenly Faye's lungs felt deprived of air while her head seemed filled with the stuff. Though she struggled to find a witty comeback, she was at a loss, bewildered by the raw sensations created by his words.

"No one is perfect," she said, and found she could no longer look at him, no longer view his boldness, his goodness, when her own failings loomed so large.

"And what are your flaws, lass?"

Guilt, harbored for an eternity, rushed in on a wave of fear. "I am a coward, for one."

"As am I."

She glanced at him, stunned by the ridiculousness of his statement. "There is no need to lie," she said, but she felt no evidence of untruth in her head.

"Courage is not the lack of fear, wee lass. Courage is fear overcome."

"Well I've not overcome."

"Do you fear me?" he asked, and suddenly she wished she could tell him the truth, that she was afraid every day of her life, that she had, at first, thought him the Devil, that she still feared him even as she was drawn to him. To his strength, to his gentleness, to his honesty.

"Should I be fearful?" she asked.

"Many are," he said.

"Perhaps my fear is overshadowed by other things."

"Such as?"

"I cannot forever hide in the comfort of Lavender House."

"You do not seem to be hiding."

"What does it seem I am doing?"

He was quiet for a moment, considering. "Mourning," he said.

She stared at him, shocked, for suddenly it seemed that he might well be right. Perhaps she *was* in mourning. Perhaps she was lamenting the life she had never had. The betrayals. The losses. And perhaps it was time to forget those disappointments. To put away the sackcloth. To move on. Perhaps then she might even be worthy of this man who rode beside her. This man with the artist's soul and the warrior's body. This man who terrified her and thrilled her all at once, so that she could barely breathe in his presence. This man who made her wish to do things she had never before considered. To touch, to feel, to—

"You must miss him a great deal," he said.

"Who?" she asked, startled from her increasingly lurid thoughts.

"Your husband," he said, and scowled. "You were wed, were you not?"

"Wed! Of course. Yes." And she was an idiot. "To Albert Leonard Nettles. Only son of Martin and Elisabeth Nettles. Born on . . ." She was acting even more idiotically than usual, and yet she could not help herself. The lies took hold of her. She refrained from closing her eyes. From passing out. "June 3 . . . 1782 on . . ." Quit. Just quit. "Why ever would you think otherwise?" she asked, breathless.

He shifted again, seeming uncomfortable, and suddenly, the truth burst in on her. When he'd spoken of his size, he hadn't been speaking about the width of his back or the bulk of his arms. He'd been referring to his . . . his . . . He must think her the most naïve widow ever to walk the face of the earth.

"And you are . . . lonely without him?" he asked.

She was ultimately grateful for the descending darkness that hid her blush, yet she was still tempted to set the quirt to Sultan's flank. To fly down the streets, away from this heart-trembling embarrassment.

Instead, she tightened her hands on the reins and tried for normality. Sultan ducked his head at the increased tension, and Faye lightened the contact with a mental apology. "Certainly I . . . miss him." Her head was beginning to ache.

"He was a good man then?"

"A merchant." The words escaped against her will. She ground her teeth and refused to turn away. She had been given the fictional details of his existence. Height, weight, hair color, home. But she had never considered his temperament. Never envisioned him in her mind. Neither had she been able to fabricate a personality. Dealing with the lies handed her was difficult enough. Embellishing them might very well have meant her death. "Textiles," she said, and closed her eyes to her own stupidity for a moment.

"It pains you to speak of him," he said.

"No," she lied, and felt an additional ache in her temple. "Perhaps a bit, but not—" She stopped herself. What had she been about to say? Had she nearly spilled the truth? Never once in all the years since her rescue had fabrications been this difficult.

"He must have been a brave man," he said.

She glanced at him. "My . . . husband?"

"To ask for your hand," he said.

"I don't . . ." She shook her head, puzzled.

"Knowing you could deny him." His face was the epitome of sincerity. "I would not have the nerve."

"You jest," she said.

Lavender House loomed above them. Sultan turned onto the cobbled drive of his own accord.

The world was silent but for the sound of the hoofbeats beneath them. Sultan's light and quick. Colt's solid and final.

"Rogan—" she began, but he spoke before she could continue.

" 'Tis late. I shall care for your mount if you like."

"No." She tried to deal with this change of pace, but she was horrific at social interactions even with the average acquaintance, and he was so much more. "I will see to him."

He dismounted with sweeping grace, then stood beside her, looking up, silver-gray eyes stunning in their moon-shadowed glory.

"You'll ruin your frock," he said, and raised his arms to catch her.

It took all the nerve she possessed to slide into his arms. All her control not to wrap hers about his neck.

He caught her easily, lowered her slowly, his legs hard against hers, his eyes earnest and devouring.

Time ceased to be. Beneath her hands, his biceps felt as broad and hard as living pillars. His fingers were against her ribs, and at each point of contact, her skin seemed to burn with the touch.

"It's a riding habit," she said. Nonsensical. She sounded as daft as a peafowl.

The shadow of a scowl crossed his features, and some long-buried yearning in her wanted nothing more than to smooth it from his face, to caress the scar that notched the edge of his lips.

"Sturdy," she murmured. "Worsted. The dark fabric doesn't easily show stains. And—"

"I'll not hold you to it," he rumbled.

The breath caught hard in her throat as she struggled for his meaning.

"You do not need to befriend me," he explained.

Relief flowed through her, but it was drowned in disappointment, in desire, in something she could not explain, had never felt before. Why was he allowing her this opportunity to renege? Perhaps he had decided to return to the maid at the inn. Perhaps he didn't find her attractive. And perhaps she should consider herself lucky that he'd given her an opportunity to retreat. But she did not. No one could have been more surprised than she to realize that truth.

"The utilitarian design makes it easy to move about," she intoned.

"You've no need to worry," he said, and loosened his grip on her ribs.

"But what if I want to?" The words came out in a jumbled rush.

He froze, so close her skirt brushed his legs. So close she could feel the warmth of his breath on her face.

"What if you wish to worry?" he asked. Cautious. Good heavens, he was more cautious than she.

"To befriend you," she breathed.

He inhaled carefully. "It has occurred to me that we may be speaking of two different situations entirely." His words were very low.

If her legs felt a little steadier, she might very well have scrambled into the stable and hidden in the loft. "What are *you* talking about?"

"To me you are perfection come to life, and I . . ." A muscle jumped in his hard jaw. "Your nearness makes it difficult to . . ."

"To what?" She leaned a little closer, barely able to hear the masculine intensity of his voice.

"Before I met you . . ." His eyes searched hers. "I was content enough."

"And now?"

He seemed to relax just a smidgen, as though he had decided on his course and would accept whatever it offered. "Now there seems to be little reason to breathe if you are not in my arms."

Shivers coursed over her, followed by an urge to burst into song. Odd. "Oh."

"I was not being completely honest when we spoke earlier."

"Oh?"

"I *am* lonely," he admitted. "But I am also aroused."

She stared at him, lips slightly parted, heart pounding in her chest. By comparison, her last two *ohs* seemed rapier sharp.

"I wish to bed you, wee Faerie."

She tried to speak, but nothing came to mind. Literally nothing but the thought of being in his arms.

"Might you feel—"

"Yes," she said. Too quick. Too eager. Too . . .

everything contrary to who she usually was. She had to slow down. Relax. Try for refinement. Or rationality. She took a deep, silent breath and steadied her voice. "My apologies. I didn't mean to interrupt."

He watched her carefully, as if trying to decipher her whimsical ways. But he was hardly the only one. There might well be a queue. "Lord Wrenwall is hosting a garden party in two days' time," he said. "I will understand if you change your mind before then."

"I shall be there," she said, and, granting him a regal nod, lifted her heavy skirts in one gloved hand before turning toward the house.

Chapter 22

Faye kept her steps slow, her head high as she made her way up the hill toward Lavender House. Her hands were steady, her expression serene.

" 'Tis late."

Faye jumped, heart thumping like a wild hare's inside her constricted chest. Apparently, her careful pretenses had reached their shallow limits.

"Did he harm you?" Shaleena asked, and stepped from the shadows, fully clothed, but still intimidating.

"Who?" Faye rasped, and refrained from placing a hand to her chest to keep it from leaping into the open air.

"The Scotsman."

"No. Why? Were you listening in on our conversation?"

"Was it terribly interesting?"

"Well I . . . No."

"Then why would I waste my time?"

Faye stared at her a moment, then turned away, but Shaleena spoke before she could escape.

"So you have agreed to meet him."

"I thought you didn't listen in?"

"If that is true, you are even more naïve than I realized," she said.

Anger welled like a fountain inside Faye, but she had little time for foolish emotion. She was confused and lost and jittery. "I just . . . am I mad?" she whispered.

Shaleena canted her head, studying her in the darkness. "For wishing to bed him?"

Faye felt the air leave her lungs in a rush. Though really, she should not have expected less from Shaleena. "I never said as much."

"Perhaps I got the wrong impression," said the other, and watched her in silence. "Perhaps the Celt did, as well."

"I didn't mean to . . ." Faye began, then closed her eyes and wished she were someone else. Or some*thing* else; hermit crabs had always intrigued her. "What am I going to do?"

"Are you asking for my advice?" Shaleena raised one haughty brow.

God help her. "I believe I am."

Even in the darkness, Faye could see the other's lips curl up with humor. But the moon-shadowed dimness made the expression look strangely soft. Not jaded or hostile, but almost self-deprecating, almost kind and longing and gentle.

Shaleena sighed and glanced toward the place where the lightning had crackled just a few nights before. "Ella would warn you to be on the alert, to determine what it is he truly wants from you before you make a decision. Madeline would tell you to think about how your life will change if you choose this path."

But she didn't want to think. "And you?"

"I would say that some mistakes cannot be undone," Shaleena said, and suddenly, for the first time in Faye's life, she felt a bottomless depth of sadness in the other woman, a well of pain covered by nothing more than a thin veneer of harsh superiority. "If you pass up this opportunity, will it be a mistake, do you think?"

"I don't know."

"What *do* you know?"

Besides fear? Very little. But Shaleena was watching her with careful intent, and she had no respect for cowards.

"I know he's . . ." Kind? Courageous? Wounded? "Large," she said.

Shaleena's lips twitched up. "Then I would suggest you read a bit of Cleland's little novel and get a good night's sleep."

"Read— Oh." Remembering the lingering folderol associated with the publication of the scandalous *Fanny Hill*, Faye felt the blush reach the tips of her toes. "I've made a terrible mistake," she said, and turned away, but Shaleena caught her arm.

"Faye," she said, startling her. Up to that point,

she hadn't been entirely certain Shaleena even knew her name. "Don't do anything rash."

"It is rash, isn't it?"

"I meant . . ." Something crossed her face. It almost looked like regret. Perhaps guilt even. She glanced toward the street again. "Do you care for him?"

She nodded, able to do no more.

"Does he care for you?"

"I don't know."

"Don't you?"

Hopes and doubts tumbled wildly in her mind. "He saved a maid today."

Shaleena canted her head, waiting.

"He . . . I think he's a good person. But . . ." She shook her head, still crazed. "In the past I've thought . . ."

"What?"

"That others were good."

"And you were wrong." It wasn't a question, which was just as well because as memories assailed Faye, she found it impossible to force out an answer.

"Tell me, Faerie Faye . . ." she began, but her voice was distant, her expression far away. "Is it worse to live as if life is good and to be proven wrong or to believe it is evil and be proven right?"

Faye stared at her. "What was Joseph to you before he came here?"

"He was nothing," she said, but the lie popped off a bright spark of pain in Faye's temple.

"You knew him," she countered, and Shaleena drew herself to full height.

"I've known many men, little witch. It does not make them important."

Faye refrained from stepping back.

"He was someone you cared for."

For a moment, a hint of honesty wafted through the garden, but an instant later Shaleena laughed. "He is someone who pleasured me for a time," she said. "Several times, in fact. But you cannot expect too much from men. Not more than thrice in one night, no matter how powerful your charms," she said, and tossed back her auburn hair. "Unless you have had the foresight to obtain more than one lively partner for the evening."

Embarrassment almost caused Faye to back down, but she had done so most of her life with little to show for her cowardice. "You cared for him," she repeated.

Something deep and earnest shone in Shaleena's eyes, but in a moment she straightened, hardened, cooled. "Indeed I did. I cared for him with each hard thrust. With each soft death. You want advice, little witch? It is this. Enjoy your Scotsman to the hilt," she said, and turned haughtily away.

Chapter 23

Rogan strode between the rows of booths and stalls that lined Long Acre. A carnival had been assembled, and every conceivable delicacy seemed to be available. The intoxicating aroma of pork pies and chocolate soufflés melded uneasily with the coal soot that perpetually saturated the city. But Rogan's normally impressive appetite was not up to his usual standards, for he was a man with a purpose. He was having a rather difficult time, however, remembering just what that purpose was. Something about a death, he thought, but the memory of a faerielike creature kept distracting him.

Had she truly agreed to meet him in Wrenwall's garden? And if so, what did that mean? Did she intend to share his bed? Or had his blatant desires driven him mad?

To his left, a small, golden-haired lass lifted her wares high beside a battered dogcart. "Buy me sausages," she said. Her voice was singsong, her smudged cheeks pinkened from the chafing evening wind. She had solemn sea-green eyes and a cherry bow mouth.

Rogan hunched his shoulders and hurried on, passing an idle pair of jugglers.

"You've power in you."

Glancing to his left he spied a bright-eyed crone behind a wooden counter covered in small, dark bottles and sprigs of dried herbs tied in hemp.

"What say you?" he asked.

She nodded once, as if answering a voice in her head instead of responding to him "Even from here I can feel it in you."

She was old and bent and knobby, standing behind her bevy of strangely shaped bottles. But he stepped toward her, realizing suddenly that this was where he had planned to come at the outset. This was where he would find his answers.

"You are the proprietress of this shop?" he asked.

"The *proprietress*?" she said, and titled her head a little, studying him with an almost girl-ish glint to her eye. "I suspect one might call me such. Certainly they have called me worse. But I did not suspect such naïveté from one such as yourself."

"Like myself?" he asked. What went on here?

"You have strength, but not just in your brawn," she said, skimming his torso.

"I am no great scholar," he said, confused, and she laughed as if she understood much that he did not.

"There are many sorts of strength. This one was given to you by another," she said, then shook her head as if drawing herself into the present. "But you did not come to hear of her. What is your question for me?"

He scowled, but focused on the problem at hand. "I but wondered if there is a potion of sorts . . . an herb, perhaps, some concoction that could cause a man's death and make it appear as if he did naught but die in his sleep."

She looked at him askance, sparse brows raised over faded eyes. "You look more like the sort to kill outright than to trust to secret herbs."

"I've no intention of killing," he said.

She watched him in heavy silence for a moment. "And yet you have."

He felt his stomach pitch again, for she was correct, and though he mourned the deaths he had caused during battle, there were other tragedies even more shameful. "I have," he admitted, for honesty was as much a part of him as the color of his eyes or the width of his shoulders.

She nodded. "But now you wish to know how another has died."

It was his turn to nod. "Can it be done undetected?"

She bent over her stall, waving him closer. He leaned in. "Any sorceress worthy of her grimoire could brew such a potion."

He drew back abruptly. "Do you say you're a witch?"

She laughed. "You, of all persons, should not be surprised to know such exist."

In fact, until that moment, he would have been. For though the Church had oft blamed the troubles of the world on the mystic, he had seen true evil and knew it to be caused by naught but greed. Yet she looked to be the very personification of a witch.

"And what about those who do not dabble in sorcery. Could they, too, obtain such a potion?"

She shrugged. "In truth, lad, the king's own surgeon would be hard-pressed to tell if a swain had died of a simple blend of hensbane and poppy or from pleasuring his young mistress."

"Hensbane and poppy?" he said, but she had turned to the right, brows crinkled, not listening for a moment.

"Would there not be signs that he had consumed poison if—"

"Prickly poppy soothes—" she began, then jerked her attention away again. "Go," she said.

"Where might one find—" he began, but she was already stepping back. With a quickness that belied her age, she slammed down the shutters that closed her inside her simple stall.

He scowled at the wooden enclosure, then turned to stare back in the direction he had come, wondering at this strange turn of events.

The young girl's singsong pitch sounded hollow and lonely. "Buy me lovely sausages. Lovely sausages to buy."

Two grand ladies passed to his left. Their petal-bright gowns brushed the street and each other's. Perhaps their frilly parasols held the city's heavy soot at bay, for their gloves looked as white as summer clouds. Behind them, a dark, liveried boy of less than ten years carried a bundle of new purchases. The underlings of London might be half-starved and much beaten, but they were often well dressed.

It was forever a city of disturbing variables. An aging woman in a pink frock coaxed a complaining ass down the rutted street, hawking the fine qualities of the animal's milk. A plump maid removed a baked apple from a charcoal stove stowed in a rickety barrow. Wrapping it in brown paper, she promptly sold it to a gentleman sporting a pristine cravat and creamy, strapped pantaloons. Nearer by, an old man sat on a three-legged stool in the mouth of a listing canvas tent.

Rogan stepped inside to peruse the titles. There were a number of books of poetry and a good many devoted to religion and science, but stashed among the weighty volumes he found a slim, leather-bound volume of animal illustrations. Leafing through the book, he was struck by the lyrical beauty of the paintings, for the artist had seen his subjects not as beasts of burden but as entities with souls and feelings that shone from their eyes. He shifted through the pages, admiring.

"Lovely sausages. Sausages to buy."

The girl's litany melded forlornly with the

sound of hoofbeats from the street behind him as the city took on a rhythm of its own. A dog snarled. A woman laughed. But the paintings were entrancing—a wolf bitch smiling at her young. A mare nuzzling her wobbly-legged foal.

"Buy me sausages—"

A dog growled again. Someone gasped. And suddenly the world seemed eerily still just as it had a hundred times on distant fields, stunned to silence by impending violence. Rogan turned in slow, silent motion, and it was as if the image before him was framed by the mouth of the tent. The tattered sausage girl stood perfectly still. Her sea-green eyes were as wide as forever against the now-pale curve of her cheeks. Her scrawny arm was lifted, wares dangling, seeming to be the only motion in a world gone still. Not three feet away stood a gaunt hound, glazed eyes fixed on the child's face. The hair along the cur's spine stood up in a primeval arc, and its fangs showed yellow beneath snarling lips.

"Dear God," breathed the proprietor, but in that instant, the cur coiled to leap, and there was no more time.

Reaching to his right, Rogan snatched a heavy volume from the nearest shelf and heaved it toward the slavering hound. The book slammed into the beast's ribs like a missile. The animal went down with a snarl, tumbling to the ground. But in a moment it had found its feet. Eyes glaring, it swept its attention back to the petrified girl, and in that moment Rogan lunged from the tent.

Grabbing the child about the waist, he swung her into the air. The dog sprang just as Rogan slammed his fist sideways. The animal snapped at Rogan's forearm, felt the crunch of knuckles, and hit the ground hard. For a moment it lay still, stunned and disoriented. Still holding the fair-haired lass aloft, Rogan shifted his feet wide and braced himself for the next assault, but the hound only found its balance, stood uncertainly, then trotted shakily away.

The world returned to normal by unsteady degrees. Sounds gradually seeped into Rogan's recognition. Colors bloomed in the flowers of a vendor's bouquets. But nothing seemed to make sense. Only memories remained. Cold and ashy in his reeling mind.

"Posie."

Someone spoke, but he was lost in the past where haunting eyes watched with silent horror.

"Release her."

Tears streaked a tiny round face capped with silken curls.

"Sir!"

Rogan blinked and stepped shakily into the present.

A woman stood before him, lips pursed, chin uplifted haughtily to gaze into his face.

"Is this your maid?" he asked.

She nodded primly.

Rage coursed through him. "Could you not find

a larger servant to abuse?" he asked, and swept an angry hand over the city at large. "This place is filled with the downcast. Why not throw some larger morsel to the hounds rather than—"

But suddenly the woman's face crumpled. She dropped to her knees and covered her face with one shaky hand. "Tell me she is unhurt."

He tightened his grip as memories consumed him. "If she is, it is because of nothing you've done to make certain—" he began, but she was weeping now, gasping nearly silent breaths.

"Posie, my love . . ." she croaked, and with the sound of the woman's voice, the girl struggled from his grip and leaped into the other's embrace. Tears streamed like rivulets down the woman's face as she enveloped the thin lass in her arms. Eyes squeezed shut, she rocked sideways in rhythm to their tandem tears.

Rogan could do nothing but watch. Nothing but stare. So he had been wrong again. The girl was not neglected. Was not left alone to fend for herself and turn over a few meager shillings to a harsh master. The girl was loved. Cherished as every child should be. As so few children were.

"My husband . . ." The woman had cupped the back of the girl's head with chapped, reddened fingers, seeming to soak solace from the feel of the child's silken hair against her skin. The girl had turned her little face against her mother's neck. "He suffers from consumption. I left Posie with the sausages whilst I brought him a tonic."

Rogan felt foolish suddenly, as if the world watched, knowing how little he understood of love, how little he comprehended of caring. "The child is too small to be left with such a task," he rumbled.

"I know, sir. I know." The mother's throat contracted, and her mouth twitched as she rose shakily to her feet, bearing the clinging child on her hip. "But I've no wish to beg for help," she said. "My husband says my pride will be the death of me." Closing her eyes, she allowed herself a moment to turn her face into her daughter's fair curls. "Better that than to lose . . ." Tightening her arm around her baby's back, she drew a shuddering breath and turned toward him again, a smidgen of her former attitude returning to her proud features. "I can never repay you for what you've done, sir, but my sausages are fresh and hearty if you'd care to take—"

"See to the child," he said, and turned away, but his legs still felt weak, his heartbeat uncertain as he strode away, memories swirling like a whirling dervish in his mind. From behind him the stench and noise made his gut clench, and finally, hidden behind a wooden stall, he stopped to grit his teeth against his roiling stomach, to cover his eyes with a shaky palm.

"Mr. McBain?"

The voice was sweet and summer soft. He turned slowly, letting his hand drop from his face.

"Mr. McBain." Faye stood before him. Her costume was perfect, an azure confection that flowed about her lissome body like sun-swept waves. But it was her eyes that captured him. For they were bright and wide and worried, as if she cared for naught but him alone. "Are you well? I saw what happened. Were you hurt? I was—"

"Why are you here?" Against the feathery beauty of her voice, his own sounded like the rough scrape of a whetting stone.

"I was . . . Rogan!" She paused, face as pale as sea foam as she stared at him. "You've been injured."

Scowling downward, he glanced at his chest, but all seemed to be well.

"Your arm," she said and sure enough when he looked to the left, he saw that his sleeve was rent near the elbow. A ragged laceration skittered a couple inches across his forearm, and blood dripped easily from the wound.

Somehow it barely registered, however, for in his mind's eye he again saw the shattered expression of a child. A child whose world he had ruined.

He glanced up, seeing the beautiful faerielike face blend with another. "Were you cherished?" he asked.

"What?" Her voice was breathy, and though he'd asked before, he needed reassurance yet again, longed to believe that she had been loved, that she had been held as the sausage girl had been held. Cuddled like a precious gift.

"As a child," he said. "As a wee lass." A muscle

twitched almost painfully in his jaw, a remnant of the terror he had felt only moments before. "Tell me ye were adored?"

"Rogan, please . . ." she said, and reached for his hand. Her skin felt like a cool balm against his. Her eyes found his in a moment, evergreen flecks against an amber backdrop. "You're shaking."

"Tell me your da doted on you."

"Where's your mount?"

"Gave you piggyback rides. Sang to you in the wee hours of the morning."

"You're scaring me," she said.

"Tell me," he said, and tightened his grip on her hand.

"I was . . . I was cherished," she said.

But she was lying. He could feel it like a bayonet to his soul and winced at the pain. "What of your mum?"

"Rogan, where is your Colt? You did ride here, did you not?"

He wanted to shake her, to demand the truth, but who was he to think he deserved that much? Nodding brokenly, he glanced down the street. In a matter of moments he was astride, but truth to tell he remembered little of the journey to his house though he eventually found himself inside.

Connelly appeared, making some sort of questioning noises. But the little faerie sent him on a mission, and in a few moments, the irritating Irishman handed over a bowl of water, gave Rogan a foolish wink, and declared he was about to leave for an important meeting. The door closed behind him. The house went silent.

"You must remove your shirt." Faye's voice was quiet but firm, bringing him vaguely back to the moment at hand.

He glanced to the side, noting the basin of steaming water. Then, turning his gaze upward, he saw her. Fragile yet strangely tough. Young yet seasoned. So bonny and fair he longed to feel her heartbeat beneath his fingertips, to know she was well. But he held himself carefully from her, for she looked pale and troubled.

"Are you feeling unwell, lass?" he asked, wondering about the water. Steam curled upward in the darkening room.

She shook her head, scowling a little. "It's you who has been injured."

Ah yes, the dog. He glanced at the wound, but it mattered little.

She, on the other hand, he could consider all day. Could spend the rest of his life watching emotions chase through her eyes and wonder if any artist could catch the mercurial moods that enlivened her elfish face.

"You look pale. You'd best sit," he said, and began to rise to his feet, but she pushed him back down.

" 'Tis you that needs tending."

He didn't bother to glance at the offending appendage this time. "That?" he asked, nodding to it.

"Yes, that. It's . . ." she began, then started as a kit popped into the doorway, dark eyes shining beneath peaked ears before scampering from sight. "Was that a fox?"

"Mayhap."

"They run . . . Never mind," she said, and shook her head. He clasped her arm, stood, then lowered her carefully to his just-vacated chair. "You're bleeding," she said, but her voice was weak.

"Breathe," he ordered.

"I *am* breathing," she said, but didn't manage to glance up.

"Do not rise. I'll fetch you something to drink." It took him only a moment to discover that the pitcher of water usually kept in the kitchen was dry. True to Connelly's debauching ways, however, there was a bottle of red wine in the pantry. Pouring a liberal dose into a marmalade jar, Rogan hurried back to her. "Drink this."

"I'm fine," she said, voice infused with indignation, face still pale as winter.

"Drink it," he insisted. She did so finally, and though her sips were ridiculously small, her cheeks seemed to take on some color.

"I can see to your injury," she said, but though her tone was defiant, he noticed with some amusement that she failed to look directly at the silly wound.

" 'Tis not necessary, lass," he assured her.

"Of course it's . . ." she began, then paused as she accidentally skimmed his arm. "I'm a . . ."

She stopped herself, exhaled carefully. "I've some small capability with healing wounds," she said.

"I can attest to that," he said.

She skittered her eyes to his as if searching his face for mockery. Perhaps his tone had implied some cynicism, but if that was the case, it was completely inadvertent. 'Twas obvious she could heal. One glance into her ethereal, wounded eyes made that clear, but he moved the collar of his shirt aside, revealing the bloodstone that caressed his skin.

"I'm not one to believe old wives' tales," he said. "But sometimes the ancients knew best. I've been healing well since the day you gifted it to me."

Her gaze seemed to be captured on his chest.

"Another scar," she said. Her voice sounded small, sweet, so concerned it made his heart feel weak.

"That?" he said, and rubbed the old wound that ran diagonally across his pectorals to his left arm. "'Tis naught to worry on."

She stared at him. "You lie," she said, and he smiled.

"'Tis naught to worry on any longer," he corrected.

"But it once was." She swallowed, worry so deep on her lovely features that he felt her concern like a balm to his soul.

"It once was," he admitted.

"How did it happen?"

This did not seem like the time to discuss old battle scars, but some of the golden color had returned to her bonny face, and surely allowing her to sit and listen was better than letting her rush to her feet and pass out at his. "I forgot lessons taught me as a lad."

"What lessons were those?"

He sat finally on a chair not far from her, watching her, for truth to tell, he still felt a little shaky. "The usual."

"Eat your greens?" she asked. "Don't venture out without your cloak?"

He chuckled. "Not those precisely."

"I believe that's the usual."

"You believe?" He met her gaze, catching a whisper of pain. "You're uncertain?"

"I'll see to your arm," she said, and rose to her feet, but he caught her hand.

"You don't know?" he asked, longing to believe the best, to trust in beauty.

"My apologies," she said, and winced as if wounded. "I wish I could say . . . I wish I could tell you what you wish to know."

He felt his stomach clench. "That you had a happy childhood."

She nodded.

"But you cannot?"

"I find it . . . difficult to lie to you."

"I don't believe 'tis your place to apologize for that, lass," he said, and gently, ever so carefully, swept his thumb across the back of her hand. It felt as soft as a sunset beneath his callused digit.

"But you want to hear it," she breathed.

"Everyone longs for favorable news, lass."

"You are wrong. Only the kind do," she said, and, dropping slowly to her knees, touched her fingers to his chest.

And it was then that the magic struck him.

Chapter 24

"Lass . . ." His voice was a deep rumble in his chest. She lifted her eyes to his, all but breathless from the potent flow of feelings that rushed through her.

The magic of his skin beneath hers made her heart race and her head light. It was nothing short of a miracle that she had found him; though she had sought him out for a reason, had questioned Connelly regarding his whereabouts not a full hour before.

" 'Tis not necessary," he said.

"You shook," she said, then slipped her fingers lower, concentrating on his top button. Her own hands were unsteady, but she would do this thing, would tend this man, would give him what comfort she could. "When the girl was attacked. You shook."

He glanced away, and although she only skittered her attention to his face for an instant, she saw a muscle work in his jaw. "I believe I warned you before that I know fear," he said.

"For others."

" 'Tis not what I said."

She found his eyes, pinned them with her own. "Perhaps you forget our time at the inn."

"Nay, I shall never forget," he said, and something in his voice made her remember the warmth of his hand on her thigh. The music of his sincerity as he confessed his desire for her.

"Then you recall that you did not shake after the altercation with the trio at the inn."

He shrugged, scowling, dismissive. "They were . . ."

"Pups," she said, remembering his words.

"Aye."

"While today there was a wolf involved."

" 'Twas naught more than a hound."

She had managed to loose the first three buttons. His skin looked smooth and dark against the stark white of his damaged shirt. She swallowed and continued.

"So if they had been *men*, fully grown and well armed, you would not have interfered. Is that what you are saying, Mr. McBain?" she asked, and glanced at him through her lashes. But even as she did so, she sensed the struggle in him, knew he wished to lie. And knew, just as surely, that he would not.

Drawing a careful breath, she glanced at the amulet lying against his mounded pectoral. There was power in the earthy stone. Power that grew daily. Still, she could not tell if it was the cause of his forced honesty. And found, in fact, that she hoped his inability was caused by naught more magical than his feelings for her. Which was foolish. He was a warrior, courageous, bold, honest. While she was . . . What was she exactly?

"I doubt a man would have made a lunge for the lassie's sausages," he said, hedging, and there was something in his voice, a sulkiness almost. Juxtaposed against the alluring sight of his massive hero's body, it seemed almost comical.

But she kept her expression somber as she tugged his shirt from his breeches. "I think the hound was dangerous enough," she admitted. His tunic was long and sturdy. It pooled in loose folds against the muscled expanse of his abdomen, the sight of which made her breath catch in her throat. Dear God, he was beautiful beyond words. "And yet you do not fear them," she said, and wrestled her gaze from his bare skin.

"I—"

"Unless another is at risk."

The muscle in his jaw tensed in concert to the rolling strength of his torso. And despite everything, she found the courage to place her hand against the straining muscles of his chest.

At the warm contact, his eyes dropped closed for a fraction of a second.

"Is that not the truth of it, McBain?" she whispered.

He gritted his teeth as if struggling to make her believe the worst. As if wishing to maintain his poor image in her eyes. His voice was broken when next he spoke. "She was just a wee small thing."

She nodded, for she, too, had seen the terror in the child's eyes, had felt the horror permeate the air like an ugly toxin.

"Unprotected." His tone was rough with emotion. A muscle jerked spasmodically in his jaw.

"But for you," she whispered.

His eyes found hers. "Bairns are meant to be nurtured, lass," he said, and there was such caring in his voice, such hopeless pain, that her heart all but broke for him.

"I am sorry," she said, and, reaching out, covered his hand with her own. Warmth seeped from his skin with the gladness of winter sunlight.

He looked down at it, swallowed, then gritted his teeth against the painful pleasure of skin against skin and raised his eyes. "Sorry?"

"That you were not."

"Ahh lass," he sighed, and, lifting his free hand, shook his head as he cupped her cheek. Hope seemed to stream across her face, lighting her soul, warming her skin. "What foolishness did Connelly tell you?"

"That there was good reason your uncle was called Stone."

"Aye, that there was," he said, and, smiling, shook his head. "But I did not know that. Not until me own beloved parents were gone."

"And when was that?"

He shrugged one heavy shoulder as if his own

broken childhood were of no consequence whatsoever. "I was never so small as the lass hawking the sausages."

"That seems unlikely," she said. "But regardless, a larger size does not make you less vulnerable."

He smiled a little, a wistful expression of kindness and caring as he turned his hand. Enveloping hers with his own, he stared at their joined fingers with aching intensity. "In truth, I believe it does, lass."

"How old were you?" she asked again. "At the loss of your parents?"

"Old enough to carry me uncle's battle gear when me father died," he said, and ran the pad of his thumb across her knuckles.

Feelings skittered across her hand even as he broke her heart with the image he placed in her mind.

"Too young to be without a mother's caring," she said.

For a moment she thought he would disagree, but finally he lifted her hand solemnly to his lips. Excitement chased hope over her knuckles, scattering terror in every direction. "It has occurred to me recently that one can never have enough hours with a kindly woman."

"She was kindly, then?" Reaching out, she undid another button.

"As are you, lass," he said.

She glanced up from her self-appointed task, face hot with desire.

"Kindly," he said, but she shook her head and swallowed. The last button fell open, revealing a swath of chest as smooth and muscled as a stallion's.

"I am not what you think."

"I think you are a woman."

"Well . . ." it was difficult to deny that, for his presence made her hopelessly aware of every aching piece of female anatomy she possessed.

"With a woman's softness," he said.

They were inches apart. His hardness called to her, and though history warned her to be cautious, his presence insisted that she forget the past, that she reach beyond the aching memories and take a chance, just this once.

Thus she remained motionless, but he, too, seemed to be waiting, eyes as intense as a spring storm as he watched her, and she knew beyond a sliver of a doubt that he would never push her. The world was hers for the taking. *Take it now,* she thought, and, reaching up, brushed his shirt aside.

The masculine beauty of him was almost more than she could bear, but she forced herself to run her fingers across the undulating strength of his abdomen.

"A woman's heart," he said, and held her gaze with his, but truth pushed its way in, insisting on being heard.

"I realize we are thought by some to be the fairer sex," she began, "to be the purveyors of . . ."

She could not go on, for the disparity between the admiration in his eyes and the pain of her failings was too much, too harsh, too real and abrasive. "I have not always been that which I should be."

"And what have you neglected, lass?" he rumbled.

"I . . ." she began, but again courage failed her. She rose to her feet. "I will see to your wound. If you'll remove your . . ." She glanced at his chest and away. "Your shirt, I will . . ." What? Tend him? Bind him? Beg for his touch. "Suture it if—"

But he was already shaking his head, already rising to his feet. "'Tis naught. Truly." But she caught his arm, trying to ignore the flare of feelings that sparked between them.

"You would not wish to deprive me of my duty, would you?"

He shook his head, and she nodded.

"Very well, then," she said, and, glancing down, reached for the button on his cuff. He lifted his arm slightly, making her job easier, and finally the little wooden orb slipped through the fabric, baring one broad-boned wrist. It was dark-skinned, sprinkled with coarse hair, powered with strength and capability. Turning, she reached for the other arm, and he gave it freely. In a moment, that wrist too was visible.

Her breathing was ragged now, her stomach a little unsteady. But she reached up to smooth the garment from his shoulders with both hands. They were as broad as a bullock's. As alluring as sunlight, bulging with taut, rolling muscle that rose like ramparts from his torso. She smoothed her hands up the taut width of his deltoids, barely breathing, barely staying upright.

His eyes seared her, but she could not meet them. Indeed, she could not tear her gaze from the banquet of strength before her, from the liquid feel of hot muscle that skimmed beneath her fingertips as she pushed the sleeves over his tight biceps, past the massive strength of his forearms. It was amazing, surreal, so unlike her own pale, weakling body that she was all but mesmerized, all but entranced by the—

Her hand touched something wet. She jerked her gaze to his wound as his shirt dropped to the floor and suddenly she remembered her mission. "I cannot bear the idea of you hurting." Her voice sounded odd, husky, almost unrecognizable. She cleared her throat.

"I assure you I do not," he said.

She shifted her gaze to his, searching for truth. He cleared his throat. "I do not ache *there*."

She felt her heart hiccup in her chest. "You were injured elsewhere? You should have told me," she said, and skimmed his shoulders, his chest, his undulating belly, his massive legs, but all seemed well. Better than well. Bursting with strength and vitality. Bulging with . . .

Her gaze stopped abruptly at his crotch. Her cheeks warmed. She jerked her attention upward, skittered it across his face. But wait, his cheeks almost looked ruddy, as if he, too, were blushing. As if he, too, were embarrassed.

They stared at each other for an eternity, and although Faye was relatively aware of her whereabouts, it felt as if a strong wind was at her back, pushing her forward. Indeed, his bloodstone seemed almost to be reaching toward her, pulling him in its wake.

But she forced her mind back to the matter at hand, her fingers to do their duty.

He didn't complain when she set the cloth to his wound. Indeed, she wasn't entirely certain he felt her ministrations as she washed the blood that stained his wrist. If she had Ella's astounding powers, she would mix the proper herbs beneath a waxing moon and brew a potion tailored for him alone. But that was not her talent.

"I am sorry I do not have a poultice to draw out the poison," she said.

"'Tis not necessary."

"I could return to Lavender House. I've a friend there—"

"No." The word came quickly. She glanced at him, and he scowled. "There is no need for you to leave. Unless . . ." His brows were lowered over his quicksilver eyes. "Unless that be your wish."

Her wishes were not the sort to be spoken aloud. "I'll simply bandage it, then."

"Don't bother yourself, lass. I'll but don a fresh tunic if you are disturbed by—"

"No. Please," she said, and stopped her own

words before she embarrassed herself beyond redemption. But the thought of him covering all that glorious muscle was hopelessly abhorrent. "Allow me to do this for you. Because of . . . your kindness to little Posie."

He scowled.

"The sausage girl," she said, and turned away before he realized her true motives. Nudity had never been so appealing. "I have no bandages," she realized suddenly.

"I shall fetch—" he began, and tried to rise.

"No," she said, and placed a hand on his shoulder. Muscles roiled beneath her fingers. Feelings tingled up her backside. "Please . . ." Please what?

"What?" he asked, reading the question in her mind.

She opened her lips though speaking seemed a terrible waste. But he was waiting. And she was a coward. Time pulsed around them like a wanton heartbeat. "Don't bother yourself. Where might I find bandages?"

"In the wardrobe. My chambers," he said finally, and she turned stiffly, happy to get away, dreading the loss of touch.

His bedroom was in perfect order but for the forest green plaid tossed at an angle across the bed. The woolen looked surprisingly soft, but she did not touch. Instead, she pulled her gaze from the expansive mattress with an effort, only to find a new sketch on the bedstead nearby. With one backward glance, she tilted it toward her.

Again, the image was of a dove. It roosted on a narrow branch. One wing drooped as if damaged, but its sleek, narrow head was high and in its almost-human eyes, there was something notable. Hope maybe or . . .

A noise sounded from the kitchen. Faye jerked toward the wardrobe and tugged open a door, only to find row upon row of bandages. Skimming them for a moment, she chose one and turned, chiding herself for her odd desire to riffle through his things even as she struggled for some witticism to lighten her mood.

"Are you preparing for battle or—" she began, but the sight of him stopped her clever quip. He was strength personified. A warrior of old. It seemed almost strange that he was seated, for a man of his magnitude should always be seen in action.

"Is something amiss?" he asked.

She shifted her gaze from his torso, trying to avoid each alluring part of him. But there was little hope. Even his fine, artist's hands were enthralling. "There were a good many bandages," she said. The words sounded gimpy and pale.

"Aye?" He waited. She felt like an idiot.

"I was but wondering if you were preparing for a battle."

"Ahh." He relaxed a bit, muscles just a shade

less rigid. "With Connelly in residence, 'tis best to be prepared."

"Does he oft become injured?"

"Not as oft as he injures."

"Not as oft as he injures . . ." She unwrapped the bandage, trying to do the same with the mystery of his words until his meaning struck her suddenly. "Surely, he would not hurt *you*."

"You needn't worry for my welfare, lass," he said.

She shook her head, bemused, holding the forgotten cloth in front of her. "Because he would bandage you himself were he here?"

His eyes sparkled as if amused, though his lips didn't twitch. "Truth be told, lass, he'd more like lop off me arm than bind it, but . . ." He paused. "Here then . . ." he said, reaching for the bandage. "I can do that meself."

She pulled it out of his reach. "But what?"

He paused a moment before answering. "He'll not hurt me."

She stared at him, the roiling muscle, the tremendous size. "He said that he could not compare to you on the battlefield."

He raised his brows, watching her a moment before speaking. "You jest."

"No. I had asked . . ." she began, and just then remembered that Connelly had been under the influence of her powers. Kneeling beside the chair, she silently chided herself for her carelessness. "I think he admires you."

His eyes had narrowed slightly. "Might we be speaking of different Connellys?"

"*Thayer* Connelly," she said, and began wrapping his wound. Her fingers brushed the taut expanse of his forearm. She gritted her teeth against the potent feel of skin against skin.

"You didn't hit your head whilst rushing me through the door, did ye, lass?" he asked.

"No, I . . ." she began, then realized the jest. She felt the blush begin at her ears and refused to meet his eyes. But the rest of him was far too tempting to dwell on; his shoulders, heavy with touchable power, his nipples dark and flat, his belly graced with a line of downy dark hair that arrowed beneath his breeches.

"Lass?" he said, and she jerked her gaze away. Clearing her throat, she pinned her gaze on the amulet she had given him. But even that seemed dangerous, for she could not help thinking how fortunate it was to lie undisturbed against the strength of him, to—

Flustered, she yanked her mind back to the topic at hand.

"Is it so difficult to believe that he admires you?" she asked, and realized suddenly that her task was finished, and yet her hand remained on the bulging strength of his forearm.

The room fell silent, then, because she could no longer resist, she looked into his eyes. They were as solemn as a dirge. As dark and mysterious as a Highland loch.

"Why did you come here, lass?" he murmured.

"I . . ." She tried to think, but it would have been so much simpler to *act*. "I had something to tell you."

Silence again. Deep and heavy.

He rose to his feet, all rolling, quiet muscle. She moved with him, transfixed by the strength of him, by the sheer masculine glory. His expression was stoic, his eyes dead steady. "You came to say you have decided against . . . befriending me."

Good heavens he was attractive. Not in the traditional sense of Regency style, of course. He was no preening dandy. Instead, he was power personified. Strength just leashed. And he wanted her. She knew little enough about men, but that much she realized. "Yes."

He reached silently for his shirt, but she stopped him with a hand on his arm. Excitement skittered through her.

"Is something amiss?" he rumbled.

Yes. She was losing her mind. "I don't think it necessary for you to . . ."

He was still staring, but she had run out of words.

She glanced away. "Put the shirt down."

He glanced at the bloodstained rent in the sleeve. "If it offends you, I shall fetch another—"

"But *that* will offend me also."

He stared and she laughed. So it had finally happened. She'd officially gone mad.

"I do not understand," he said, and scowled as he took a step toward her.

Her heart knocked hopefully in her chest. "I just . . . I don't . . ." She glanced around, searching for help. But it was nowhere to be found, thus she turned back and felt her breath catch fast in her throat. "You're beautiful," she rasped.

He stopped in his tracks, brows raised. "What say you?"

"You're the most beautiful man I have ever encountered." There. That sounded much better than, 'I want to tear your clothes off and have my way with you.' Though really, she wanted to tear his clothes off and have her way with him. This madness was rather liberating.

"I . . ." He still hadn't moved. "Do you jest?"

"No, why . . . No," she said, and felt the world settle gently around her. She'd set her course, mad as it seemed.

"Then why did you come to—"

"I've changed my mind. Again."

"So you wish to . . ."

"Yes," she said, but even to her own ears, the single word was inaudible.

"My apologies," he rumbled. "I do not believe I heard you correct—"

"Yes!" she said, and, grabbing him by the belt, rose on her toes to kiss him.

Chapter 25

Something flipped in her stomach as he kissed her in return. It quivered up her sternum and shivered over her nipples. She slipped her arm around his back. Muscles shifted beneath her hand and against her breasts. But in a moment he drew back.

"Lass are ye—"

"I'm sure," she breathed.

He delayed for a momentary eternity, then scooped her into his arms and pulled her against his chest. She wound her arms breathlessly about his Herculean neck, and he bent that strong pillar to kiss her again.

Their breath melded as he carried her through the house. Their gazes caught, but the shifting strength of his chest called to her, and she lowered her head to kiss it. His eyes fluttered closed for an instant, then he stepped into his bedchamber. The door closed behind them as if by some kind of unknown magic. His eyes were like brands upon her face. He kissed her again, slowly now. She slipped her fingers into his hair, then down, over his ear to his bulging neck and the hard slope of his chest.

His eyelids stuttered down, lashes downy against the firm skin of his cheeks. "Lass . . ."

"Perhaps you should put me down," she whispered, and he scowled as if he had forgotten he still held her. Releasing his right arm, he let her feet swing to the floor, and there they stood, inches apart, his torso so bold and beautiful it all but stole her breath.

But the room was too dark to appreciate his full beauty.

She glanced at the fireplace. In the hearth, a charred log shifted. Embers caught and flared. Perhaps she should have been surprised at her awakening powers, but if the truth be known, she felt as if she could set the entire world ablaze with the heat of her desires.

He turned to the fire, surprised, searching for answers to unspoken questions. "Perhaps it caught a draft."

She knew she should lie, should make up some story, but firelight was dancing across the breadth of his chest, illuminating the scar that sliced beneath her dangling amulet. She winced at the sight of it, then reaching out, brushed it with her thumb.

"What happened here?" she whispered, and, raising her eyes, realized that his had fallen closed again.

"Nothing of consequence."

"I disagree. Anything that mars your beautiful chest is surely a sin," she whispered.

"Me chest is not beautiful, lass," he said, watching her. "While you—"

"It is to me," she said, and slipped her hand up the slope of his hard pectoral. "As is your shoulder." The scar there was small but angry. She kissed it gently and felt the muscles twitch restlessly beneath her lips. "And your cheek." The mark there was merely a nick. "Your throat." Completely unscathed. She ran her thumb down his sternum and felt him shiver in the wake of her touch. His excitement fueled her own, and she pushed her fingers lower, down the bumpy path of his quivering muscles. "Your belly," she whispered. But he caught her fingers tight in his.

"Lass." He bore her hand slowly upward, eyes intense. "You set me ablaze like yon fire," he rumbled, and she almost smiled as she tugged her fingers from his.

"Which parts?" she asked, and skimmed her fingertips back down his abdomen.

It was the first time she ever heard him curse, a low hiss of feelings so deep and masculine she felt something clench in her gut.

"I think you may have other areas just as beautiful," she whispered.

His eyes were half-closed, dark and solemn and steady.

"Do you mind if I look?" She could barely force

out the words. But neither could she hold them back.

"Lass . . ." he murmured, still watching her with those soul-dark eyes.

"Yes?"

"I think you may well be delusional."

She chuckled, heady with power, then leaned forward and carefully kissed his nipple. He jerked as if shot, but she was already bumping her fingers along his ribs. Following an aged laceration, she stepped around to his back, marveling at the width of him as she spread her fingers out to fan across his rippling strength. He turned his head to watch her, but his eyes were heavy-lidded, as if in ecstasy, and it was the sight of him thus that most fueled her own sizzling lust.

She found his spine and slipped down the groove between his powerful muscles, then shifted her hands along his sides to skim across the hard expanse of his belly, but her fingers struck his belt buckle and she stopped, breath held.

He watched her, face solemn past his endless shoulder, sable hair caressing his bronzed skin. "I will not hold you to this course," he said.

"You think it is not what I want?" she asked, and brushed her fingers breathlessly through the downy arrow of hair that graced his belly.

He hissed a careful breath through his teeth. "I believe I mentioned how I fear for your state of mind."

She leaned her face against the smooth strength of his back and smiled as she moved her hands lower. Compared to his hot flesh, the metal buckle felt cool and out of place. But she maneuvered it easily enough, easing the leather from its keeper, pulling the strap wide. She paused, drawing away a hand's breadth, needing to breathe, but he neither rushed her nor stopped her. Instead, they stood together, still, unmoving. Fire crackled in the hearth, casting light and darkness with loving care across his rugged features, and with that encouragement, she slipped her hand over the bulge of his erection. He was hard and long beneath the fine fabric of his breeches. She swallowed, drew a careful breath, and eased open the top button of his trousers. His penis eased out, hot and throbbing against her palm. She pressed her breasts against the heat of his back and pushed her open hand against the length of him.

His groan seemed to escape from the very earth, and with that primal sound, she slipped her hands into the waistband of his trousers and pushed downward along his lean hips. The fabric moved slowly, as if loath to leave him, and she could hardly blame it, for he was beautiful beyond words. Powerful and lovely and tempting. Indeed, she felt the need to move back the slightest degree, not only to allow the garment to slide down his buttocks but also to glance down, to see his furrowed spine flow into the mounded hillocks of his posterior. They looked powerful and foreign in the shadows, and she eased her hands down his body, filling her palms with them. They tensed against her skin, perfect, hard, eager. She pressed downward, following the powerful length of his thighs with her hands, feeling every taut muscle, every hard fiber, until finally he stood all but naked before her. Gathering his breath, he pried off his boots with his feet, then leaned down to release himself from the binding garment.

She watched as he bent, watched as the firelight glowed along the broad sweep of his back, watched the turgid curve of his testicles peek out, just visible for an enticing instant before he straightened. She held her breath as he turned slowly toward her, power personified, desire come to life.

She felt her throat tighten, felt the core of her sizzle as she skimmed her gaze down his body, viewing the massive power of his full erection.

He watched her unblinking, seeming frozen, waiting.

"You are . . ." She paused, caught her breath, swallowed, found her nerve and continued. "Large."

His brows dipped the smallest amount. "My apologies."

She almost laughed, but her mouth was too dry. "I do not think it a bad thing in and of itself."

"Even though you are small?"

"Shaleena said . . ." she began, but even the memory made her blush. Repeating it seemed impossible. But he was scowling his curiosity.

"You discussed the size of me . . ." He paused. "You spoke of me to another?"

"I have never . . ." She paused, remembering to shadow the truth. "I have been without a husband for a long while. Hence I find I am a bit . . ." She flickered her gaze down again. His erection stood tall and hard against his belly, leaning slightly to the left as though the weight of it was too much to support.

He eased his fists open beside the bulging power of his thighs. "You are what?"

"Nervous," she said, and pulled her hot gaze back to his face. "And what of you?"

"Would it seem unmanly to admit I might well pass out?"

"I believe it might well be charming."

His scowl deepened the slightest degree. "You will tell me when you decide for certain?"

She smiled. Perhaps it was his own nervousness that dulled her own. "Do you often pass out in these situations?"

"Nay," he said, but his answer sounded uncertain. She stepped up closer still and placed her palm flat against his right pectoral. The muscles bunched eagerly beneath her hand.

"How many times?" she asked, and slipped her hand down his body, taking her time, letting herself absorb, feel, think, revel in this agonizing ecstasy.

He lifted his chin and gritted his teeth. "There has not been a woman like you, lass."

"Like me?" she whispered, and skimmed her fingers, featherlike down the coiled strength of his abdomen.

His breathing escalated, but it was the leashed desire in his eyes that allowed her to continue, to travel lower still, to fill her hand with him and find that her fingers would not quite fit around his girth.

He jerked against her touch, then stiffened, holding himself perfectly still. "Irresistible," he said, and found her eyes. "Powerful." She tightened her grip the smallest degree. "Bold," he ground out.

It might be the strangest thing that had ever been said to her. The strangest, and oddly, the most flattering. "You think me bold?"

He raised his brows in an expression that was almost arrogant, but when he spoke, his tone was low and flat. "I seem to be naked, lass."

"You do that."

"While you are fully clothed."

"Is that wrong?" Unusual? Untimely? Fantastic? She knew so little.

"Far be it from me to pretend I know much of these situations, lass, but I would guess it is not the norm."

She scowled. "Had you so desired, I think you could have fought me off," she whispered, and lowered her gaze to catch the strength of his chest once again.

"I rather doubt it."

She raised her gaze back to his. "I did not mean to take advantage of you," she said, and stroked him gently, just to feel the effects of it in her own clenching body.

His head fell back the slightest degree. "I shall try to forgive you."

She froze, uncertainly flooding her. "Have I hurt you?"

He made some sort of choking sound. "Nay, lass."

"You . . . enjoy it?"

"Aye."

"Then why did you not . . ." She fought for breath, for strength. "Why did you not initiate this exchange?"

"I wished to allow you a chance to change your mind when you saw . . . the whole of me."

"And now?"

He gritted his teeth again as if holding himself back. "Now I await your decision."

She kissed the bottom of his jaw. It was as high as she could reach without rising on her toes. "Tell me, Mr. McBain, are you always so patient?"

"Patient," he said, and rumbled a laugh. It seemed to begin beneath her feet, to shake the very foundation of her world. "I am near to exploding in your wee hand, lass."

Embarrassment rushed over her, but it was spiked with desire, fused with need. "Because of me?" she asked, and shyly drew her hand up over the plum-ripe edge of his head.

He shivered at her touch but never lost contact with her eyes. "There is none other, lass. Thus, I would know—"

But in that instant a tiny droplet oozed from the tip of his cock. She felt it on her fingers and glanced down.

"Your intentions," he continued, voice guttural.

"I fear they may not be honorable," she breathed.

"Thank God," he rumbled.

"What say you?" she asked, and jerked her gaze to his.

"The decision is yet yours," he said, "though I am not certain how much longer I will be able to say the same."

His words intrigued her, sizzled through her. "What will happen after much longer?"

His brows quirked a little. "You are certain you were once wed, lass?"

She could not lie. Not when he was naked. Literally and figuratively. Not when he was hard and heavy in her hand. So she remained silent.

"Tell me lass, was he human?"

She scowled.

"To resist you while you . . ." His voice was breathy. "Handled him."

"Oh." So it was hard . . . *difficult* . . . for him to wait. Is that what he was saying? "He was not as large as you." That seemed a safe bet.

"I do not see what that has to do—"

"Nor so tempting," she said.

For a moment their eyes met, then, with the slowness of a winter sunrise, he kissed her.

"I need you," he growled, and she found she could not answer. "Now. But I shall try to . . ." He glanced down, drinking her in. "They say 'tis best to take one's time," he said, and, reaching forward, swept her hair from her neck. The air felt cool against her throat. His lips felt warm and supple when he kissed her there. Tingling sparks raced downward, igniting her nipples, her belly, her core.

"*Who* says?" she asked. Her voice sounded oddly guttural to her own ears.

"*They*," he said, and paused for just a moment before he kissed her shoulder.

She shivered at his touch.

"Have you been speaking to Shaleena too?"

He chuckled as he turned her. "I am not as brave as all that," he said, and, lifting her hair, kissed her back. She stifled a moan and let her eyes drift closed. His fingers felt steady against her spine as they undid a button.

"Who then?" she persisted.

Air rushed against her flesh, replaced by tender kisses. "I meant 'they' as a collective sort of knowledge."

"So you do not know firsthand?" she asked, and glanced over her shoulder. Her gown had slipped lower. She held it to her breasts and hunched her back. He kissed her again, as soft as a butterfly's caress.

He cleared his throat. "Connelly—"

"You spoke to Connelly?" she asked, and jerked her gaze to his.

He scowled, but his tone evidenced some emotion. Embarrassment perhaps. "I felt certain after all these years that he must be good for something," he rumbled.

She stared at him, and found, once again, that she could not resist. Twisting slightly, she kissed his lips and felt as if she would surely melt like molten wax against his skin. "And was he?" she breathed.

"He said that if I did not take you to bed, I did not deserve to breathe."

"And here we are."

"But still not abed. Which makes me wonder if slowness is indeed all it is—"

Loosening her arms, she let her gown fall and turned fully toward him, unbreathing, unthinking.

"So there is a God," he said, and let his gaze fall slowly down her body.

Embarrassment struck her, fused with excitement, heated with longing.

"You are perfection," he said, and with his fingers drifting over her nipple, he weighed her breast in his hand as he moved closer still. Between them, he bucked with impatience, but his hands were still slow as he trailed his thumb with trembling gentleness over her taut nub. She shivered at his touch, then he was kissing her again, covering her lips with his as he urged her slowly backward. She felt the mattress touch her legs and sat down. In a moment, he was kneeling before her. His chest brushed her legs, and she opened for him, breathlessly inviting him closer. He leaned in. His cock brushed the inside of her thigh as he kissed her breast. Feelings sizzled like comets through her ravenous system. His hands captured her ribs and slid downward until they met the edge of her pantaloons. His fingers moved toward the center of her waist, found the drawstring, and paused.

"One final chance to change course," he said. Perhaps his words were meant as a warning, but to her they sounded like no less than a promise.

She shook her head, scared but exhilarated, and he sighed as he tugged the string loose. The garment pooled gently around her hips. His broad hands followed, pushing the cotton down. She raised herself slightly, allowing him access as he slid the garment over her buttocks. She scooted onto the mattress, and he followed, his right thigh brushing the insides of her knees as he moved with her. She lay back against the pillows, watching his face, waiting for the fear to come crashing in on her, but he was so careful, so slow, so strong and patient and caring as he stretched out half atop her that she could feel nothing but desire. He throbbed against her belly, kissed her, then slid his hand along the outside of her quivering form, along the curve of her waist, the flare of her hip, the length of her thigh, tilting it up slightly as he settled against her.

Firelight crackled along the hard lines of his chest, setting his skin aflame, his eyes alight.

"You are beauty come to life, lass," he breathed, and soft as thistledown, skimmed the flats of his nails along the back side of her leg.

She shivered in the wake of his touch. His coarse-haired thigh had settled snug and hot against her wet center.

"Soft and firm and moist."

Embarrassment pursued her. Surely this was not the time for conversation. "Why are we talking?" she whispered.

"You've no wish to talk?"

"I can . . . I can think of other things to do." Which was true in an abstract sort of way.

"But they say . . ."

"Perhaps *they* do not have your magic," she whispered, and with that, he gently grasped her hips and rolled her atop him.

Her hair cascaded down, spilling over his shoulders and onto the pillow as she shifted her legs around him.

"You are the magic, lass," he whispered. "Wonder come to life. Touchable music."

"You talk a great deal," she whispered, and pressed against him. Their gazes locked, and, with slow deliberation, he raised his hips. Muscles coiled as he slipped inside, easy, hot, fluid.

She arched into him, welcoming more, and he gritted his teeth against the bursting feelings, rocking slowly against her.

"I've no wish to rush you, lass," he rasped.

Tightening her knees against his sides, she let her eyes fall closed, let her head drop back.

He clasped her buttocks in gentle hands, squeezing. Desire roared through her, driving her faster. Clasping his pectorals, she bucked against the strength of him, head thrown back, breasts thrust forward. Her hair swished against her back, brushing his thighs, his hips, his balls.

He hissed against the wispy sensations and pressed into her. Controlled. So demmed controlled.

Impatience boiled within her; there was a banquet beneath her, waiting to be shared. Dragging her fingers down his rigid chest, she leaned forward and, with slow deliberation, sucked his nipple between her teeth. He cursed with raspy impatience and jerked against her. She sat up straight, propped against his chest, feeling the burning excitement build as he held her hips and stoked the flame with hard strokes, pushing to the hilt, taking her with him on a wild flight.

She gasped, felt the primal, snarling release, and contracted around him. He pushed again, every muscle taut beneath her, then shivered, still pulsing, as he let his hands soften on her hips.

She fell to his chest, heart racing against his as she struggled for breath, for sanity. Good heavens, did others realize how this felt?

His fingers trembled slightly as he pushed the

damp hair from her neck. "Are you well, lass?" His voice was breathy, uncertain.

She managed a nod but could not quite trust her voice.

"I did not hurt you?"

"No." She was embarrassed suddenly, cowed by her own wild feelings, her own noisy actions.

Shifting her gently to the mattress, he captured her chin with one broad hand and caught her gaze. "You are certain?" he breathed.

She forced herself to hold his gaze though a dozen tantalizing parts of him called for exploration. "If you'd hurt me, I would not wish to do it again," she breathed.

He blinked. "Are you saying . . ." He paused, uncertain, possibly holding his breath. "What is it you're saying?"

"Perhaps I owe Connelly my thanks," she whispered. Against her breasts, his chest felt as hard as sun-warmed marble.

He scowled, and for a moment she thought he would protest, but finally he spoke. "You wish to do it again?"

"Don't you?"

"I do, lass, yet I do not think I can immediately—" he began, but she let her hand trail downward, easing along hardened muscles, heavy bone, reawakening desire. "My mistake," he rumbled, and kissed her.

Chapter 26

Five times. Not that he was counting. But for such a delicate lass she seemed extremely . . . energetic. They lay now in the aftermath, his arm curled about her body, his torso pressed tight to the smooth length of her narrow back. Between the taut curve of her buttocks, his manhood remained semierect as if it saw no reason to retract at this late date. His legs cradled hers. She was a marvel to him, every nook and cranny, every thought, every sigh. A small, perfect, kindly angel sent for him alone.

"You are well, lass?" he asked, and felt the rumble of his words seep into her back. She turned her head slowly, sleepily. Summer gold hair spilled across his arm, bright as an angel wing against the sun-stained skin.

"I do not think *well* is quite the word," she said, and he tensed.

"Is something amiss? Did I press you too hard?" he asked, but she turned in his arms, her face seeming to shine with solemn beauty.

"Hush," she said, and placed a single finger across his lips. "I am beyond well," she said, and smiled shyly into his eyes. Her face was slightly flushed, and with this change of position, his arm fell across the snowy curve of her breast. He felt himself harden again, though his desire was no longer the ravenous beast that had consumed him earlier.

Taking her hand in his, he kissed her fingertips. Her lips parted slightly, passion-reddened and curving as her eyes darkened with renewed desire. And in that moment life was too good, too full, too hopeful to be true.

He pulled her hand to his chest, feeling his heart fill. "You are desire itself, lass. Beauty and grace and kindness all bound together like a Yuletide gift. Yet it may be best for me own health and well-being if you do not gaze at me like that just now."

"Oh." The thick fringe of her lashes flickered downward. Her face colored again, as pink as a spring sunrise. "I am sorry if I was too . . ." She paused, seeming unable to go on.

"Too what?"

"Demanding," she said, and he laughed, for he could not help himself. His heart was too full, his soul too happy. But she pursed her lips, a silent reprimand for his humor.

"I do not think this be something that can be demanded, lass," he murmured, and, leaning forward, gently kissed the corner of her mouth. Feelings flared through him like a velvet spear to his heart. " 'Tis freely given or is not give a'tall."

Her gaze flickered away again, fleeting on the wings of a scowl. It was almost as becoming as her smile.

"Shaleena said not to expect more than three times unless . . ." She paused, cheeks autumn-apple red.

He raised his brows, curiosity nudging aside his contentment.

" . . . unless you get plenty of sleep," she finished, and studied his amulet for an instant before turning her eyes away.

"Shaleena does not possess your magic, lass," he murmured, and, touching his knuckles to her chin, raised her gaze to his own.

For a moment, her eyes looked almost frightened, but in an instant she calmed whatever misgivings she harbored, and her expression could only be called adoring. The sight of her thus made his heart twist.

"And you are like none other," she breathed.

Her statement eased into his soul like a balm, and yet there was a niggle of something else. A hopeless prickle of foolish jealousy. "Not even your husband?" he asked.

"Not even he," she said, but she could not hold his gaze as she spoke, and with that lack of eye contact, she looked so suddenly sad that his heart cracked quietly in his aching chest. Better far to take a rapier than to feel such emotional pain. But he kept his tone steady, kept his fists unclenched.

"So you miss him still," he said.

Time ticked silently away. She tugged her fingers from his hand and placed them ever so gently on the amulet that lay against his nipple.

He closed his eyes against the pleasant torture.

"I would share a truth with you," she whispered, and raised her eyes to his.

He braced himself, for he knew these perfect, pristine moments were too fine to last, and so he steeled himself against the upcoming pain. "There is another," he guessed, though it was nearly impossible to force the words from his lips. But she did not collapse into tearful agreement. Did not admit that he was right. Instead, she scowled, brows lowering over ethereal eyes.

"What?"

A flicker of hope lit his soul, but he damped it, put it out, scattered the tinder. " 'Tis clear you still feel deeply for your husband." He tried to look away, to fake nonchalance, but there was no hope. She was all-consuming. "That you miss him."

Her lips parted again.

His muscles ached with sudden tension. "A lass such as yourself, so filled with fire, you would not have delayed . . . this . . ." He nodded vaguely toward the bed, toward the magic they had just shared. "Unless you felt some loyalty for another." The truth struck him suddenly, as painful as a blade to the ribs. "He is yet alive," he deduced.

She blinked.

"Your husband," he said, voice roughening with emotion he could not quite resist. "He is yet alive, is he not?"

She shook her head, but he would know all now before he could no longer bear to hear the words.

"You can tell me the truth, lass."

"I am," she murmured, but he continued on his headlong course, certain beyond reason that he was right.

"Has he found trouble somewhere? Is that why you came to me?"

She shook her head, and he watched her, wanting to believe. But he could feel the untruth in the base of his soul.

"Tell me true, lass. I will help if ever I can."

"I . . ." She exhaled softly as if overwhelmed, and he waited, tense with grinding anticipation.

"I but ask that you do not lie to me," he said.

"I'm sorry," she whispered. There were tears in her eyes. Tears shining like dewdrops in her precious-jewel eyes, and though he was certain he was right, that she would betray him, he found he wanted nothing more than to see her smile. To set her world aright.

"Where is he, lass?" he asked. "Incarcerated? Hiding from an enemy?"

"It's not like that."

"Is he someone I know?"

"No."

"What sort of help does he need? Brute force, I assume since that is—"

"I was never wed." Her words came out in a rush.

He stopped. Stopped talked. Stopped breathing. Stopped thinking. Merely let his heart beat a steady tattoo against his ribs, as if to remind himself that he yet lived, that this was not a dream.

"What say you?" He said the words quietly, steadily, lest the world evaporate around him.

"You were correct. I lied." Her words were no more than a whisper. "I have never known a husband."

Relief was a shy blossom in his chest. He spoke slowly. "So this man you care about—"

"There is no man."

Joy bloomed like a winter rose in his soul, but he kept it in the dark though he knew, was *certain* that if there was none other, he could mend whatever troubles plagued her. "You are not a widow?"

"No."

"And you do not cherish another?"

"No."

The relief was so poignant it actually hurt, but a new problem came to him. He scowled. "But there have been other men. Other lovers."

She inhaled as if she were breathing in strength. She was gripping the amulet in her right hand. "No other lovers." Her eyes flickered away.

He scowled. Was it a lie? "Then I should have been slower. More careful, more . . ."

"Any slower and I would have taken you down like a wolf on a lambkin." Her cheeks were pink, her gaze still lowered.

He remained absolutely silent for a moment, considering. "So you do not resent my . . . impatience?"

"Is that what you call it?"

He could breathe properly again and reached out, needing to touch her, to feel her angel-soft skin against his own. "But why the lie, Faerie Faye? Why the fictitious husband?"

Her eyes fell closed for a moment. "I was once . . ." He could barely hear her and leaned closer so as to catch each pearlescent word that fell from her lips. "My past is not what it should have been. There were troubles."

"Of what sort?"

"What I told you before of my parents . . ." She winced. "It was untrue. I, too, was left alone at an early age. But not . . . not entirely alone. There was a man . . ." She shook, trembled like a chilled goddess. Her face was pale suddenly, as white as death, and he pulled her into his arms, skin against skin, wrapping his strength around her. Still she spoke, spilling the words quietly onto his chest. Her breasts felt like warm magic between them. Her tears were hot against his skin. He closed his eyes against her pain and cupped the back of her silken head with his palm.

"What was this man to you, lass?" he breathed.

"He was a noble. Lord Tenning." She swallowed. "He liked for me to call him Uncle Max."

He waited, stroked her hair, and forced himself to breathe.

"But he was not my uncle. Not my kin. I was given to him," she whispered.

He waited for more, dreading yet needing to know, but she did not speak for many seconds, and when she did, the words struck him like a blow.

"In actuality, he won me in a game of chance."

Rogan gritted his teeth against the truth and tightened his grip, holding her as if he could shield her from the agony.

"He was not a good . . ." she began, then paused. Another tear fell, scalding him as it squeezed between them, heat on heat. "For years I believed he meant me no harm. *Wanted* to believe as much. But . . ." She ran out of words. He stroked her back. "He cared for me for a long while. Sheltered me. Clothed me. Educated me. What difference did it make that he did not allow me to venture from the house? That sometimes he touched me in a way that . . ." She swallowed. He felt the constriction of her throat against his skin. "Or watched me with a strange expression in his eyes. He knew I was . . . different. Had from the start. Said I was gifted. Special. Always wanted to know what I sensed of people. Wanted to know the truth." She winced. "He warned me never to lie to him. Said there would be consequences if I disobeyed his wishes." She hunched her shoulders, seeming smaller, more fragile than ever as she continued in a whisper. "Perhaps he wouldn't have harmed me." It seemed almost that she no longer spoke, that he could but feel the force of her memories through the heat of her skin. "But he was so angry. I had never seen him thus. Not even when I tried to escape." She laughed. The sound was breathy, eerie. "I knew he would be, of course. Knew he would . . . if I did not do his will." She swallowed. He felt the contraction of her throat against his chest. Felt her body tighten and tremble before she tried to force herself to relax.

He held her close, as if they were one, his thigh between hers, their hearts in unison. "He forced you to . . ." He clenched his teeth, trying to remain calm, to understand. She had said there were no former lovers, and he longed to believe. But now he realized there were other options that were far worse. "To do his will?"

"Force . . ." She breathed the word, then stiffly shook her head. "There was no need for force. I was too much the coward to resist his simplest command. Nay . . ." Her lashes brushed his chest with dewdrops as her eyes dropped closed. "I would ruin lives at his whim."

Silence slipped into the room, echoed there in uncertainty.

"You are joy itself, lass," he said finally. "I am sure you could not harm—"

"Bartholomew Langley was a decent man."

He tightened his jaw against her pain and ran his hand down the length of her hair, pulling her nearer still, as if he could take her agony if they were close enough. "Langley?"

"Decent. Wealthy. A doting father. A loving

husband." Another scalding tear slipped between them. "But he had a weakness."

He didn't press her.

"For men."

Somewhere in his soul he knew what she was about to say, but he waited for the words.

"Tenning . . . learned of that weakness and . . . He was not above using secrets," she whispered. "There are times I believe he was not above anything."

"There is evil in the world," he said.

She nodded brokenly, then drew a deep breath, filling her lungs, though when she next spoke, her words were no louder than a hopeless sigh. "At times I can see . . ." She paused, seeming to search for strength. "There are times I sense things. Inexplicable things."

He shook his head, not understanding, then stopped, remembering as he felt the heat of the amulet on his skin. "You knew I was wounded. Knew and took steps to heal me."

"Yes. But—"

"So 'twas *your* powers the crone felt on me," he rumbled.

She raised her gaze to his, questioning.

"An old herbalist I visited at the carnival," he said. "She looked to be the very essence of a witch. Like—"

"How do witches look?" she asked, searching his eyes, and he remained silent. Thinking.

"You are . . . gifted," he said, the truth of the words finally seeping into his consciousness.

" 'Tis no gift," she whispered.

He wanted to disagree, to argue, for surely every part of her was as precious as a gemstone, but she would not believe it. Not now.

"Or perhaps it could be." Her voice broke, and she shook her head, lowered her eyes. He felt a muscle tic in her cheek. "I told Tenning of Langley's indiscretions."

Rogan could see the picture in his mind, for he knew the workings of evil. "And he told others."

She shook her head. "He but threatened," she whispered. "He would not have followed through. Not if Langley had continued to pay."

"Blackmail."

"There had been others." Her voice was little more than a wisp of pain in the crackling darkness. "Others who were broken. Others whose lives I tore apart, but none who took their own lives." She pulled in a shuddering breath. "I couldn't do it again."

"You told him so."

"I said I didn't care what he did to me." She shivered again. He tugged the blankets over them, though his own flesh was overheated. "Didn't care what Lucifer did."

"Lucifer." Dread leaned hard against his soul, but she no longer heard him.

"I lied." Her voice was almost inaudible now. Little more than a whisper of terror against his chest. "If I had not cared, I would have let him beat me."

"No, lass," he breathed, and felt rage and fear and horror flow through him like a swelling river. "No."

"I could have run," she whispered. "Lucifer was not fast. Not . . ." Her words failed. "There is no such thing as demons in human form." The words were no more than a breath. "Just men."

Rogan kept himself still. "I would know it all, lass, if you can tell me."

Her nod was short, jerky. "We lived on a country estate. Alone but for the servants. I was not allowed to venture outside the house for fear of . . . molestation."

"From whom?"

"Tenning said Lucifer waited outside." She shook her head. "Maybe he was a field hand. Maybe . . . I don't know. I'll never know. But he was real. I'm certain of that."

"So you remained confined."

"Usually." The word was little more than a breath. "Sometimes I would convince myself to run. I would shimmy through the window or slip through an open door. But in the end I would always falter."

Rogan waited.

"Until the day I began to . . ." She swallowed. "I knew next to nothing of the ways of nature. I was confused, disoriented."

He scowled, but the meaning of her words dawned on him in a moment. "When you became a woman."

"There was a good deal of blood."

"And you were frightened by it."

"Yes. But there was more. Things were changing. My *gifts* were out of control. Things moved without . . ." She shook her head. "I was embarrassed. Frightened. *Frightening.* I needed to escape. To leave before Tenning returned but . . ." Her words fell away. "Lucifer. He was so big," she whispered, and Rogan felt his own size like an open wound. "I hid. In the woods. In a log." She was breathing hard. "But someone loosed the hounds."

"Tenning."

"He kept a lock on the kennels. None other had a key."

Rogan kept himself very still, muscles rigid, mind fuming. He would kill them both. Slowly. Patiently. And on their dying breath, they would know why.

"He pulled me out by my feet. I was too scared to fight."

Silence fell between them, heavy and hard.

"He raped you," Rogan said.

Tears again, hot and steady. "There were no lovers, Rogan. Only the Devil."

His arms ached to do damage, but he remained very still, waiting for the rest.

"Tenning found us immediately after. Or so I thought. But he was there the whole while. Waiting. Watching. Yet he was so gentle when he treated my wounds." A sob broke from her. "There were tears in his eyes. Like a father who—"

"Do not say those words to me, lass."

"He was only trying to protect me, he said. To show me the error of my ways."

So the bastard had told his giant to keep her there whatever the cost. Had insisted that he punish her if she tried to escape. And all the while he'd pretended to be her doting protector. Anger mixed with venom in his gut. "How old were you?" he asked.

"Ten-and-four perhaps."

Rage boiled anew. "This Tenning, where does he live?"

She shook her head. Perhaps she could see the killing lust in his eyes though he tried to hide it.

"I would but speak to him," he said. It was the first time he had lied in some years. It would not be the last if that is what it took to obtain vengeance.

"You cannot," she whispered.

"You did not deserve to be hurt, lass," he said, and tried to keep his tone level, his muscles unclenched.

"Yes I did."

"Nay," he said, and felt rage soar anew. "You were but—"

"I killed him," she whispered.

The breath stopped in his throat. "What?"

She was holding his wrist in a desperate grip though he had no idea when she had taken hold of him. Her eyes searched his. "My mother would have been ashamed. She had the power, too. Father knew it, tried to keep it quiet. Thought it . . ." She was breathing hard, speaking fast. "But she was not evil. I know it. She told me to use it for good, but Father . . . I think he was happy to be rid of me. And Unc—*Tenning*, he was just as happy to have me, and I wanted to please him, but . . ." She drew a deep breath, shuddered. "The last time he ordered me to assist him, I . . .

"I'm not very strong. He always told me as much. I didn't mean to hurt him. Just drive him back. Keep him away. But he tripped and fell. There was an armoire behind him, and his head struck . . ." Her voice broke.

"So he's already dead," Rogan said, and felt the disappointment burn through him like a flame out of control.

She had ceased breathing. Her eyes were huge, devouring him as she nodded.

"And the man called Lucifer?"

"He did not find me. Lord Gallo did."

"Lord Gallo." He nodded, feeling his heart unclench the tiniest degree.

"I was broken," she said. "Hiding. Waiting to be found. Waiting to die."

"'Twas he what brought you to Lavender House."

"He saved my life. Gave me family."

"The others then," he said, deducing carefully. "They are . . ." What were they? What was *she*? ". . . injured also?"

"More than I. Ella is perhaps the most gifted. But

she was also the most . . . I am a terrible coward by comparison."

"A coward!" he said, and croaked a laugh. "You killed him, lass. Took his life." His fists tightened in her hair, but he forced himself to relax. "If . . ." Memories assailed him. Memories of a tiny girl with haunted eyes. "Justice." Justice tortured him. He gritted his teeth. "I, too, have killed. Pointless battles. Unjust duels." He winced as the ghosts of the past brushed him. " 'Tis fortunate for me I suppose that Winden had none like you to avenge his death. None but wee Cat to mourn—" He stopped, drew a hard breath.

"What are you talking about?"

He glanced down. She was staring at him as if he'd gone mad. He brought himself back to the present with a start.

"You'd best be getting home, lass," he rumbled. "Connelly is sure to be returning soon."

Tugging the blanket over her breasts, she sat up. "I know it was wrong," she said.

He watched her, seeing her as a child, as an innocent. Scared, broken, abused. He could not bear to look.

"What I did. All of it. I know it was wrong," she said, and though everything in him longed to pull her close, he could not, for he would never deserve her.

"You'd best be dressed," he said, and, rising from the bed, left the room.

Chapter 27

What had happened? Faye's head spun with uncertainty. Originally, she had sought Rogan out to dredge up his carefully protected truths. But instead, she had spilled her own, dropped them like precious droplets of blood. Had said things she should have kept to herself until her dying breath. And why? Because he had plied her with sex? Hardly that. Indeed, in the end she had all but begged for his touch. What kind of earthy magic did he possess? Some kind she could not understand surely. Could not resist.

Not in all of her years had she admitted the truth of her past . . . of her powers. Though the lies had pounded her brain like the beat of wild hooves, she had used them like weapons, stabbing them forth whenever necessary.

Until now. Until him.

Now she had endangered the coven. The sisters of her heart. And since their time together, he had not spoken to her, had not contacted her in any way. She had bared her questionable soul, and he had turned aside. Why? What was he planning?

She had spent the day shut up in her chambers. A full day followed by a sleepless night during which she had reviewed every moment of their hours together. Not that she had to try to recall how his hands felt against her skin, for that perfect torture was indelibly etched in her mind. As was his expression as he had all but tossed her from his home.

She had tried to remember the conversations she'd shared with him. Indeed, she had combed through every word spoken and after a seeming lifetime, had recalled the name Winden.

She had paced the length of her bedchamber until her feet throbbed in time with her head, but she knew what she must do. It had taken all her quivering courage to take her news to Lord Gallo. And he, in turn, had gone to the committee.

They had learned what they could in record time. Had, in fact, found the location of Winden's widow. But she was no longer known under that name. She was Lady Mullen, second-time widow and noted philanthropist.

Mild as Mullen.

Faye had prepared nothing to dredge the truth from her. What would be the purpose? The woman was known to London as all but a saint. Besides, Faye's powers were growing stronger, surer. Despite the headaches that had plagued her since leaving McBain's town house, she would learn the truth.

She stood now on the stoop of a well-groomed

home in a good section of Bloomsbury. Not a whisper of breeze disturbed the topiary that surrounded the house. In a moment, Faye was admitted inside. The high hallways echoed as she was escorted to a sitting room, and in a matter of minutes, a lady joined her. She was tall and slim and lovely. Some might have said frail, but she held herself erect as she crossed the hardwood floor, heels rapping.

"Mrs. Nettles?" she asked, and Faye stood, nerves jumping like scalded cats.

"Yes. Thank you for seeing me without notice."

"Certainly," she said, then, pausing momentarily, motioned in a servant who stood in the doorway, already bearing a tray of tea and biscuits. He was a handsome man, straight-backed even when he poured the steaming liquid into two fragile cups. Without a glance at his mistress, he disappeared, closing the double doors quietly behind him. "But tell me . . ." she began, and, handing over a cup, waved elegantly toward the settee. Faye forced herself to take the tea, to sit, to act as if all was well. "Are we acquainted?"

"No," Faye said. "But I believe we may have a mutual . . ." What did she call him? An acquaintance? A lover? The man who held her soul? Her hands trembled slightly. "Friend."

"Oh?" The lady's lips quirked up the slightest degree as she lifted her cup. "And who might that be?"

No use delaying. No hope of skirting the issue. "Rogan McBain," she said.

For a moment the woman froze, then the cup trembled from her hand, falling to the floor like a felled dove. "How could you be so cruel?" Lady Mullen whispered, and sat back, ignoring the spilled beverage, face as pale as ash.

Faye's heart quivered in her chest, but she would know. Would learn the truth. "So you are acquainted with him?" The question fell drunkenly from her lips, for she had hoped against hope that that would not be the case.

"Know him!" Lady Mullen exhaled a breathy laugh, devoid of humor, of tone. "He is my husband's murderer."

The world stopped. "What?"

"Are you . . ." She paused, winced, hands atremble even as she clasped them together in her lap, ignoring the tea that soaked the carpet beneath her feet. "You're in love with him, aren't you?"

Faye shook her head. It was all she could manage, for her mind was roiling.

"But of course you are." Her eyes were sad. "He is, after all, a master seducer."

The world felt strange. Off kilter. "You must be thinking of another," she said, but in a manner of speaking Rogan *had* seduced her. Had broken through her well-fortified barriers as none other. So seemingly innocent. Almost shy.

Lady Mullen rose rapidly to her feet, body stiff, movements jerky. "So he's done it again."

"Done . . ." Faye shook her head. The movement made it throb. Had she been duped by a man yet again? Had she believed in the goodness of his soul merely because she had wished to?

"Made another believe his toxic lies."

"I don't know what you're talking about," she said, but she lied, for she knew she had been weak. Had been willing to believe for the sake of his touch.

"I was wrong. I'll admit that. I was young and unhappy." She twisted her hands. "My first husband . . . he was more interested in his club than in me, and Rogan made me feel . . ." Her words ran aground, but she found the current and cleared her throat. "He must have known how I longed for love, for . . ." She shrugged stiffly. "When he looked at me, it was as if I were the only woman in the room. In all of the world. It became so that I could think of nothing but him. How his fingers felt against my skin. How his . . ." Her hands trembled as she sat again and brushed an imaginary fold from her skirt. "I did not want my husband dead. I swear I did not."

"You must be thinking of another—"

"They did not call it murder," she said, and laughed. " 'Twas a duel, they said. But Gregor . . ." She shook her head. Tears brimmed in her wide, expressive eyes. "He was no match for Rogan. Not with a sword. Not with anything. But he had a heart," she said, and clasped a loose fist to the center of her chest.

"Surely you're mistaken," Faye whispered, but the other only gave her a sad glance.

"Rogan McBain," she murmured. "A man to make you forget all others."

"No. He's gentle, kind . . ."

"So you've slept with him."

Faye felt her cheeks flame. Felt her tongue tie and her wits scramble.

"Tell me, Mrs. Nettles . . ." Lady Mullen began, and raised her chin as if facing the world. "Are you wealthy?"

"I don't think . . ." Words failed her. She had already spilled too much truth and dare not do more damage.

"Neither did I," she said, and smiled ruefully. "Not until after Catherine's disappearance."

Faye felt her heart clench, felt the world shudder. "Catherine?" The name was little more than a breath on her lips.

A single tear spilled from an azure eye. "She was little more than an infant then. Two years of age. As bright as a butterfly. As sweet as a rose."

"What happened?" Faye could barely manage to push out the question, for every fiber of her being ached with the misery of her failure, of her foolishness.

"A portion of my husband's fortune would have passed to her after his death."

"Are you saying—"

"But if she *and* my husband were dead, Rogan would have had only me to contend with."

"But he would know you would not condone murder."

"Tell me, Mrs. Nettles, have you not lain in his arms and found yourself willing to say anything, to *do* anything to remain there? To feel his strength. To know his love?

"There is no need to answer," Lady Mullen said. "I can see the truth in your face. And I cannot blame you. For perhaps he would be living off my husband's fortune even now." She closed her eyes for an instant. "But for Catherine."

"What happened to her?" Faye could barely force out the words.

"She disappeared. Two days after Gregor's death, she vanished."

"Surely you cannot think Rogan had a hand in this," Faye said, but how many years had she believed Tenning's lies?

Lady Mullen smiled grimly. "He murdered my husband, Mrs. Nettles. There is no reason to believe he would not do the same with a child. Indeed, that is why I do what I can for the Foundling Hospital. To atone for my part in her death."

"I'm certain you're wrong," Faye breathed.

Mullen looked sad, forsaken. "He has duped you completely. And now you come to me. The only question that remains, is why."

Faye's lips felt numb, but she forced out the dreaded words. "There has been a death."

Lady Mullen clasped her hands tightly, squeezing until her knuckles went absolutely white. "So he's killed again," she said, and Faye trembled, shaken by the depth of her own weakness.

Chapter 28

Faye spent the remainder of the day in agony. She had fled Lady Mullen's house as soon as she could marshal her senses and escape. Shame and confusion plagued her. Pain pounded her head. She was supposed to be strong. Wise. Gifted. But instead she'd been weak and needy, wanting so desperately to believe herself worthy of a man's love that she would risk not only her heart but her sisters. And he had used her. Indeed, he most probably planned to use her again, to exploit her gifts to gain his own ends as Tenning had done.

But what were those ends? If he was Brendier's and Lindale's murderer, what was the purpose? For a time she had imagined he had killed Lindale to avenge the attack on her person, but perhaps that was wishful thinking. Perhaps on some level she had wanted him dead. Perhaps she was no better than McBain. Perhaps, in fact, it had been he who had molested her at Inver Heights, despite the gentleness he had shown her just a few nights before. Despite the adoration in his eyes.

Men could be conniving. But so could she. And she would learn the truth.

Thus she sat in Lady Lindale's drawing room. The widow had been as gracious and kindly as ever. They sat facing each other, a small platter of cucumber sandwiches between them.

"And what brings you by, my dear?"

"I've been worried for your welfare," Faye said, and felt not a tingle of pain for her lie. She was beyond that now, cold, driven. "I wished to stop by to ascertain your well-being."

"I'm well enough," she said, and poured the tea. The stream followed a graceful arc, making barely a ripple as it fell into a gilt cup painted with ivy. "Mots has stayed on."

"Your nephew."

"My husband's. Yes. A sweet boy. But honestly a few moments of solitude would not be unwelcome."

"I'm sorry to bother you."

"Oh no, please," said Lady Lindale, quickly setting her cup aside. "I did not mean to insult you. It is simply that young men are so . . . young," she said, and smiled.

"Is he planning to live here indefinitely?" Faye asked.

"Not indefinitely, I'm sure. He became master of a lovely home in Park Lane, after his father's death."

"So he inherited nothing from your husband?"

"Not at all true," said Lady Lindale. "He received a fine snuffbox and a writing desk he long admired."

Faye scowled. Could the desk be significant? Or was she only hopelessly trying to find another to take the blame for Lindale's death when she knew the true culprit all along.

"But you needn't worry," Lady Lindale said, tilting her head. "Mots will be perfectly capable of keeping a wife in fine style."

"I didn't mean to imply—"

"He's a good catch for any woman looking to make a match."

"I'm certain he is."

"His great-grandfather was the Baron of Warton."

Something stopped whirring in Faye's head. Even she had heard of Warton. It was one of the most prestigious estates in England. "Who is the current baron?"

"A younger son I believe. Though I'm not entirely certain."

"And he's in good health?"

Lady Lindale raised her brows. "I assure you, Mrs. Nettles, Mots will make a good husband even though he'll not inherit the barony."

"Of course. Of course he will," Faye said, and, excusing herself, hurried from the house.

She spent the remainder of the day speaking with Brendier's staff. His wife was staying with her mother for an undetermined amount of time, so there was no help to be found there, but a young woman named Ada remembered McBain's visit.

"Oh aye, a great pillar of a Scot," she said, eyes bright. "I remember him well."

Faye squelched a half dozen unwanted emotions. "He visited the day prior to your master's death, I believe."

"Aye, it could have been. It could well have been the day before."

"How did they get on?"

"Well enough I suspect, though the master was never a mean drunk."

Faye felt her heart clench. "They were drinking?"

"I didn't mean nothing by it. It wasn't like my lord was a sot, but he was in some pain, and the wine eased his discomfort."

For a moment Faye couldn't speak, for suddenly she remembered the herbalist McBain had mentioned in passing. The very essence of a witch, he had called her. Why had he visited her? Might he have been buying some toxic blend? Hensbane or nightshade or mandrake?

But no. It was foolishness. Rogan McBain was a warrior. If he wished someone ill, surely he would have no trouble causing their death. But perhaps he was too clever for that. Poison was said to be a woman's revenge. What better way to turn suspicions aside?

"Where did he acquire the wine?" Faye's voice sounded odd to her own ears, but the maid seemed not to notice. She shrugged.

" 'Tis impossible to say. The master kept a full cellar."

"Did McBain bring it?"

"The Scotsman? I wouldn't say so, but truth to tell, I may not have noticed. He had them eyes, you know. All solemn, brimming with truth and earnestness."

Faye questioned the others, but most of them were male and remembered little of the Celt's visit.

She returned to Lavender House exhausted but sleepless. Her eyes felt scratchy, her body achy on the following day. Nerves jumping, she made a journey to Hookums Lending Library. Flipping through the pages of a giant tome, she finally found Warton's lineage. It was an old line, but she was hardly interested in a match. She was interested in murder. According to Lady Lindale, her husband's nephew would inherit nothing with the old baron's death. But someone would.

Faye noted the names and pictures. Both Brendier and Lindale might have eventually inherited the title of Baron of Warton, but it was a long road, though the current patriarch was well into his seventies.

Faye scowled, frantically searching for more information. Apparently Warton had had no sons of his own. Thus, his nephew, a round-faced man named Theodore, was poised to inherit upon Warton's death. What did that mean? Was he doomed to suffer the same fate as Brendier and

Lindale? Or was it Warton himself who was at risk?

A portrait struck her consciousness. Chiseled jaw, dark, unruly hair.

Dread pounded in her head as she skimmed the text. Gerald Franquor. She glanced at the portrait of the woman beside him, and there, staring up from the page, were Rogan's eyes, all but identical except for the sky blue color. The world slowed as she read the caption. Elizabeth Skye Franquor had been born to the McBain clan, but had married an Englishman. She'd died in childbirth, bearing a son about whom no further information was available.

She searched frantically through the remainder of the book, but there was little point, for she knew the truth; Rogan McBain was Lord Brendier's cousin. Rogan McBain stood to gain a fortune and a title if but two more men died. Rogan McBain had deceived her.

But he would not do so again. She was no man's pawn.

She would go to Theodore Franquor first, and if necessary, she herself would keep him safe. She touched his portrait, making a vow. And it was then that she felt a tiny sliver of danger slice through her veins. She jerked her hand away, breath tight in her throat. But this couldn't be. She had no gifts for sensing danger. But perhaps Rogan McBain did.

Memories of him lunging from the bookseller's tent stormed through her mind. How had he

known little Posie was in trouble? How but some
battle-honed premonition? Had he known Faye
was just outside? Is that why he had acted, to influence her even further? Perhaps he was far more
clever than she knew. Perhaps he had been able to
curtail the truth-seeking attributes of the amulet,
but maybe this power of his had seeped from him
to her. Or was fatigue finally bringing on the madness she'd fought off for so long?

Tentative, breath held, she touched the portrait
again. Danger sizzled through her, unmistakable
now. She jerked to her feet and hurried toward the
door. But she did not even know where Theodore
Franquor lived.

It took her nearly half an hour to reach Bow
Street Magistrate's Court. By the time she raced
inside, she felt breathless and frantic.

"There's going to be a death," she said.

The man behind the desk turned slowly toward
her. "What's that, madam?"

She tried to calm herself, to portray some semblance of sanity. She smoothed her hair back
behind her ear, but there was little hope. She had
ridden hard to get there. "I have reason to believe
Theodore Franquor's life is in danger."

"Mr. Franquor of Medville House?"

"You must send someone immediately."

He was watching her carefully. Was this how
her contemporaries became locked away? Not
crazy at all, but frantic. Or perhaps she was confusing the two.

"Of course," he said. "But it's a long ride to Southwark. "Why not take a seat for a bit and I will—"

She never waited to hear the rest. Instead, she turned and flew back outside. It took her two hours to find Medville House. But Theodore Franquor was not there. A fat doorman with a hooked nose informed her that he was at his estate in Bournebridge.

The night was as black as sin as she raced through the streets of London. Rain slapped her face. But she spurred Sultan on, riding astride, leaning hard over his straining neck.

Franquor's second estate was little more than a hunting cottage. Built of native stone, it stood alone in the midst of a broad stand of hawthorns and elms.

Faye slowed Sultan to a walk. It was dark. The rain had dwindled to a drizzle. A curl of smoke twisted from the chimney, suggesting habitation, warmth, and yet those were not the feelings that emanated from the building.

Fear, nurtured from infancy, crept up her spine, tingling along her nerve endings, freezing her breath. But she would not quit. Not now. She had shielded herself from the truth in the past. But no more.

Her legs felt wooden as she slid to the ground and wrapped the reins through a hitching post. Sultan's breath warmed her sleeve as he blew, and for a moment, Faye was tempted almost beyond control to remount. To ride away. But truth was everything. She knew that now.

Her boots were all but soundless against the graveled walk. Not a noise disturbed the quiet. Her knock at the door seemed ungodly loud, but no one answered. She knocked again, the sound hollow and piercing in the stillness.

Instincts crowded in, insisting she had done all she could. That she could leave now, conscience clear. Indeed, she almost turned away, but in the end she could not.

The handle felt cold against her fingers. The door creaked inward.

"Sir." Her voice shook. "Mr. Franquor, I would have a word."

No sound answered.

She forced herself to move. To do. To step inside. A fire crackled in the fireplace, and in a moment she saw the body. It lay at an odd angle, crumpled at the foot of the stairs. Fear flooded in, almost drowning her, and yet she did not stop. Instead, she stepped toward it, heart hammering, feet silent on the carpet until she stood only inches from the hand that lay outstretched as if reaching—

A scrap of noise sounded from the entry. She jerked her gaze up, heart pounding, and he was there. Rogan McBain, face as somber as death.

"No," she rasped, and suddenly she realized the truth. She had not come here to prove him guilty, to make him pay for his crimes. She had come to keep him from killing again. To hide his sins, to keep him safe.

"I feared you'd come." His words were little more than a rumble of sound.

But even as he said them footsteps echoed outside.

Rogan lurched toward her. She meant to leap away, to save herself, but she was frozen in place, and in an instant he had grabbed her arm, propelling her across the floor, all but tossing her into the hallway.

"Go," he ordered. "Out the back and away."

She shook her head, but even as she did so a voice bisected the silence.

"What goes on here?"

Rogan turned slowly toward the man who stepped inside, praying with silent urgency that Faye was gone. Safe. Well away from this place that had drawn her.

The constable was a lean, red-faced fellow with heavy side-whiskers and a blue greatcoat that reached to his knees. A second man, not as tall, but youthful and quick, rushed in behind him. His scarlet waistcoat seemed strangely incongruous against the somber, firelit darkness. He delayed not an instant.

"Cranton! Look."

They turned toward the body in unison.

"We were told there might be trouble here," Cranton said, and pulled a club from beneath his voluminous coat. He was neither powerful nor well armed.

Rogan raised his hands, gladly surrendering.

Had she gone? He had no way of knowing and strained to hear her footfalls, to know she was safe. But there was no noise from behind him.

"He's dead," said Redbreast.

"By your hand?" Cranton asked.

And so it came to this. To the spot where they would learn of Rogan McBain's true mettle.

The world seemed to stand still, awaiting the verdict. Outside, in the cool open air, rain dropped with rhythmic brilliance from the night sky.

"We argued," Rogan said, and found it was not difficult after all to find the lie to save her. Indeed, he would do far worse to keep her from harm. To keep her safe and free.

"And you pushed him down the stairs?"

He didn't answer immediately. Instead, he turned toward the body. Is that how he had died? There was a broken wine bottle near the wall. The floor was wet beneath his head.

"Search the house," said Cranton. "There might be someone hiding in—"

"I was in a rage," Rogan said. The lie seemed to rumble through his very soul. Redbreast hustled upstairs and was back in a heartbeat. "When he turned away, I struck him from behind."

"It's a lie," Faye said, and winced as she stepped into view.

"Lass." He found her eyes with his, locked on

them. They were as sad as eternity, as deep as forever. "Why are you yet here?"

Cranton shifted nervously. Perhaps he sensed the power that emanated from her. The power Rogan himself had missed for so long. But he felt it now. Like a sizzle of lightning, it seemed to scorch his very soul. But it mattered not if he burned, for she was everything. Aye, she might have killed. But if that was so, the victim deserved to die. 'Twas as simple as that.

"Who are you?" Cranton asked, but Faerie Faye's eyes held Rogan enthralled. Calm and brave, she watched him for an instant. Then, almost smiling, she turned toward the elder Redbreast.

"He died by my hand," she said.

"No, lass," Rogan rumbled, and clenched his fists.

"What?" The older officer was scowling, carefully shifting his gaze from one to the other. The younger left the stairs to stride through the lower level, knife clenched in a steady grip.

"I killed him," she said. Her voice was as clear as morning.

Cranton's gaze flitted from one to the other. "The Scot said he was to blame."

She smiled a little. "Rogan McBain is a warrior, sir. A decorated soldier. And a hero. He would do no such thing."

"Then why did he—"

"He's protecting me. Mr. Franquor and I were having an affair."

"And . . ."

"He threatened to leave me."

"That hardly seems a reason to kill a man."

She did smile now. The expression was beatific, carefree, kindness, and light. "Have you ever been in love?" she asked, and suddenly her eyes filled with tears, though her perfect face remained absolutely unmoved. "Have you ever been willing to give all?"

"Lass—" Rogan rumbled.

"No," she said, and shook her head before finding his eyes with hers. Her brow was smooth, her eyes clear. "There is much I don't understand. But you are a worthy man, Rogan McBain."

"I've done things that—"

"I know truth," she said. "And I know goodness. You'll not suffer for your affiliation with me."

"I believe you'll both come with me," Cranton said, and in that instant fear flickered in Faye's earth-stone eyes. It was more than Rogan could bear.

He stepped forward, placing himself between her and the constable, just a few feet from the door.

"You'll not take her," he said.

The captain spread his legs. The boy with the knife had returned to the stairs, but he stood a goodly distance away. Rogan could take them both down if need be.

"What's this then?" asked a voice.

They jerked their gazes to the doorway as a slim youth stepped inside.

"Cur!" Faye hissed.

"Who are *you*?" snapped Cranton.

The boy lifted his head the slightest degree, almost as if he were testing the scents. "Well, *I'm* not the killer," he said, and glanced from Faye to Rogan, brows raised.

The constables were looking nervous. And for good reason. There was something eerie about the boy, something unearthly and rare and capable.

"Who might you be?" Cranton asked, but he kept his distance from the boy. He was not, apparently, a foolish man.

"Have you searched the house?" Cur asked.

"There's none other here," said the youth.

"Are you certain?" Cur asked, and strolled leisurely down the hall.

He raised his nose again, narrowed his eyes, then bent to study a drop of scarlet that marred the white wall.

"Have you tried there?" he asked, and pointed to a door placed under the stairs that led to the upper floor.

"It's too small," Redbreast said.

"Try anyway," Cur insisted.

Cranton nodded. The boy stepped cockily toward the pantry, opened the door, and glanced inside. "As I said—"

"Farther back," Cur said. The words were almost a growl.

Crouching, the boy stepped inside, but suddenly a form hurtled past. He stumbled out of the way, and a woman sprang forth, eyes wild, hair frazzled.

A moment of silence lapped the room, then, "Lady Lindale." Faye's voice was raspy and hushed.

"What happened?" she asked, then turned toward the body, eyes wide and already tearing. "No. Not dear Theodore."

"Who are you?" Cranton asked, but it seemed to take a moment for his words to register in her shaken mind.

"I am Lady Lindale. Of Inver Heights. Is he . . . " Her voice broke, but she rallied. "Is he dead?"

"I fear he is. Might I ask why you are here?"

"Yes. Of course." Her face was pale, her eyes wide and limpid. "I . . . I had heard Theodore was feeling poorly." She turned her head slightly, then closed her eyes and shuddered before seeing the body. "I came to visit him. He is, *was*, my husband's cousin."

"Yes," Faye said, but there was an eerie calmness to her voice as though she was quietly delving for truth.

The lady's gaze skittered to Faye, seeking solace there. "My poor dear Henry. Taken too early from me. It is too unfair to lose another man for whom I cared."

"What happened?" asked Cranton.

"As I said, I but came to make certain he was

well. I brought him a bottle of burgundy. He only drinks French. Says local wines insult his palate. It sounds haughty I know, but really—"

"Perhaps we could discuss his preferences later."

"Of course. Yes." She shuddered, but did not let her gaze slip to the body again. "It hardly matters now. The point is, I came alone. When he did not answer the door, I stepped inside. There was a noise from up above. I planned to ascend the stairs. But suddenly . . . " She turned as if seeing it all again, one hand lifted dramatically. "Someone grabbed me from behind. The bottle flew from my hands. It must have broken, but I barely noticed, for someone was propelling me across the floor. I was pushed into that alcove and locked inside."

"You poor thing," Faye said, and, stepping forward, gently pulled Lady Lindale into her embrace, her sensitive hands spread against the lady's back.

"It was terrible. Terrifying." Her voice was broken, trembling.

"I'm so sorry."

The constable stepped forward, examining the clasp, turning it easily. "You say it was locked."

"I was so scared," Lindale mewled.

"Of course you were. Of course," Faye said, and, pulling away just slightly, found the older woman's gaze with her own. "But why did you do it?"

The lady's face gradually went slack as her attention pinned to Faye's eyes.

"You did not stand to inherit even with Franquor's death."

Lindale's eyes looked strangely blank. "But Mots did," she said.

"You said Lord Warton yet lived."

"But for how long? He's an old man with a failing heart. He will die of his own accord."

"So you killed the others first, thinking none would think the deaths connected."

The older woman smiled, as if blandly sharing secrets with a friend. "Not many know how to mix horse nettles and bloodroot to their greatest potency. But I have not always had access to an apothecary, you know." She shook her head, and in that moment, Rogan caught a glimpse of the beauty she had once been. "I made my life on the stage. Never has there been a greater Lady Macbeth."

"You killed three times so your nephew could inherit?" Faye murmured.

"My *husband's* nephew," she said. "We are not kin."

"You are having an affair with him."

"It's not an affair."

"You love him."

Lindale smiled. The expression was innocent yet terrifying. And in that moment, Faye caught her first glimpse of true madness. "I had no wish to give birth to Henry's offspring. There are ways to cause barrenness if you know your herbs. I was thrilled when he turned to others. Let his wanton slatterns bear his children.

"It was he in the library," she said. "It was he who attacked you. There are secret passageways throughout the house. When inebriated, he would think himself quite clever, sneaking about, spying on me, pawing the servants. I accepted it for a host of years, smiling at his antics as if he were a coddled child. But when he began molesting guests . . ." She shrugged. "I knew I could not keep his debauchery secret much longer. I had worked too hard to become a laughingstock." She raised her chin. "He was a worthless shell of a man, more than willing to drink whatever poison I infused in his wine. It was a pleasure killing him," she said, and in that moment Faye could bear no more evil. She stepped back, breaking contact.

The woman's blank expression faded. Reality settled in gradually. She raised her hand slowly. In her fist she held a pistol. Its brass scrollwork glistened in the firelight as she aimed it toward Rogan. "Out of the doorway, oaf."

Silence slid in. Rogan shook his head, and in that moment Faye leaped, forgetting pain, forgetting fear, and magic. Action was all there was, and in that instant Lindale swung toward her.

The world exploded. Agony slashed Faye like a knife, but it hardly mattered. Even as she fell, even as she heard the Redbreasts pull Lindale to the floor and felt her own consciousness slip away, she smiled.

Rogan McBain would suffer no more scars.

Chapter 29

"I'm sorry, lass. So very sorry." His words were a rumbled prayer whispered in the darkness. His hands were a tight belt around her own. "I knew better than to think you were for the likes of me."

Pain hammered through Faye, catching her breath, tearing her muscles. She lay still, listening. Upon her chest she could feel the warmth of the bloodstone he had placed there. The cord felt slim, the amulet heavy. It was doing demmed little good.

"'Tis me own fault you are here." Firelight flickered. She could sense it through her lowered lids and wondered if Ella had left some magic to keep it glowing. "I should have warned you of the curse that plagues me. Had not my guilt been so heavy, I would have done so. Would have shared the truth." He lifted her hand. Hot tears smeared across her knuckles. "'Twas I what caused me mum's death. My size . . .'Tis unearthly. The midwife said as much. 'Twas then, long ago, that I knew I was not meant for a maid's tender company. I tried to keep meself private, to spare the fairer sex, but Charlotte . . . Lady Winden . . . she was a golden torch, searing my mind. I could think of nothing else, and when I saw the bruises . . ." He paused.

Faye waited, wanting to open her eyes, to ease his pain, but needing to hear his words, to let him spill the toxic truths.

"I meant only to save her from her husband's temper. Or at least I told meself as much. But I wonder now. Perhaps I but wanted her for meself, and in so doing . . ." She felt a muscle contract in his jaw, brushing her nails. " 'Twas I what issued the challenge. Perhaps he thought it a gentlemanly contest where none would be injured. But I knew better. Indeed, I feel little remorse . . . but for the child." His voice had dropped to the thinnest of whispers. "Winden's bairn by another marriage. A wee wisp of a maid. Silken curls and eyes as bright as a summer lochan. I knew Charlotte had created no bond with her. But I did not understand . . . did not even consider the evil that was in her. The babe died of fever in the days following her father's death, she said. And I've tried to believe it true for me own soul's sake. But I do not. I think she took the bairn's life with her own hands." He inhaled shakily. "Had I known . . . had I seen her wickedness, I would not have fallen for her beauty," he said. "Or that is what I've told meself these past years. But perhaps the truth is not so gentle. Perhaps, had I known all, I would still have forfeited the child's life for my own pleasure. Just as I forfeited my mum's life for me own." Another hot tear dropped onto her knuckles, and with its liquid heat, Faye opened her eyes, heart breaking.

"No, Rogan. 'Tis not true."

"Lass." His haunted, silver eyes found hers. His hands tightened around her fingers. "I have not killed you."

" 'Twas not your fault. It was my choice to make. My choice—"

"Nay." He shook his head. A muscle ticked in his unshaven jaw. "Had I explained myself after our time together, perhaps all would have been well. But when you told me of your youth . . . your abuse at the hands of others . . ." Rage shone like a blaze in his dead-steady eyes, and for a moment, she was almost afraid. "I wanted nothing more than to kill. To feel my hands on their throats. I could not bear to see you for the heat of vengeance in my soul." He relaxed his grip on her fingers slightly, inhaled carefully. "But I see now that you are safer without me than with me."

She shook her head, but he continued.

"Look at me, lass."

She did. He was beautiful beyond words. Kindness and goodness and strength.

"A beast some say." His voice was low. "An ogre. Yet I failed to keep you safe. Had it not been for me, you would not have gone to Franquor's cottage. Had Brendier not been me own kin, perhaps even he would be alive."

"You didn't cause his death, Rogan. You know that," she said, but he shook his head.

"Those around me suffer, lass. *That* I know. Have known for a long while. But me uncle thought it time to mend relations. To seek out me father's family. Thus I ventured here. And though death followed, I thought mayhap the curse was broken. For I found you." His fingers tightened on hers. His eyes shone like quicksilver.

"The curse *is* broken, Rogan," she whispered, but he shook his head.

"Not so long as I am here, lass." Kissing her hand with hot reverence, he rose heavily to his feet. "I'll not risk your magic, wee faerie."

Dread flooded her, drowned her. "No!" she said, and clung to his hand, but his eyes were steady, his features stern.

"I've set my mind," he said, and, turning, left her in agony, alone again.

"Faye."

She awakened slowly, not particularly caring to. He was gone. She knew that, felt the absence of his truth in her soul. There was little point to consciousness.

"Are you improving?" Ella stood beside the bed and reached for her hand.

"Yes." Her voice sounded strange, dry, guttural, as though she'd been crying.

"Good," she said. "Because I've been waiting to see you toss a teapot cross the room with nothing but your mind again. After some discussion, Maddy and I think you may have the ability to absorb the powers of those around you." She sat on the mattress beside her. "Thus I hoped you would be up and about by now. It's been three days." She smiled and touched Faye's forehead, sweeping back the hair. "I used my best potions. Hogweed and tetterwort stirred with a cypress wand and boiled under a gibbous moon."

"You've done well," Faye said. "My thanks. 'Tis simply that—"

"She's weak," Shaleena said, and sauntered in, uninvited and arrogant.

"What are you doing here?" Ella asked, and squeezed Faye's hand before rising to stand protectively between them. Would she forever need a protector? Would she forever be so frail? "I thought you were busy hiding in your chamber."

The redhead drew herself up. "I do not hide."

"Oh? Then you've spoken to Rikard?"

"That is *not* his name," Shaleena hissed.

"Are you certain? I was sure it was Rikard Baranyi III, eldest son of—"

"I know what you've done!" Shaleena rasped. "You've crafted a potion to make him pretend he is Rikard. To pretend he yet lives. To drive me mad."

"You are wrong, Becca," Joseph said, and stepped quietly into the room.

Shaleena backed away, fists clenched, eyes wide. "No."

"You *are* wrong," Ella agreed. "I mixed a potion to bring the love of your life. Myrtle and gardenia grown with a lodestone in the shadow of the rowans. Very potent," she said, glancing at Faye.

"No," Shaleena said again, and shook her head.

"I searched for you," Joseph said. "When I realized my father's lies."

"You didn't want me. Admit it." There was rage in Shaleena's eyes. Rage and tears. "I was *odd*." She winced, scorning the very thing in which she took such pride. "I was a *szolga*."

"You were gifted. As were my antecedents. There was pride in that knowledge. And I did not care that you were a servant," he said, but Shaleena laughed.

"You don't lie any better than you did as a boy," she hissed, and he winced.

"I lacked the strength you deserved," he said. "That I admit. I longed to please my sire. Certain I was that I could make him see the error of his way. But I realize now the mistakes of my youth. Indeed, I have paid dear for them, Rebecca. But we've been granted another chance."

"You're wrong. There are no more chances."

"Why?" he asked, and anguish filled his face. "Why can you not forgive?"

"Because I'm no fool! Because—"

"Because she doesn't deserve happiness," Faye said. Reality was like a spear in her side, forcing her to acknowledge her *own* mistakes. Allowing her to understand another's.

Shaleena turned on her with a hiss. "I deserve everything this world has to offer."

"Do you?" Faye asked, and eased her feet to the floor, barely wincing at the pain. "Then it's because you're weak."

"I am not weak."

"Yes you are. You're—" Faye paused, waiting for her head to cease its spinning. "You're afraid. Afraid of chances. Afraid of *him*." She nodded toward Joseph, but didn't glance that way lest she fall face-first onto the carpet. Truth was soaring through her like a wild dove, and she dare not shake it off. "Afraid of happiness."

"Happiness." Shaleena's voice broke. "I *was* happy. He took it from me."

"Then take it back," Faye said, and, realizing her every shortcoming, shifted carefully to her feet. The world wobbled. "Or don't."

"How can I?" she asked. "Too much has passed."

"You are wrong, Becca," Joseph said.

"Truly? Can you retrieve the years?" she asked. "Can you bring back our son?"

"Not the years," he said. "But our son . . ."

The world fell silent. Even Faye managed to look up.

"What are you saying?" Shaleena rasped.

"Our child yet lives."

Not a soul breathed.

"He lied." Shaleena's voice was no more than a whisper of pain. "Your father . . ."

"*Igen*. Yes."

Her face looked as pale as death. "I should have known." A muscle ticked painfully in her jaw. "Perhaps I did. But I was young. Alone." A tear slipped down her alabaster cheek. "I'm sorry," she whispered, and he went to her, drawing her into his arms, pulling her against his chest.

"He forgives you." He stroked the back of her head, almost smiling, eyes closed. "Or he will . . . in time."

Shaleena looked up, eyes wide and desperate. "You know him."

He nodded. "As do you."

She shook her head, fingers tight in his simple shirt.

"We should have expected some . . ." He paused. "Irregularities. What with your gifts and the unusual history of my family so near the Carpathians."

"Irregularities. What do you mean? What's wrong with—"

But in that instant, Cur stepped through the door, dark eyes snapping, lips turned up in a wolf-ish grin.

" 'Ello, Mum," he said, and for the first time in as long as Faye could remember, Shaleena looked as if she was about to swoon.

* * *

Faye sat in silent stillness upon the room's faded settee, hands folded in her lap, waiting.

Five days had passed since they had discovered Theodore's dead body at the foot of the stairs. Three since Rogan's tortured confessions by her bedside.

She had not stayed there long after his departure. Ella's healing skills were legendary. But perhaps more therapeutic than all else was the full realization that her life was her own, to ruin or rejoice in. She had found she preferred to rejoice.

Thus she had returned to the modest house in Bloomsbury. And there, she found the strength to touch Lady Winden's hand. Things seemed perfectly clear now. Exact. Faye no longer doubted either her own powers or Rogan's goodness. It was a simple thing to pull forth the truth. It spilled from the widow like cheap wine.

Her husband had been a pale insect of a man. A drunkard, too weak to make his debtors pay their bills, surely too weak to beat her as she had told McBain he had done. But it had taken so little to convince Rogan of the opposite. A few bruises. A blackened eye. So little to plant the idea of a duel in his head.

Thus Rogan had fought to save a woman who needed no saving, a woman who was cruel and conniving.

But 'twas not that knowledge that Faye needed

to garner. Nay, she knew as much by now. It was what came after that had kept her sleepless and hopeful. It was what came after that brought her here to the frayed and faded sitting room of a foundling house many miles from London's bustling streets. It was what made the air stick tight in her throat as she waited in tense silence while footfalls echoed down the bare hall.

Finally, able to wait no longer, Faye rose to her feet, breath held.

The door opened. Two people stepped inside. A thin woman with a drawn face and a pale, emerald-eyed child. Barely four years of age, she clung to the woman's hand, but the other pried the girl's grip loose.

"This is she," she said simply, and, turning, left the room, closing the door behind her.

The child half turned too, as if cast adrift in an uneven sea.

Faye cleared her throat. "What is your name?" She knew it, of course, knew Lady Winden had left the child on a midnight street some miles from here. Knew a local farmer had found her that very night and brought her here to this moldering house with the tumbling chimney.

The girl glanced at her, eyes wide, face solemn above her tattered gown. She was too thin, too pale, too frightened. She shook her head, barely able to manage that much, and Faye's heart lurched.

"I'll call you Catherine," she said, and squatted, tears filling her eyes. "*He'll* call you wee Cat."

* * *

It was the following day that the two of them stood on the stoop of Rogan's town house. Connelly opened the door, grinned into Faye's face, then lowered his gaze to the tiny girl who clung like a burr to her hand. She was dressed all in white, her dark curls tied back in a bow.

"Yours?" he asked.

"Yes," Faye said, and, brushing past him, stepped inside, drawing Catherine with her. With a few whispered words, she left the child in the foyer and paced into the great room. Already she could hear McBain's footfalls. Her heart felt heavy in her chest, tight and oversized, but in a moment he was there. Emotion flared in his eyes, but he quelled it, making his face a flinty mask.

"I thought you understood that I would not be seeing you again," he said.

She lifted her chin. "You made that clear."

He nodded. A muscle jerked in his scruffy jaw, and he turned away.

"There is no curse," she said.

He glanced back at her, torture in his eyes. "You do not understand, lass. Those—"

"I *do* understand, McBain. There is good. And there is evil. You are good."

"You're wrong," he began, but in that moment tiny Catherine abandoned the foyer. She crossed the room like a tiny angel, eyes wide, cheeks pale.

McBain's gaze fell to her like a rock. Pain contorted his features as the child reached for Faye's hand and ducked her head, hiding it against the sweep of the other's gown.

"Little Cat," Faye said softly, and did nothing to draw the girl into the open. There were times to hide and times to be brave. She knew that now. "This is Rogan McBain." The child shifted slightly, peering past the folds of Faye's lavender skirt with one shy eye.

"He's . . ." The girl's voice was no more than a lisped whisper. " . . . scary."

"At times," Faye agreed, watching him. "But he is also gentle-hearted and brave. Though he doesn't yet know it." She squeezed the child's hand and looked down into the hopeful spring of her eyes. " 'Tis our task to teach him."

Silence echoed in the room.

"Catherine." Rogan's voice was a rumble of dark emotion. "Catherine Winden."

Faye nodded.

Rogan's throat contracted. "She yet lives."

Tears stung Faye's eyes. "Yes."

"Wee Cat . . ." His voice broke. He cleared his throat. "You found her."

"Yes."

"For me."

"For us all," she said, and he hit his knees as tears welled in his stormy eyes.

Epilogue

The room was dark, the night quiet. Rogan kissed Faye with a quiet passion reserved for her alone, and she kissed him back. They'd not yet been married a full year, but she could feel a babe stir in her womb. A wee sister for little Cat.

New life was sharpening her every sense, honing each unearthly power. Or maybe it was simply her newfound security that strengthened her. Oh aye, she had learned she did not need a protector to keep her safe, but she had also learned that she very much enjoyed having one.

"I love you," he rumbled, and she smiled, knowing it was true, knowing it would always be true.

"I love you too," she murmured, "but I will still see to this mission alone."

"You'll not," he said, but they both knew she would do what she would. 'Twas the way with Les Chausettes.

A sharp-nosed vixen pointed her nose in the room, sniffed, then trotted through. Two others followed. Just part of the family. Cur had had a word with them. They were quite well behaved. Better than Cur, according to Shaleena.

"A member of Parliament has gone missing," she said. "Lord Gallo believes a Mr. Barton may know something of his disappearance."

His hand roamed her back, pulling her closer. "Then Lord Gallo should question him," he said.

"But *I* am the one who can garner the truth," she said.

"Give me ten minutes alone with him I am fair sure I can do the same," he rumbled ominously.

"As it happens, they still want him alive at the end of the day. Besides, Lord Gallo is uncomfortable with tears."

"I would try to keep him quiet."

"I meant yours," she said. What had she done before she had him to tease? To love. To touch. To ease her headaches with his quiet earnestness. "It seems you are weeping each time I turn about."

"I do not cry," he rumbled.

There was happiness like music in her soul "Only when little Cat falls and scrapes her hands."

For a moment she thought he would deny her words, but he scowled finally. "They're such wee little things," he said finally, and she laughed again as she turned away, but he caught her fingers in his fist, pulling her back.

"You are my life," he said.

Hope flowed between them. Hope and love and so much more. "And you mine."

"You'll be careful?"

"For you," she promised, kissing the back of his hand before stepping away. "And the baby."

"There's a bairn?" he rasped, and she laughed as tears filled his ethereal eyes.

*At Avon Books, we know your passion
for romance—once you finish one of our
novels, you find yourself wanting more.*

May we tempt you with . . .

- **Excerpts** from our upcoming releases.

- Entertaining **extras**, including authors'
  personal photo albums and book lists.

- Behind-the-scenes **scoop** on your favorite
  characters and series.

- **Sweepstakes** for the chance to win free books,
  romantic getaways, and other fun prizes.

- Writing **tips** from our authors and editors.

- **Blog** with our authors and find out why they
  love to write romance.

- **Exclusive content** that's not contained
  within the pages of our novels.

Join us at
www.avonbooks.com